KISS OF DARKNESS

CURSE OF THE GUARDIANS BOOK ONE

TAYLOR ASTON WHITE

DARK WOLF
PUBLISHING

Edited by Alexander Small
Cover by MiblArt

www.taylorastonwhite.com
Official Taylor Aston White Newsletter

DEDICATION

This is for everyone who gave me a chance. I would never have believed in my wildest dreams I could have such a crazy career, but because of readers like you I'm able to write and support my family. So thank you for letting me talk to the imaginary voices in my head and creating these weird, and wonderful stories.

P.S. Nan, I've warned you not to read this.

Also by Taylor Aston White

Alice Skye Series

Witch's Sorrow
Druid's Storm
Rogue's Mercy
Elemental's Curse
Knight's War
Veil's War

Alice Skye World

Witch's Bounty
(Newsletter exclusive)
Chasing Shadows
(Midnight Magic Anthology)

Curse of The Guardians

Kiss of Darkness
Touch of Blood

DISCLAIMER

Kiss of Darkness is an enemies to lovers paranormal romance. The story contains explicit content, graphic violence, profanity, and topics that may be sensitive to some readers.

Trigger warnings:
Graphic gore/death, torture, threats of sexual assault, sexually explicit scenes.

BREED INDEX

Celestrial - Also known as 'angels.' Can lose their powers and wings, known as 'falling'

Magic class - Unknown

Origin realm - Unknown

Other - Once a celestrial has fallen, they're rumoured to be as weak as humans, but none have openly confirmed (See Fallen Angel)

Daemon - Druids who choose to ascend into black magic. In return for more power, they sacrifice their bodies and sanity

Magic class - Black

Origin realm - The Nether (also known as Hell)

Other - Once imprisoned in The Nether, they now freely move between realms

Druid - Born male, druid genes are inherited from the fathers

Magic class - Natural/Arcane. Can be strengthened with Ley Lines

Origin realm - Earth Side

Other - Breed governed by the Archdruid. When they come of age they must tattoo a syphon, known as a glyph, around their wrists to better control their arcane

Guardian - Druids who were cursed to share their soul with a 'beast.' Their bodies, including their 'beast' form, are designed to battle Daemons, with increased strength, agility and ability to survive severe damage

Magic class - Natural/Arcane. Can be strengthened with Ley Lines and glyphs

Origin realm - Earth Side

Beast - Unknown

Other - The Archdruid made the deal with Hadriel, the Fallen Angel who powers The Nether, creating the curse in return for soldiers

Fae - Umbrella term for anyone from Far Side. Includes faeries, selkies, pixies etc. Split into two castes, light (Seelie) and dark (Unseelie)

Magic class - Wild Magic

Origin realm - Asherah of Far (also known as Far Side)

Other - Never say thank you, and be wary of gifts (Fae stuff seem to have a mind of their own)

Fallen Angels - Celestrials that have 'fallen'

Magic class - Unknown

Origin realm - Unknown, but now reside on Earth Side

Other - Hide themselves amongst humans, always trying to regain their wings

Ghoul - Name for a failed vampire transition. Primal instincts only

CHAPTER 1
KYRA

ONE YEAR LATER

Death threats were often made anonymously, the words designed to intimidate and scare. Kyra wasn't scared of pieces of paper. She'd seen more horrors and monsters in her twenty-eight years than most would in their lifetime. But after six months, and numerous letters, the envelope she tucked beneath her arm scared her, the threat darker, more graphic than those before.

It had been personally delivered to her home, the generic white envelope missing a stamp and an address. She wouldn't have even opened it, if not for the gift inside.

"He'll see you now," Bane said, the tall Fae gesturing from behind his desk. "You're lucky he has a break in his schedule."

Kyra nodded, flicking her long black braid back over her shoulder. She knew never to thank the Fae. Just one of the many complicated rules when dealing with them. It was why she preferred to work with the dead. They had no rules, and they never wanted to engage in awkward small talk.

"Why, if it isn't my favourite black witch," Frederick Gallagher, the voice for the Triumvirate, and therefore the Magicka, said with a slanted smirk. "Miss Farzan, what do you need?"

Bane took his time closing the door. Kyra waited, hit attention lingering before he quietly excused himself. This wasn't a conversation she wanted to hold before a crowd.

Hesitating, Kyra swallowed hard. She tried to do everything without the assistance of the Magicka, the governing body for all witches and mages. The very organisation that usually slaughtered people like her.

"Well?" Frederick prompted when she remained quiet. He moved from his chair, dramatically tugging the ruffles that draped down his shirt like a romanticised pirate. He sat on the edge of his desk, letting out an irritated puff.

Kyra carefully held out the envelope, waiting until he had taken it before she explained. "That's the fifth letter I've received, but the first with the death charm."

Frederick tipped the contents into his hand, eyes bright as he read the words that had made her stomach twist into knots, rising bile that burned her throat. He only gave the severed finger with a broken nail freshly painted black a brief glance.

"It's not active," he said, tossing the digit onto his desk. "And this letter is nonsense. We both know you're under my protection. No one would ever hurt any witch considered mine. You're being dramatic."

"Dramatic?" Kyra echoed, having to concentrate to keep her voice even. "Someone's written, in detail, how they wanted to slice me open from neck to navel and use my organs for spells. I think that warrants some concern."

Organs used in black magic weren't uncommon, which was only one of the many reasons practicing magic that specialised in blood and death had been outlawed by the Magicka long ago. There were exceptions, like herself. She was granted special privileges, but only under strict supervision of Frederick himself.

If Kyra had been luckier, she would have never revealed herself, but it was Frederick, one of the three witches who ruled her Breed who'd recognised her unique chi and understood what she was. She was left with little choice but to agree to his protection, and the conditions that came with it.

"Don't play me for a fool," he said with a chuckle. "I wouldn't be surprised if it was fake, and this was just an excuse to get out of our arrangement." He slipped off the desk, moving closer until she could clearly smell the ozone that radiated off him like some narcissistic cologne.

"It wasn't fake." She knew, she'd smelt the sulphur come off the finger when she'd tossed it carefully into salt water to dissipate the black charm.

"Whatever you say," he said with a crooked smirk. "But it's a peculiar time to receive such threats, especially after I've asked you for assistance with my little project."

Kyra clenched her hands, nails digging in. She knew she'd have little crescent moons indented into her palms. "I've always done exactly what you've asked, but you have no idea what you're messing with. I won't do it, ask one of your other witches."

He had enough under his control, being the main voice to the Triumvirate, the three witches who ruled The Magicka. Frederick Gallagher made the laws, and as she'd found out only a few years ago, he could also bend them.

"I don't think you quite understand our situation." He bowed down, his hooked nose only inches from hers. "Bane has made you an appointment at the market to pick up the correct supplies. Make sure you're not late."

Kyra controlled her chi as it flared out in response, her magic reacting violently as the crystal she kept flush against her skin began to burn. "Frederick –"

"You'll address me as Councilman," he corrected. "You seem to be a little unstable at the moment, Kyra. Carry on and you may need a babysitter."

Kyra froze, anxiety wrapping itself around her chest.

"You *will* do exactly as I ask, as that's our agreement," he said, his smile darkening. "We wouldn't want your secret to get out now, would we?"

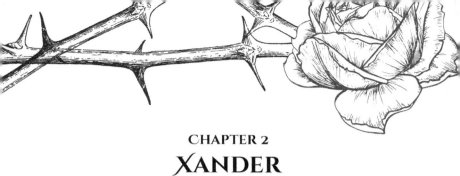

CHAPTER 2

XANDER

X ander fucking hated cemeteries.

"Stop sulking." Axel smirked at him as they both walked past the darkened unkept graves. "They're already dead."

"It's not me who's sulking," Xander grunted, ignoring the howls of the spirits that wanted his attention. He kept his eyes straight, careful not to acknowledge any one of the spooks. Otherwise they would never leave him the fuck alone. "Titus was scheduled to go hunting tonight, not me." He stayed away from the Troll Market if he could help it, the underground bazaar not the best place for a man who could see the dead. "What happened between you two? You have a fight again?"

"Nothing happened, he's just an arsehole." Axel's face tightened as he scrubbed his hand over his short, brown hair. "Now, are you gearing up or not? I need a good fight."

Xander wanted to press the situation between Axel and Titus, two of his fellow Guardians, but knew better than to ask. They were all brothers, chosen not blood, except Axel and Titus who were actually cousins. They grew up together, their bond strong but complicated.

"You know there won't be a fight, Pretty Boy," he said, readjusting the leather cuffs at his wrists. "Not at the market."

"There definitely will be if you call me Pretty Boy again." Axel pressed his slightly too full lips, his cheekbones an envy to most models. "You may want to put your shades on, the entrance is just ahead."

Xander reached for his sunglasses, the mirrored aviators protecting his sensitive eyes. He could see perfectly fine, regardless of the level of light, but preferred the darkness. His mother had always told him he had the eyes of the dead, so pale blue they were almost white. His best friend Riley had always thought that comparison was amusing considering his ability.

The Troll Market was the largest underground place to buy weapons, drugs, black spells, as well as a few other questionable products and services. While named by the trolls, it was run by two Fae High Lords, ruthless bastards who bought and sold whatever they wanted. They had created specialised doorways to the market beneath the largest cemetery in the city, with temperamental portals connecting to other parts of the country. It was cleverly designed, the portals only able to operate if you had the right token, which you could only acquire through some serious money or services. Once you owned a token it would forever follow you, appearing in your wallet, at home or in your car only hours after leaving the market. Convenient, really. It kept the police and paladins out, and allowed everyone to sell their wares without risk.

Xander hated it just as much as the cemetery.

"You ready?" Axel asked as he produced the token from his pocket, the small golden coin imprinted with a jawless skull on either side. There were several entrances to the market, including two within the cemetery itself. The one they stood before was a large headstone with three concentric circles, the patterns engraved in each one mismatched. "You first."

"Fuck off," Xander snorted. He knew exactly what would happen once they touched the stone.

With a quiet curse Axel moved to the left, carefully moving the outer circle until it matched the patterns and clicked into place. His body was rigid, his teeth clenched when Xander pressed his fingers against the second circle. The heavy vibrations that paralysed Axel shot up his arm like lightning. It was harder to move the middle circle, and the longer it took, the worse the pain became.

"Xee?" Axel said, barely able to release the word.

With a last push Xander forced the circle into place, completing the pattern. The centre sank into the headstone. A slot matching the exact same measurements of the token appeared. "Why did we choose this entrance again?" he asked, flexing his hand as the remnants of the stiffness wore off.

"Because the other door has a Cockney ghost who talks in riddles." Axel sighed, clicking his neck. "You think you're smart enough to answer some stupid brainteasers? Because I doubt I could," he huffed. "Honestly, what is with the Fae and fucking puzzles?"

Xander nodded in acknowledgment. "Can you hurry the fuck up?" He could feel the individual energies of the spirits around him. It was becoming increasingly difficult to ignore their cries for attention. "I have a date."

"What, with your hand?" Snorting, Axel inserted the token. The ground behind the grave opened to reveal stairs. Wooden, crooked and squeaky. Fae folk had an allergy to everything iron, and because one prick decided to hide iron inside a silver blade one time, they'd decided to remove *all* metal.

Rumour has it that the guy had been quickly devoured by a particularly pissed off faerie. At least, that was what the statue in the centre displayed. Unfortunately, it now meant dangerous timber stairs, and no weapons of any kind that contained metal.

Not that they needed weapons, but blades, guns and anything else sharp and pointy usually made people hesitate before they had to resort to violence.

Xander reached the stone floor, gaze sweeping to note every corner and exit. The market was an assault on the senses, hundreds of wooden stalls, all in various bright colours, had been set up in the high-ceilinged mausoleum, with loud peddlers pushing their wares. Xander hoped the scowl that was his go-to expression was enough to keep the shopkeepers from hassling them to buy their shit. He didn't need the skull of a siren to help with his love life, or a kidney, freshly harvested according to the sign.

It was also the place where glamour magic was nulled, which meant everyone who worked and shopped looked exactly like they did when their mother birthed them, or hatched or whatever. It meant there were humanoids with every skin tone on the spectrum, pinks, blacks, greens, blues as well as feathers, scales and more. Fae in general had the most diverse looks of all Breed, the term Fae itself only an umbrella term for those who weren't born of earth, and instead came from Far Side. Not that Asherah of Far was accessible anymore, not since the veil between the realms was locked tight by the dark king himself.

"Are we here for anything specific?" he asked, eyes scanning across the stalls. Crystals, exotic fruit, armaments and spells that could easily take a life. Assassins stood and sold people their services, succubi their bodies in exchange for secrets, and bookies offered bets in the fighting pits. The ceiling was decorated with cages, again made from everything but metal. Many holding specialised artefacts that Xander itched to learn, as well as small animals and even a few pixies.

Xander's attention settled on the only metal allowed in the room, the weapons displayed in a carefully protected shield. The bubble around them shimmered, the stall owner the only person able to handle the deadly pieces.

Food, mostly grey in colour was being sold beside him. Flies buzzed hungrily around the meat. A troll was trying to convince anyone who walked too close that the food was edible, and that the mould was an added delicacy.

"Riley mentioned that activity has increased down here," Axel said quietly, not wanting anyone to overhear as they pushed themselves through the heavy crowd. "There's a stall selling Daemon horns which he asked us to look at."

Xander didn't need to ask where. A sign ahead written in a very friendly blood red stated clearly that they were selling 'The freshest Daemon horns around!'

It wasn't exactly a surprise that Daemons had started to infiltrate the Troll Market. The Undercity was exactly where Breed famous for death and corruption would enjoy. It would only be a matter of time before they made a play for control, and then it would get real interesting.

"You sir, with the sunglasses!" an old woman called, her hand snaking out to wrap around Xander's wrist. "Druid, please may I read your fortune?"

She looked at him, her single beady eye widening before she released her grip. Reaching up to her shawl, she wrapped the fabric tighter around her shoulders, the bright colours at odds with the black velvet of her eyepatch.

"Please, let me read your fortune." She sat herself back down behind a rickety old table, a large crystal ball in the centre surrounded by tarot cards, discoloured and well used.

Axel crossed his arms beside him, nudging Xander. "This could be interesting."

The old woman touched her crystal, the opaque ball brightening between her fingertips. "I can tell you anything you wish to know."

Her chi brushed against his, powerful but full of death and decay. It felt like pins and needles across his aura, the sensation choking as he fought the memories that tried to resurface.

"Then you would already know I have nothing to pay," Xander said. The whole Undercity had their own currency. The black onyx coins were patterned with different creatures depending on their value. Ravyns ranged from one-hundred pounds, to one million. The lesser depicting an imp on the polished black crystal, while the highest value was a dragon.

"It's only a single Ravyn," she said, pulling up her eyepatch.

Xander didn't bother to hide his disgust. The witch had sacrificed her sight in return for black magic. The dark socket empty bar a shrivelled raisin.

"I'm the best there is."

"I'm sure you are," he said as he began to turn away. "But I'm still not interested."

A slim hand snatched his wrist. "Your home is calling!" she said, releasing him with a hiss when he shot her a caustic glare. "They need you to go home."

Xander stilled, shoulders rigid before he turned back into the crowd, careful not to nudge the tall troll who was more brawn than brains. They had a tendency to start a fight with anyone, which was why there were anti-violence wards painted onto every wall in the vast mausoleum.

They constantly pulsed, the patterns darkening when they absorbed any physical, or magical violence. With a crowd as big as there was, Xander knew the wards wouldn't stop all fights. A single punch would pass with little repercussions, but if there was a full-blown attack, the wards would kick in and neutralise both parties until they could be removed from the premises. The Overseers didn't care what happened outside the market, as long as no one drew attention to the doorways.

"What was that about?" Axel asked quietly. "She talking about the community?"

Xander just gently shook his head. He never discussed where he grew up, or the woman who'd birthed him. Especially somewhere with so many ears. The spirits were just as heavy down there as they were above, their moans nothing but static compared to the overwhelming shouts of the market. The stronger ones could pass as living, corporeal enough to move small objects. The weaker ones could only grow in substance when they had someone to focus on. Xander was mindful of avoiding contact, not wanting to strengthen any of the dead enough that they could solidify their bodies and cause havoc.

"Over here."

The stall they needed was called *'All Things Hell!'* The contents on top of the dark red velvet something you could find in a novelty Samhain store. Axel picked up the horn labelled Daemon, the hardened shell well made, but fake.

"How can I help you guys?" the slim Fae asked when they approached his stall. "I have fresh fish eyeballs, newts and snakes. I've also received a shipment of Daemon horns, tails and wings."

"Wings?" Xander asked, eyebrow raised when the shopkeeper unfolded what was supposed to be a Daemonic wing. Except it had no bone structure, and the leather was stitched together with thread.

"Yes, only the finest for all your spelling needs." His

smile widened, showing off a row of sharpened, silvery teeth. The shopkeeper could have been any number of the types under the term Fae, and Xander couldn't have cared less which one.

"Do you know what's interesting?" Axel crushed the horn in his hand, its substance crumbling easily.

"Hey, what do you think you're doing?" the Fae screeched, trying to catch the falling fragments.

"Daemon horns aren't just made from keratin like other horns, they're also made from bone. Neither would break like that." Axel tossed the remnants to the table.

"They also don't have tails," Xander added with a casual shrug. "So it's impressive that you're selling them."

"You don't know that," the Fae said. "When's the last time you saw a Daemon?"

Axel began to laugh, and Xander couldn't help as his lip twitched. Daemons weren't officially classified as Breed – which was everyone not entirely human – and were so rare they'd only recently been recognised by the Council. They were once trapped in the Nether, commonly nicknamed Hell, where they could only leave if summoned. Until recently.

It wasn't really Hell, at least, not what the humans believed, but a dark, dangerous realm enclosed in powerful magic. The gates that kept all the fuckers below had broken, and now that it was repaired, it was the Guardians job to hunt down the Daemons, and creatures that had escaped.

"This was a waste of time," Axel muttered, wiping his hand down his skin-tight shirt.

Xander had to agree, his beast not picking up any sort of Daemonic energy. He could feel the beast's presence inside his head, but unlike his brothers, his beast was always silent, happy to just observe.

He guessed it was a bonus considering the stories the

other Guardians told about their own beasts, but then again, he wasn't sure if any part of their curse was really a bonus. He would rather have been alone in his head any day.

"You need to pay for what you broke!" the Fae said, his voice raised enough others looked towards them curiously. "You need to –"

"Or what?" Xander interrupted. He had no patience left and just wanted to get out of there so he could go sit and relax in the dark. "You're selling fake products, I'm sure the Overseers would be interested in that." Not that he had any idea if the Overseers gave a shit about what was sold.

"Hey, hey I don't want any trouble," the Fae said, holding his hands out in surrender.

Axel pulled against his shoulder. "Come on, Xee, this guy's a waste. We should check out –"

A commotion drew their attention, the voices loud enough to break through the general hum.

"Hey, is that –" Axel began, his voice lost amongst the rest. Xander began to move through the crowd before he'd even realised, the small female familiar.

Her dark hair was braided, and his beast was fascinated with how it sat perfectly against the centre of her back. It took a minute for her scent to reach him, and as soon as it did, Xander felt his face tighten with his usual scowl.

Of course *she* was there.

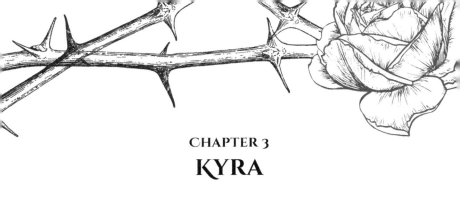

CHAPTER 3
KYRA

Kyra tried to keep her composure, the frustration harshening her tone. "No, accept something else."

Bludrial laughed, the sound like little bells in the wind. They crossed their arms, pearlescent lavender eyes enlarged in a symmetrically oval face. "Bane already agreed the price." Their smirk darkened. "Now give me a vial, or you don't get the supplies requested."

Kyra let out a steady breath, trying to calm herself. Bane, which meant Frederick, had agreed a vial of her blood as payment. That was something she would never have agreed. Blood was the catalyst used within black magic, and hers was more potent than most. She couldn't risk anyone using it.

"No, it's not possible," she said again. "You'll accept a Ravyn."

Kyra knew Bludrial was a faerie, not only because of the androgynous characteristics popular with many of the twenty-odd faerie kinds, but because Bludrial had acknowledged themselves as such. Unusual amongst any Breed to give away knowledge that could be used against them.

Although, it wasn't like either of them could hide behind glamour within the walls of the market.

"That was not the deal. One vial for the supplies," Bludrial said, smile disappearing altogether. Their words came out in a harsh bark, drawing attention Kyra didn't want, or need.

She kept herself quiet, voice straining even as she fought the frustration, and anger that tightened her fists. "I'm sure we can come to some other arrangement, but I can't give you a vial of blood."

"You will, as that's the deal agreed." Bludrial's eyes glistened mischievously, snake-like tongue flicking out. "Although, actually, don't worry, I know a fun way to collect my payment."

Bludrial snapped out his hand, the sharp pain stinging her cheek. She must've been unable to stop the revulsion from creasing her face.

"Touch her again, and lose the hand." A growl, one in a rich timbre that had her straightening.

"Xander?" Kyra pushed at the hair that had escaped her braid with shaking hands. "What do you think you're doing?"

She would be blamed for this, she knew it.

Xander ignored her, adding pressure to Bludrial who looked like a pretzel, their arm pressed into their back and face crushed against the wood of the table.

"Get this blood bag off me!" they snarled, struggling to escape.

Another male moved closer, his face strikingly handsome with cheekbones that would make an angel weep. "Kyra, you okay?" The Guardian's stare darkened with concern. "Kyra?"

Right. He'd asked her a question. "I'm... I'm fine."

She recognised his friendly eyes and military short hairstyle, but not his name... *Axel!* She finally remembered. *That's his name!*

How hard had Bludrial hit her?

Kyra stopped herself from cupping her face, copper on her tongue. She'd worked with the Guardians once, all large men heavily roped in muscle designed for both strength and speed. Fascinating black and red tattoos decorated their skin, the patterns intricate enough she caught herself staring at the exposed lines on Axel's wrists.

"What do they feed you all?"

Axel stilled, eyes widening when she met them.

Oh, bloody hell! She'd asked the question aloud, and not just inside her head.

"Excuse me," she mumbled, the words more of a squeak as she quickly grabbed the package.

"Hey!" Bludrial shouted, their face still pressed against the table, arms twisted painfully. "You haven't paid for that!"

Blindly reaching into her pocket she grabbed a Ravyn, not even caring how much it was. She left it beside Bludrial's face, not daring to look back as she rushed towards the exit. The anti-violence wards glowed against the walls, not yet activated, but ready to intervene.

Heart racing, she found a vacant portal, turning the dial until the incantation showed the outskirts of the city. The Troll Market was connected by carefully constructed doorways. For a price, they could take you further than a few miles from the cemetery. It was relatively new magic, banned by both the Light and Dark courts of the Fae, and yet the High Lords who ran the market cared very little when it could make a profit.

Wild magic was notoriously unpredictable, as were the portals. Normally Kyra would never have trusted them, even though they were convenient, but she couldn't face the man who seemed to hate her on sight.

She grabbed another Ravyn, checking the value before she found the slot beside the dial.

"You shouldn't be here." A hand struck out, carefully circling her wrist with enough pressure to stop her, but not enough to hurt.

Kyra paused, the coin at the edge of the slot. She looked up, and Xander removed his sunglasses. The dark shades had done little to stop the animosity radiating from his pale blue eyes, but without them, it was like icicles across her skin.

"Shouldn't I?" she said, trying to tug from his grasp, her pulse a violent beat. "According to you, this is probably exactly where *I* should be." A knot formed in the pit of her stomach when she remembered their last interaction.

There was a reason she only met with Alice when the Guardian wasn't around.

Xander's mouth twisted, eyes narrowed as he released her wrist, only to grip her jaw. He angled her face against the light, her lip stinging when she frowned.

"What you doing here, Kyra?" His white silver hair, just long enough to cover his unusually dark brows moved across his forehead, partially concealing his expression.

"Minding my own business!" she snapped, but the steel behind her reply lessened when she met his gaze and flinched. "Don't touch me." The words came out quiet, desperate.

His eyes had been blue, she was sure of it, yet she could see her own reflection in his irises. Liquid silver.

His fingers opened, and she stumbled back, breathing heavily. She needed to get out of there before she suffered a full panic attack. Xander was just too much, his gaze too direct as she tried to look anywhere but him.

"Black witch," he grunted, as if she were tainted.

Which she wasn't, but she couldn't explain why he was wrong. He wouldn't care either way. His opinion on her already set in stone, and had been since they first met. Black witches were seen as evil because of their ability to gain power from death, and while many embraced that sordid side of magic, it didn't mean they were all evil. It did, however, make them illegal.

Ignoring him, or, at least trying to as he seemed to press himself closer, always pushing her boundaries, she inserted the Ravyn into the slot. The portal opened with a flash of light. He said nothing as she stepped through, the package hugged tight to her chest. As soon as the portal closed behind her she released a sigh of relief.

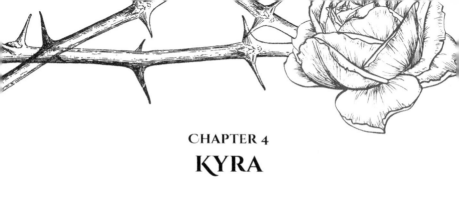

CHAPTER 4
KYRA

*Y**ou disgust me.*
That was what Xander had whispered to her the night she attended Alice's celebration. His words had echoed, and she could still hear them as clear as day inside her mind.

You disgust me.

He'd watched her the whole evening, a silent shadow in the corner, his face carefully composed to reveal nothing but impenetrable ice when she dared raise her eyes to meet his. She wasn't sure why he'd watched her in such a way, mostly ignoring everyone else who danced, and drank, revelling in honour of Alice and Riley.

During the limited times they'd met before, they hadn't exchanged more than a word or two. So she was surprised when he'd approached, only for him to curse her very existence before slanting his lips over her own. The air had electrified between them, his face carved in desire when he pulled back, only to shift to self-loathing.

You disgust me.

So she'd sworn to herself that she'd stay out of his way, not wanting to know why that even in the depths of his disgust he'd still brushed a finger down her arm as she'd said her goodbyes. Had frowned when she backed away from his touch.

Kyra took a slow, deep breath. Her vision blurred, so she closed her eyelids tight as she fought the tears that threatened. It had been years since her heart had thudded so violently inside her chest and since her palms had been slick with sweat. She thought she had control of her reactions, but clearly that wasn't the case.

She wasn't even confident what had set her off exactly, but then again she could never really predict when she would suffer an attack.

It was him, she thought, her mind sluggish as she tried to recall exactly what had happened. It had been his hand too close to her throat. Logically she knew Xander wasn't hurting her, his grip only on her jaw, but her mind had been reminded of situations she would rather forget.

"What took you so long?"

Kyra snapped herself straight as Bane appeared by her side, silent in his movements.

"Have you been following me?" she asked, her voice surprisingly strong and devoid of any remnants of the attack that still tightened her lungs.

His left brow arched. "No, should I be?" His eyes dipped to the package, then to her cut lip. "Councilman Gallagher's concerned with your recent attitude."

Kyra knew better than to reply, her sharp response not worth the hassle or possible repercussions. She had planned to run, to hide as she had for over ten years, but she knew there wasn't really anywhere she could go without them finding her. Her magic was rare, and Frederick wouldn't risk losing someone who made him more powerful.

"What are you doing here?" she eventually asked when

his scowl didn't fade, the wind picking up around them. "You don't usually come to the cottage."

Bane had purposely chosen a vague glamour, one that would blend in seamlessly with any crowd with his generic face, brown eyes and dark blonde hair. She had no idea what he really looked like beneath the magic, or what type of Fae he was. All she knew was he could control wild magic, something usually exclusive to those that came from the Fae Side.

"I'm your escort," he said as he reached for the package. "I wanted to make sure you arrived... safely," he added absently. "I'm sure you're testing their patience, you were due over an hour ago."

Anger flared, but she kept herself calm. "I was negotiating the price. It took longer than expected."

Bane's upper lip twitched. "Well, it looks like you succeeded. Shall we go?"

The portal behind her began to glow, the runes along the floor brightening beneath her feet. It had taken her to just outside London, the busy city merging effortlessly into the countryside of forests, fields and farmland. She would usually travel to the coven's cottage by public transport, but she was grateful the portal had taken her to within a mile of her destination. The walk was a way to calm her nerves.

The castle just down the road shadowed the surrounding greenery, the old structure the base for the Magicka. Breed governed their own, and it was the Magicka that oversaw all witches and mages. Three witches known as the Triumvirate were elected to run the organisation, with only one being given the title of Supreme. While all three were equal in the decision making, the Supreme was the voice, and also held a position within the Council of six.

Breed, whether born that way or changed, had their own governing council. Despite Breed and humans living together peacefully for over three centuries, there was still a subtle divide. Frederick stood for all witches and mages in Europe, while the other seats were occupied with representations from the vampires, Fae, shifters, druids, and celestrials.

It was the Magicka who'd made black witches illegal, blood magic the most powerful of the three classifications. Every classification, whether it was arcane (the ability to concentrate your chi), natural (the use of plants in low level spells and potions) or black, there was always a sacrifice. Whether it was a level of your chi, a plant, or a life, the larger the sacrifice, the more powerful the outcome.

Life, especially those of human or Breed was the largest sacrifice of all. The power it created could make cities crumble. Not many witches were born with a large enough chi to be able to handle that much power, but it didn't stop them from trying.

If a witch was caught practicing, they were sentenced to a specialised Breed prison. If found guilty of conspiring with blood magic, they would be sentenced to death. However, Frederick craved more power, which was why he'd always had a coven of black witches close to the bastion he called home. He twisted the laws that had been written long before he was born, allowing those under his personal supervision to practice the same magic that scared others.

A select few were allowed with Frederick's permission, so it made sense that the black witches that were granted authorisation were all placed into one, conveniently located coven. They were given a license, one that protected them from the primal, and outdated laws.

Under normal circumstances Kyra would have been forced to join the coven whether she'd wanted to or not, because that was the only way she could practice the magic of her birth. Except, she couldn't. Not without the others figuring out her secret. She was grateful for that at least. She could live alone, and have some sort of life as long as she did what she was told.

Like a pet.

"Hurry up," Bane said, his brisk walk forcing her to jog up the drive.

The cottage was beautiful, ivy wrapping itself around the old brick and the surrounding gardens full of life. The lounge beyond the front door was spacious before it branched out into a labyrinth of different doors, rooms and stairways. Fire crackled in the oversized hearth, the black cauldron that usually swung freely above nowhere to be seen. In fact, the room had been emptied of all the furniture, the armchairs, rugs and shelves gone, the scarred wooden surface etched with an elemental circle that spanned the entirety of the floor.

The inverted pentagram, which usually consisted of a star within a circle, had been adapted. At each point of the star a separate circle had been added, just big enough for someone to stand inside.

Kyra paused at the edge, dread a sour taste on her tongue.

"Ah, there you are," Frederick said with a flippant wave of his hand, his expression impatient. "Where's the package?"

Bane stretched forward. "Councilman," he greeted with a gentle nod of his head. "She came through the north western portal."

"Portal? I'm surprised you would risk such arbitrary magic, Kyra," Frederick said as he ripped the outer layer, upper lip lifted in disgust at the blackened vampire heart inside.

Usually when Vamps died – the second time – their bodies decomposed at an alarming rate. Bludrial had done something, a magic that they weren't familiar with for the one wrapped in plastic to still be intact.

"Wild magic doesn't obey any law," he continued. "It's probably why your kin, Bane, are struggling so much to reopen the doorway to Far Side. It's positively primitive compared to our magic." Frederick smirked, and Kyra ignored the heart when he held it out.

"Can I speak to you... privately?" she added when Bane remained by their side.

Frederick handed the heart back to Bane before adjusting the sleeve on the velvet green jacket. "Speak."

"I will never use my blood as payment. Don't offer it again." She had kept her voice quiet, not wanting the coven to overhear. Blood was usually a coveted trade, especially from a black witch.

Out of the six Breeds, four were classed as magic-bearers. Celestrial and Fae were complicated, and neither Breed cared to share information on how their kind was able to adapt magic to benefit themselves. Witches, as well as druids to a lesser extent, had the ability to harness their aura, creating a chi. It created a specialised enzyme in witches' blood, a reagent that reacted to the spells, essentially making them work. Certain spells required a larger number of enzymes, so the more powerful the witch, the higher chance of success.

Blood could also be traced, which was the reason she would never offer it.

Frederick's expression remained hard. "Who do you think you're talking to?" he whispered back, pressing forward until his breath was an unwelcome warmth against her face. "It's because of me that you're not hunted down like a dog, that you're not harvested for your body and sold at the same market you've just visited."

Kyra couldn't stop her flinch.

"Or is that what you want? To be imprisoned by some-one, and used daily in rituals against your will? Maybe it would be a man who finds you and takes pity, then you could be used in other ways too." Frederick paused, a cruel smile curving his lips. "You live as freely as I wish, Kyra. I own you, don't ever forget it."

"We're almost ready," Adeline said from the corner, her dirty brown eyes watching. "Kyra, go help Cassandra finalise the circle."

Kyra dipped her head, the gesture out of necessity rather than respect. "Of course, High Priestess."

Adeline had just been promoted to the position, her predecessor having gone missing almost two years before. It wasn't a surprise. A lot of witches went missing from the coven. She suspected they hadn't simply disappeared, but she had no evidence. Not that she could do anything about it, not when Frederick was a law unto himself.

"Hurry now," Adeline added. If she had overheard the conversation, she didn't acknowledge it, not that Kyra expected her to. She was just as trapped, as were the other witches who made up the rest of the coven. Some enjoyed it, while others fought to be free. No one succeeded and lived.

There were always a minimum of four members at all times, never less. Four black witches or mages were needed for many of the incantations. Kyra was always called for the more difficult spells.

"I don't need any help," Cassandra snapped from her position by Earth. "Just get to your own position, Kyra." She tugged at her box braids, long enough they tangled by her ankles.

Kyra bit her lip, not surprised by the acerbic response. She stepped back, checking the markings on the floor anyway.

Witch magic was centred on the five elements, Earth, Fire, Water, Air and Spirit. However, black magic depicted the elements slightly differently than their earthen magic classifications. With normal magic, the elements were represented as various squiggly lines, while black were all different triangles. Earth, which was where Cassandra stood, was an inverted triangle with a horizontal line through the centre. Beside her was Faye, the teenager barely looking up from the floor. She represented Water, simply an inverted triangle with no line.

Opposite stood Saul, the only mage in the coven. That was strange enough. Mages were seen as inferior to the Magicka because they had no direct links to their chi, essentially humans with a recessive gene from a distant witch relative. Saul was in his thirties, at Kyra's guess, but she couldn't ask because he had no tongue, having cut it out to use for a spell before he was forced into the coven. It made him powerful, powerful enough that Frederick thought he deserved a place there despite his lack of chi. Saul stood for Fire, a triangle.

"Hurry up, Kyra!" Adeline said as she took her position at Air, the element a triangle with a horizontal line through the centre. "Get in your position, we're already behind schedule."

Kyra was the last element, Spirit. As the pentagram was inverted, she stood in the bottom circle, with Fire and Earth as the fixed points to her left and right, and Air and Water as the flow points opposite.

"You all know your roles." Frederick's voice was smooth as whisky as he handed Saul the first candle, the wick already lit. Saul held it tightly in his fist, not making a sound as the scalding wax hit his bare skin.

The next candle went to Cassandra, who hissed at the slight pain as she accepted hers.

"It's important we anchor the circle," Frederick continued, "we don't want to have an accident, do we?" A dark chuckle as he handed Faye the third candle. She still hadn't looked up from the floor, but Kyra noticed the tears that glistened on the young girl's cheeks.

"We shouldn't be doing this," Kyra whispered.

Bane, who'd stood silent by the door moved closer, but she ignored the Fae.

"You know I'm right," she said louder. "What do you think you will gain from summoning a Daemon?"

Frederick moved his attention to her, his smirk still in place. Without breaking eye contact, he handed Adeline the fourth candle before slowly making his way back to her. Spirit was the element that closed the circle, so Kyra was prepared for the last candle when Frederick handed it to her, and for the dagger that sliced across her left palm to leave a smear of blood.

The wax melted against her skin, hot enough to burn while the cut on her palm stung, blood pooling at the wound. She left it relaxed, lifting her hand so the blood dripped down her arm rather than onto the markings at her feet.

"Ignite it," he said, stepping back behind Bane who'd created an outer salt line. The salt acted as a barrier, protecting anyone who stood behind it from the magic within the circle. It left all five of them within the circle vulnerable, but only if they broke the connection once activated.

There had always been stories of horned creatures pulled straight from nightmares, who tricked those that summoned them with their lies and deceit. And most people lived their whole lives not believing that Daemons existed. Unfortunately, the stories were true, just not what was written in the human testaments. In reality they were a dark and cruel Breed, once forced to live in the darkness of Hell, but that had recently been found roaming the city of London freely.

She was about to summon one, and it wasn't even the first time.

"I said ignite it!"

Kyra waited until the vampire heart had been tossed into the pentagram before quickening her candle's flame with her blood. The connection was immediate, a dome made from all of their auras appearing around the central pentagram, but not around their individual circles.

The flames flickered, one by one like a heartbeat. Kyra felt it through her body, wave upon wave of noxious murk that wrapped around her like tightly wound vines as Adeline began the summoning. Her words were in Latin, a language Kyra was fluent in, yet she struggled to focus on the High Priestess's calls. All she could concentrate on was the pulse that vibrated up from between her feet, all the way through her body until it rattled her teeth.

The magic burned across Kyra's aura, the atmospheric film that surrounded every living being. The ability to harness her aura into a chi was what made her a witch. She kept her chi tight, the pain sucking her energy until she locked her knees to stop from falling. Each word spoken was like blades against her skin, and as the crescendo came, she knew that the sudden relief of the spell would only be fleeting.

The opaque dome was made up from shades of dark blues, purples, blacks and greys. The smudged appearance created by all four witches, plus Saul's auras, swirled together to form the protection shield. In normal circles, it would be them who stood inside. Except with a summoning it kept the one being summoned contained within. The only way to break it would be if one of them touched the dome, their aura rebounding back and breaking the connection.

Smoke began to fill the space, starting from the centre of the pentagram before engulfing up the sides to obscure the view.

A scream echoed, deep and full of such wrath that the walls began to tremble. "Who the fuck called me?!"

The smoke started to fade, allowing everyone to see the Daemon who stood, trapped amongst the glowing runes carved into the wooden floor. He was tall, around seven-foot with wide shoulders built to support the leather-like wings at his back.

"Who knows my name?!" he screeched again, his naked chest pumping violently. His skin was ashen grey, his irises red and full of a fire that blazed.

Kyra immediately dropped her eyes, not wanting to draw attention. It wasn't the first time she'd met a Daemon, or even worked with one, but that didn't mean she wanted to deal with a pissed off one.

It was Adeline who responded. "We don't know your name," she said in her strongest voice, the one Kyra referred to as her 'disappointed grandmother' voice. "We called out, and you were the closest –"

"Who the fuck are you, you little cun –"

"Daemon," Frederick interrupted, stepping in between Kyra and Saul to press closer to the dome. "I apologise for the abrupt disturbance to your day."

"Disturbance?" the Daemon echoed, the first hint of a smile touching his lips. "You call this a disturbance? What the fuck do you want, you little maggot?"

Faye let out a sob, loud enough that the Daemon turned his head towards her.

"Tell me your name," Frederick demanded. "I have a –"

"You," the Daemon grumbled towards Faye. "How have you summoned me without knowing my name?"

Faye's shoulders shook, the candle dropping slightly in her clutched palms.

"It was a generic summoning spell," Adeline replied instead, trying to control the situation. "It would summon any Daemon who happened to be within the required distance." It also meant they had no power over him, and he knew it.

"Did I ask you?" he snapped, his attention remaining on the young teenager.

Frederick clapped, the sound making Faye recoil, her hand gently shaking.

"It was I who summoned you," he said, voice like a whip. "So you answer to me."

The Daemon's shoulders trembled with laughter. "Do I now?" he asked, pressing his hand against the circle. Sparks burst, but the dome shaped itself around his palm, rather than repelling him like expected.

Faye's eyes widened, unable to look away from the hand that reached to touch her face, his nails long, black, and razor sharp.

"Stop it!" Kyra snapped. "Leave her alone!"

Frederick ignored her outburst, instead reaching over to wrap his hand in her braid. "An exchange," he began when the Daemon turned his head. "This witch for your knowledge."

Kyra sucked in a pained breath, almost dropping the candle that still flickered like a heartbeat.

The Daemon paused, his neck turning at an inhuman angle to get a better look. It began to crease, turning one-eighty degrees while his nostrils flared. His large horns, similar to a ram's, curled past his ears, growing until they touched his square jaw.

Kyra cried out, her head being pulled with such force her neck clicked. Power tingled her fingertips, her chi awakening but she couldn't risk fighting back, not with the circle so close.

The roar that echoed made even Frederick withdraw, and as Kyra gasped she knew it was too late. Faye jumped with a cry, her arm swinging and accidentally touching the dome. The circle fell with an audible pop, everyone's auras rebounding back like an elastic band. Faster than anyone could react the Daemon reached forward, his palm closing over Faye's face before she could even let out a scream.

A bone curling crunch, and then both the Daemon and Faye were gone in a burst of smoke.

The sudden silence was deafening.

Frederick let go of Kyra's braid, and her knees collapsed beneath her. She landed heavily, hands slapping against the wood to stop her fall.

"It seems we need to summon someone else to bargain with," Frederick said absently, wiping his hand against his jacket.

Everyone else remained still, all staring at the space where Faye once was.

The anger that Kyra felt earlier had gone, replaced with a hollow pain. She hadn't known the young witch well, but no one deserved to suffer like that.

Bane stepped forward, reaching for the vampire heart that lay untouched in the centre. Kyra had forgotten he was even there.

Frederick kneeled beside her, gently brushing the stray hairs from her face. "Don't worry, I wouldn't have actually allowed the Daemon to take you," he whispered before returning to his feet. "You're much too useful to me alive."

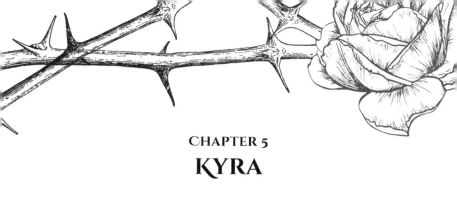

CHAPTER 5

KYRA

Kyra slowly climbed the stairs, body aching from the black magic that polluted her chi. It never lasted, fading over a few hours. Her aura worked to push out the poisonous Grimm, a physical materialisation of the magic. It was what made her different, the ability to process black magic without a lasting effect. The darkness and Grimm slowly ate away at the minds of others who used the same magic. Until they were nothing but a hollow shell devoid of everything that made them, them. It was one of the reasons familiars were first created, so black witches could push that effluence into their pets rather than take the cost. It was also why familiars were quickly made forbidden, because it wasn't just pets being used.

The queasiness had settled to a slight stomachache as she approached her building, the front door broken. Always broken.

Her flat was cheap, which meant it was small. There were no lifts, only the gruelling metal stairs that made such a racket, every step rattling down the halls to upset resting neighbours. Her knees protested, but she finally made it to the fifth floor, her place the furthest down the hall. The wallpaper was several decades out of date, and the carpet was an ugly green and mostly threadbare, but she couldn't complain. The landlord was friendly enough, and the flat itself was clean. But, most importantly was the natural light, with every room, except the bathroom, having a window. It was something she craved after being kept in a dark, airless room her whole childhood.

It was her little bit of freedom.

A screw you to those who had tried to keep her down.

Her phone buzzed just as she reached her front door.

'*Good luck tonight, not that you need it!*' Eva, her best friend, sending a million eggplant emojis along with a smiley face. '*Don't do anything I wouldn't do!*'

Kyra smiled down at the screen, typing a quick reply before opening her front door. '*It's a first date. Trust me, no eggplants tonight.*'

She'd barely had time to step inside before she felt the next vibration.

'*This is your first date in… forever! Ride that eggplant!*'

Laughing, Kyra set her keys on the side before lifting her rug to check the protection wards beneath. They'd worn, but they'd be fine. She carefully placed the rug back down to hide the damage and mentally made a note to redo them within the week. The magic was both complicated and simple, as were most wards. Complicated because it was temperamental. While the spell kept those who wanted to do her harm from crossing the threshold, it only worked if they had those intentions *before* they stepped over. If they decided *after* inviting themselves inside that they wanted to hurt her, the ward would do nothing but look pretty.

Heading to the bathroom, Kyra paused by the long mirror. Touching the bruise blossoming on her cheek, she traced her tongue over the cut on her lip. Marks on her skin weren't an uncommon sight, but they weren't something expected on a first date. Probably the reason why she didn't go on many first dates. Definitely not any seconds.

With a sigh, she turned on the shower until the water was hotter than Hell itself. A date was a nice distraction. Maybe she would treat herself to a couple of glasses of wine to help her forget, just for the night. Forget that she wasn't really free. That at any moment, she might have to do something that would go against everything she believed in.

XANDER

Xander paused when he found the correct door. He'd needed to convince Alice to give Kyra's address with some bullshit story about returning a lost purse. Alice hadn't believed him, especially when he couldn't show her the purse in question, but had given him the address anyway.

His knock seemed to jangle down the hallway, loud enough it made him cringe. It highlighted how cheap the wood was, the door thin enough he was sure he could punch through it with not much effort. There was magic there, a slight tingling against his chi as he stretched it out. A ward, he would guess, but nothing special. Nothing that would stop him if he was really determined.

The second knock was louder, his impatience darkening his mood as he lifted his fist for the third time. He had shit to do, and checking on the woman he didn't even like – a *friend* of the Guardians, apparently, – wasn't a priority. Especially after staying out of her fucking way for a year.

"Hello, I'm just –" Kyra stood in her ridiculously high heels, black boots that reached her knees, leaving only a slight flash of bare skin before the hem of her skirt started. "What... what are you doing here?" Her amber eyes brightened with surprise as she checked down the hall, noting he was alone. "Xander?"

His eyes skimmed across her face, one that contorted with confusion. There was no bruise, nor cut. He'd needed to make sure she was okay after the incident at the market, but clearly, he shouldn't have been concerned.

She probably sacrificed a cat or some shit, he thought. *Healed herself by taking another's life.*

Kyra waited with her hair neatly braided, in a black dress so tight it showed off every fucking curve and dip. Her sleeves were long, arms crossing in defence that only pushed her breasts up like some sort of fucking invitation.

"Why aren't you wearing the red?" he asked.

"Red?" she asked, her frown creating a delicate V between her brows.

Xander's eyes lingered a few seconds too long for his liking, sweeping along her skin until he noted the complexion charm nestled in the hollow of her throat. "Lipstick." So she hadn't sacrificed some poor kitty, she'd just used a pretty common glamour charm to hide her injuries.

Kyra blinked, the confusion shifting to annoyance. "I haven't worn that since –" A sound of frustration. "Look, I'm already late, so unless this is important..." She grabbed a small bag from behind her, waiting for him to step out of her way. When he did, she turned to close the door.

"Late?" Xander asked, unable to stop the question, curious at where she was going wearing *that.*

Why the fuck was he so curious all of a sudden?

Pursing her lips, Kyra flung her bag over her shoulder and made her way down the corridor. His long strides caught up in seconds, their silence awkward as they descended the squeaky stairs that surely had broken several safety regulations.

"What are you doing?" she asked when he continued to

walk with her, ignoring his car which was illegally parked outside her building.

What was he doing?

His eyes dipped to her dress again, at the expanse of thighs on show. "It's winter, you know."

A slight tightening of her shoulders, the wind catching the wisps of hair that framed her face. "Is there anything I can help you with?" she asked with a frustrated snap, the busy city glittering behind her. "Because I have a date, and I –"

"Wait, your date hasn't bothered to pick you up?" Xander stopped, and Kyra turned to glare, fire in her eyes that sent heat curling through his stomach. "Sorry, Princess, he sounds like an arsehole."

Xander knew she wanted to curse at him for the nickname, the defiance in the twitch of her lips. Was almost disappointed when she didn't.

A fight was something he needed. A fight was something he wanted. Better than finding his attention drifting down the slope of her slim, brown throat.

"Bye, Xander," she said, dismissing him without a second's glance. "It wasn't nice seeing you."

CHAPTER 6
KYRA

K eys clattered, Kyra's hand shaking slightly as she inserted hers into the lock. Of course her date had cancelled as soon as she'd arrived at the restaurant. The embarrassment of being stood up was lessened by the fact she hadn't had to sit alone at the table, waiting for a man who wouldn't turn up.

The front door swung open with little effort, and her heart clenched.

Kyra's flat was in shambles.

Her second-hand sofa had been overturned, the cushions ripped to pieces as stuffing left little clouds amongst the glittering glass. She wasn't sure what the glass originally was, but they were quickly forgotten when she noticed the note pinned to her fridge.

YOU FUCKING WHORE.
I CAN'T WAIT TO BREAK YOU IN MYSELF.
PREPARE TO BECOME MY LITTLE TOY.

Kyra stepped inside, her initial anger quickly turning to dread. The note was the least descriptive she'd received, but it had been left inside her home without any evidence of a break in. The large window in her open-plan home was still bolted from the inside, the runes undisturbed beneath her feet. The front door had been double locked, and undamaged, which meant whoever had entered her home had a key.

Broken shards crushing beneath her heels, Kyra ran towards her bedroom. The second ward she'd carved into the windowsill was intact. Her bed had been pulled apart, her sheets shredded, and the mattress sliced. Like they were looking for something hidden inside.

The syphon crystals she'd kept on the dresser were gone, as were the jewellery attachments.

"No, no, no!"

Her wardrobe was built into the wall, the mirrored door cracked. Pushing the clothes to one side, she reached up to the shelf she'd hidden with a plank of wood.

It wasn't there.

She was always prepared, the black duffel bag full of spare Ravyns, pound notes, a fake passport, as well as clothes in case she needed to leave quickly. It was her escape plan if things went wrong, and now she'd lost it.

"Please, no!" She reached on her tiptoes, searching in the space for anything left.

"Kyra, you home?" a familiar voice called from the hall. "That guy's a cock, so I've brought over –"

Kyra placed the wood back against the shelf, moving out of the bedroom just as Eva appeared at the threshold. "Hey," Kyra said, her voice hollow and on the edge of tears. "I'm sorry about the mess."

"Holy fucking shit! What happened?" Eva asked, stepping over the glass. She knocked the door closed with her hip, a takeaway bag crushed tightly to her chest. "Has this just happened? Have you called the police?"

"There's no point. I don't think anything's been stolen." Nothing she would admit to having, anyway. "They'll just give me a case number which will be filed somewhere, and then forgotten."

Eva narrowed her bright blue eyes, framed in thick lashes, and a little residue of glitter from work. "Who did that to your face?"

Kyra absently reached for the complexion charm around her neck, realising she must have knocked it off in her panic. There was a bruise on Eva's throat, the colour a painful purple and yellow. "Who did that to *your* neck?"

Eva pouted her naturally thick lips, painted a soft pink that brought out the rosy tones in her fair skin. "Here," she said, thrusting the warm bag at Kyra before carefully adjusting the sofa. The cushions were ruined, but enough stuffing remained that they wouldn't be sitting on the frame. "Lucas wouldn't take no for an answer," she said after moving to the kitchen, crouching to a lower cabinet to grab the dustpan and brush.

"He hurt you?" Kyra asked, having met Eva's boyfriend a few times. He was a vampire, one who liked control. She wasn't a fan and had made Eva very aware of it.

Eva didn't answer, but her silence was enough. She slowly swept up the broken glass, her golden-brown hair hiding her expression. "I sure pick them, don't I?" She laughed without humour, the usual sunshine overshadowed by frustration.

"Where's he now?"

Eva straightened, flicking her hair over her shoulder. "It doesn't matter, I dumped his arse as soon as he laid a hand on me. You were right." A dramatic eye-roll. "As you always are," she added with a grumble.

Kyra settled the bag in the corner. "I'm sorry."

"Don't be," Eva replied. "Now we can grow old together

and watch those terrible reality TV programmes you love so much. You may need to grow a penis though, I'll definitely miss that part of the relationship."

Kyra smiled, the easy conversation almost making her forget the note. Until she saw Eva stiffen, her hands clenching around the dustpan and brush. They had been close friends for years, having lived next door to one another for over half a decade. She could predict exactly what Eva's reaction would be.

"It's nothing," she explained. "Probably a prank."

Eva's eyes were furious when she turned. "How many threats is that now? And don't you dare lie to me. Just because I'm human doesn't mean I can't sniff out your bullshit," she said.

"It's nothing –"

"Kyra Farzan!" Eva let out an angered puff of air. "That's enough of your casual dismissal of this shit. You can move in with me until it's safe."

It wasn't the first time she'd asked, and it probably wouldn't be the last. "I can't just run from this."

"Has this –" Eva gestured wildly to the mess, "– got anything to do with your lip?"

Kyra shook her head, even the small movement hurting. "No, that was just a misunderstanding at the market."

"Misunderstanding?" Eva parroted. "Are they dead?"

"Eva!"

"Do you want them to be?" she continued, trying to keep a straight face. "Kyra, this has gone too far. If you won't call the police, you need to hire someone to investigate the threats at the very least." She bit her lip, eyes swinging back to the note. "Maybe we can hire a paladin? They deal with this sort of thing, right?"

"With what money?" Kyra wasn't sure how much hiring someone from the Supernatural Intelligence Bureau would be, but she knew she couldn't risk them investigating without the chance of Frederick finding out. She'd already asked for his assistance, and he'd laughed off her concern. If he found out she'd sought help somewhere else... She had enough to deal with without Frederick's anger.

"I have some savings since I've been doing double shifts, and I'll find the rest if it's more. It doesn't matter," Eva said, carefully placing the glass she'd collected on the counter. "You're worrying me. I know you're a dark witch and can defend yourself, but there are so many crazy people out there."

Kyra knew she was right. The threats were nothing when they were just pieces of paper, but first someone had sent her a severed finger, and now they'd entered her home.

"I can't hire a S.I. paladin, not when I've worked so hard to build relationships at The Tower." It wasn't technically a lie. Black witches didn't get hired because of fear of repercussions. "And we definitely can't hire someone private."

She'd been able to convince the commissioner to take her on as a specialist, one that paid more than the other jobs she'd been forced to take over the years to survive. She could conceal her chi and pretend she was an earth witch, but even humans could tell she was different.

"I'll sort it, don't worry," she continued, her smile forced. "I promise."

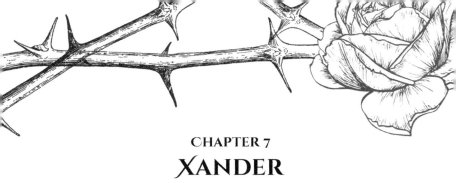

CHAPTER 7
XANDER

Xander inhaled, savouring the smoke before exhaling it out his nose. He dropped his eyes to the ground, the cobbled stone dark and wet beneath his thick, leather boots.

"Freshy?" Axel's joint glowed a bright orange at the tip. It reeked of ashroot, the weed one of the stronger brands.

Xander nodded, not wanting to vocalise the spirit's existence. The newly dead liked to stick around, moving in familiar circuits until they eventually faded, or walked into the white light. At least, he assumed it was white. He'd never seen it for himself.

"That sucks." He stubbed the joint out on the wall before balling it up in his palm. "You not figured out a repellent yet?"

Xander remained silent, his mind racing with images of a black witch with bronzed brown skin and enchanting dark amber eyes. *A fucking date.* How could she get dates when all he had was his hand?

Sythe grunted, his knee bent with his foot flat against the wall behind him. "You guys done? I'm bored."

"Then go back inside," Xander said, trying to rid the

thoughts of a certain witch. "We're not keeping you out here."

Sythe took out a small dagger and began spinning it in the air. "Riley and Alice are dancing." The music from The Blood Bar echoed, quieter through the closed door.

Axel chuckled. "You're just jealous."

"Don't lie, and say you're not," Sythe grumbled.

Xander laughed, unable to control the hollow sound. They were all jealous, so much so it physically hurt to see the love and affection that was once out of their reach.

As children they were warned that strong emotions could force them to shift. Each time they did, they would lose a part of themselves to their beasts. It was something they'd accepted a long time ago, that they could never love. The inevitable was that if they allowed themselves to get lost in emotions, one day, they wouldn't come back from a shift. They would be monsters forever.

Except that knowledge had been twisted to control them. The truth was arguably worse. They *could* shift without repercussions, find their soulmate, and fall in love just as their leader, Riley had. But it was no longer their own beasts they feared.

Because now there was a time limit, and if they couldn't find their soulmates within their first one-hundred years, they would still become monsters permanently. Except they would be forced down to the Nether realm, to be slaves to the same man who'd cursed them.

Bind themselves to someone, or live for eternity down in Hell.

Either way, it was bullshit.

All the Guardians were so happy that Riley had found the person who made his heart beat, but it was still something that the rest of them needed to adjust to. The idea of being soulbound, mated to another person, was terrifying when they were already bound to their beasts. Yet, Riley had risked everything for his mate.

"Fuck off, all of you," Sythe muttered, his lip lifted into a snarl. "You're all a bunch of –" His eyes widened.

Xander felt the same ripple of awareness across his chi.

"Bloody hell!" Axel shouted, head swinging towards the mouth of the alley. "Is that what I think it is?"

Xander moved before the thought even registered, his instincts taking him towards the quiet late-night road. Headlights flared, only for a brief second before the car passed further into the city, but it was enough to illuminate the woman who stood across the street.

"Xee, you see that?" Sythe said, coming to a stop beside him.

"What the fuck?" Axel cursed.

All three of them stared across the short distance to the old woman. She was barely five-foot, her well-worn walking stick forgotten at her feet as she stood at an awkward angle, her left foot bent, broken. She seemed to be waiting.

"She's... not right," he continued.

Xee frowned, the awareness of the Shadow-Veyn like sharp prickles across his senses. A shadow, not created by the streetlights circled around her, rolling up from the pavement like a darkened wave. Solidifying into a rat-like creature, smoke drifted from its nostrils. Bone was exposed through its black fur, skull and ribs a splash of white.

Shadow-Veyn were nightmarish creatures not from their realm. They were wild in nature, attacking and feeding just as any animal would, but they could also be heavily influenced by Daemons, such as the one who currently used the woman as a puppet.

"Isn't this the third possession this month?" Sythe asked, fist gripped around his small blade. "You would think the

50

fuckers would stop with this creepy shit now that they're technically free."

The older woman rolled her shoulders, the click, click, click of her bones loud enough to carry across the distance. Her shawl looked hand-knitted, not that any of them had any experience with knitted garments. It hung loosely from her arm, exposing the floral shirt beneath, barely thick enough to protect her from the bitter wind that whipped at her neatly pinned white hair. She made no move towards them, but nor did she move away as the rat sunk back into the pavement.

"Leave it," Xander said as the Shadow-Veyn shot in the opposite direction. The rat was a classification A, the least dangerous of all the creatures that had escaped their prison from the Nether. It wasn't worth their time compared to the woman. Rats, named because of their long tails and snouts, were scavengers and spies compared to the hounds who hunted and feasted on the general populace. The increase of disappearances was nothing in a city of millions, but the authorities were going to notice soon enough when more corpses turned up, torn to shreds and pumped full of venom.

"Let her go," Xander demanded as he slowly approached, his brothers tight on his heels. He had no weapons, but that didn't mean he was unprepared. The Guardians were trained in killing Daemons, it was the sole reason of their existence, the reason for their curse.

As children, they were forced to receive their beasts, sharing their soul with a monster not too different from the Shadow-Veyn they were trained to slaughter. It made them stronger, faster, and more resilient to wounds that would usually kill a man. Which was fucking great considering Daemons were aggressive bastards capable of destroying someone with their magic alone.

A laugh echoed, the sound deep, disturbing coming from such a frail old woman. "Or what?" the voice asked, although her mouth didn't move with the words. She seemed to wheeze when she turned, bone at her ankle piercing through her delicate flesh as she ran. It didn't slow her down, her movements almost blurred as she disappeared along one of the many dark alleys that interconnected through that part of the city.

Xander chased after her, moving in powerful strides as he followed at a similar speed. Blood spotted the pavement, easy enough to track.

"Fuck off!" the voice barked from the darkness.

Xander turned at the last minute, the ball of arcane burning across his chi only an inch from his face. The sting was sharp, short, but enough to piss him off. At least they knew the puppet was a witch. Information that may, or may not have helped.

"Easy Xee," Axel said as he dodged past. "You know she isn't worth the cost."

His beast stirred, the pressure to shift and take the woman down increasing. But the woman wasn't a Daemon, she was just a shell. "Hit high," he said back, his voice deepening as his beast fought for control in his mind.

A burst of light, followed by a feminine scream. Xander followed the sound, jumping through the open window into a bright kitchen. He squinted his eyes as he followed the shocked family's pointed fingers towards the hall. A frying pan appeared in his vision, his reflexes able to twist out the way, the pan swinging above his head as the woman screamed obscenities at his back.

The front door hung off its hinges, Sythe running past from a different direction.

"Frying pan?" he asked once Xander had closed the distance.

Xander grunted. "It's always the fucking frying pan."

"Nah," Sythe laughed, following the blood splats towards the front entrance. "Last month I got a rolling pin to the head. Hurt like a bitch."

"Everyone's so grateful," Xander muttered as they found the trail on the opposite building, blood smeared up the side of the brick, the wetness glistening against the moonlight.

"What is she, a fucking spider?" Sythe sighed, scanning the quiet residential street. "What the fuck did she even grip?"

Xander touched the blood, the temperature surprisingly hot against his fingertips. "I didn't sign up for this shit."

Sythe rocked back on his heels, the tattoos that decorated both his arms glowing. "Wait, you signed up for this? Because I sure as hell didn't."

They circled around the building, trying to find an entrance. The front had been boarded up, the name of the developer obscured by graffiti.

"Hey, this guy has some serious talent," Sythe said as he tested the boards at the door, gesturing to the graffiti. "Look at the veins along the shaft, and the detail in the tip. Honestly, the artist is wasting their talent."

The boards would easily budge, but not without making a lot of noise, which was something they couldn't risk in a sleeping residential area. All they needed was a civilian to get caught up in the chase, and then they wouldn't have any choice but to take out the innocent old woman who happened to be in the wrong place, at the wrong time.

"Shut it, and find a way up," Xander said quietly. "Axel's probably already up there while we're discussing the details of a bright green dick."

"You should appreciate the *art*," Sythe muttered as he

knelt onto one knee, his hands cupped in front of him. "You wanted a way up, your highness."

Xander followed Sythe's eyeline, realising there was scaffolding a few floors up that lead to the roof. The metal frame looked sturdy, strong enough to support him.

"Ready?" Without waiting for an answer he ran, trusting his brother to brace himself. He hit perfectly in the centre of Sythe's hands, the upward momentum launching him high enough that he could swing onto the platform.

"Don't worry about me," Sythe mumbled. "I'll just wait down here like a good boy."

Xander ignored the comment, climbing the scaffolding quickly. The building wasn't tall, at only five or so floors, but the wind was ravenous as it battered against him at every turn. Cursing, he pushed his hair away from his eyes, his ability to see in the dark better than any of the other Guardians. Hands hooking onto the flat roof he pulled himself up, finding Axel only meters from the old woman. Her smile spread from cheek to cheek, so wide that it looked like the skin was ready to split.

"How nice of you to join us," she said in a strangely masculine voice. A puppet with a hidden ventriloquist. Her foot was gone, a bloody stump remaining while the tips of her fingers were red raw. Her head was cocked, compensating for the length of the missing limb.

"What do you think Xee?" Axel asked, never taking his eyes from the threat. "They want us to choose the darkness."

"Now, why would we do that?" Xander said as he joined Sythe, arcane burning his palms. Raw power, a physical manifestation of his chi. "I don't think growing bat wings, and being forcibly summoned sounds like a good time to me."

"Immorality, and power beyond your imagination," the

woman snapped, throat unmoving as her eyes brightened until they were as red as her fingers. "You could join us in the uprising, a new era."

The arcane burned up to Xander's elbows, bursts of green, blue and white that was untouched by the wind. "What uprising?"

The woman's smile widened impossibly further, her once white teeth covered in a black tar. "We have been imprisoned long enough down in the dark. Now we're up here in the light, it's our time to rule. Join us, or burn to ash along with everyone who resists."

"Yeah, we have our own shit to deal with," Axel said. "So it's a hard pass."

The cackle that erupted from the woman was wet, the black tar leaking from her lips to drip onto the roof. She took a step back, the crunch of bone uncomfortable. "Then you've chosen your fate."

Lifting her arms like wings she thrust herself back, and thudded to the hard pavement five floors below.

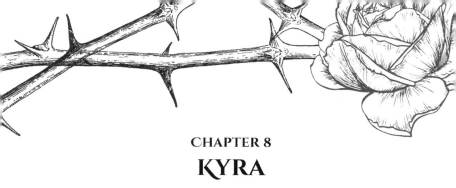

CHAPTER 8
KYRA

"Your locks still haven't been changed," Eva said, tapping her nail against the side of her steaming mug. "I know, because I checked if that little scratch was still there. You know, from that time you were blackout drunk."

"I wasn't drunk." Kyra winced, hiding it behind her own drink. It had been the first time she'd ever indulged in alcohol, now knowing her limit. Being drunk wasn't something she had any interest in repeating, not when she'd spent the next day decorating her bathroom.

"You so were," Eva sniffed, adjusting the straps of her dress. "You couldn't get the key in the hole."

"The key slipped," Kyra continued, tugging her braid. "Anyway, I've told Mr Meylor, but he hasn't gotten back to me yet."

Eva's gaze sharpened. "You know Mr Meylor takes three to five working days to reply to a bloody text. This is serious, Kyra. It's been two days. Who knows whether the creep will come back or not?" She reached for her bag, pulling out her phone. "Look, I'll sort it out right now for you."

"Eva, it was a joke. Of course I've called a locksmith, they're supposed to be here later today."

Eva stared, her upper lip twitching. "You're going to give me a heart attack. Remember I can die from stress, you know!"

"Witches can die from heart attacks too."

"Yeah, but you can use your woo woo magic." Eva wiggled her fingers with a giggle. "Remember you're always welcome to stay with me."

Kyra cradled her mug closer to her face, her smile disguised behind the hot mocha. "The locks will be changed by tonight, I promise."

"I'm not even joking, if those locks haven't been changed by tomorrow, I'm moving your stuff into mine, whether you like it or not," she warned.

Kyra reached across the table to squeeze Eva's hand. She hated the fact she felt unsafe in the one place that was supposed to be hers. She had redone all the wards, and barricaded the front door the night before. Yet she hadn't slept. Couldn't without worry coursing through her thoughts.

In any other situation she would have taken Eva's invite, but she could never risk her friend. It wasn't just because of the threats, although that didn't help. It was because if her secret was ever revealed to the wrong people, those closest to her would be in danger.

"Do you have time for another coffee before your job?" Eva asked.

Kyra checked the time, knowing she had over an hour before she was required at the cemetery. "Don't you have to get back to work yourself?" Eva had taken her lunch break to sit with her, and Kyra was sure her time was almost up. She rarely worked during the day, but Eva had explained she was training a new dancer.

"I have time for one more," Eva said, winking as she made her way towards the barista at the bar.

Kyra finished her drink, savouring the last drops.

"She's cute," a male voice said from behind. "A friend?"

Kyra dropped the mug, ignoring the crack it made against the wooden table. Bane took Eva's seat, a leather-bound diary held tightly to his chest. He looked like any other generic human, with dirty brown hair, cut relatively short to his ears, and matching brown eyes. His face was round, cheeks full with undefined cheekbones, and a strong brow. His nose was slim, but otherwise ordinary. Forgettable.

"I don't have any friends," Kyra replied, keeping her voice low. "What do you want?"

"Well, clearly you have friends," he replied with a professional smile. "Otherwise why would she be spending time with you?"

"She's nothing, just my –"

"Your neighbour," he interrupted, his eye contact unblinking. "Eva Morgan, twenty-five from a small town in Kent. Both parents are deceased, a car crash when she was sixteen, and she has no siblings. She's a dancer over at The Dollhouse." He turned towards the bar. "I wonder if she offers extras? I guess there's one way to find out."

Kyra froze, pulse a heavy thrum inside her head.

"Your landlord, Mr Gary Meylor is fifty-three –"

"Stop," Kyra breathed out in a whisper, her stomach clenching. "Eva's just my neighbour, we talk sometimes, but that's it. She doesn't know anything, I swear."

"This isn't about her," Bane said, turning back to face her completely. "This is about you. Councillor Gallagher's made note that you seem to be more disobedient than usual, questioning his decisions in front of the coven."

"I didn't –"

"Do not interrupt me." Bane lifted his hand, his lips pressed into a thin line. "You seem to forget who allows you your freedom."

Kyra waited a beat before replying, sweeping her gaze to Eva then back again. "He doesn't let me forget."

Bane nodded, setting the diary onto the table. "You have a meeting, I'm here to make sure you attend."

"I'm not aware of any meeting."

Bane opened the diary, pointing to the date. "You would know if you'd answered my call this morning. Councilman Gallagher is very displeased at your lack of communication."

Kyra shuffled in her seat, hoping Eva was still distracted. "My phone died," she lied. "Frederick knows I work with the Supernatural Intelligence Bureau, I've been called on a case."

"Then reschedule. This takes priority." The diary slammed shut. "He's requested you speak to an old colleague of his. Apparently she'll be able to advise you regarding the most recent... event."

"I can't," she said, her voice breaking. "Please, I can't do that again."

Bane's face hardened, his somewhat friendly smile turning cruel. "Your reluctance has also been noted, but we both know that's not an option," he said as he leaned forward with his brows pulled together. "Why would you risk losing your license by disobeying?"

"Please," she whispered. "It's dangerous, it'll get us all killed."

"What will happen, Kyra?" he said, emphasising her name. "What will happen if Frederick takes away your licence to practice?"

Kyra nibbled her lip, aware of the busy coffee shop that surrounded her. "I'll become illegal." She would lose everything. She couldn't even pretend she didn't practice dark magic, because it was imbedded into her very existence. It wasn't something she could control. She, along with every other witch born with the specialised chi were marked for death at their very birth.

Bane nodded, settling himself back in the chair. "I've been able to speak to Frederick on your behalf. While I appreciate your worry over these letters, I must remind you that you still must assist when asked, regardless of personal problems. I'm sure you don't need me to stress the importance of your tasks, and the time constraint that we're under."

His attention moved over her shoulder, then quickly returned.

"Frederick understands, and because of your position in our operation he's asked me to look into moving you into a protected area. Somewhere closer to him, where you can feel safe and secure."

"No!" Kyra replied, the word coming out louder than expected. "No, it's fine, I'm sorry. He was right, I'm sure it was nothing."

Bane's pupils swirled, and Kyra could taste the wild magic that leaked from him. "You could achieve amazing things with your natural born ability. Councilman Gallagher only wants to help you."

No, he only wants to use me.

"Kyra?" Eva walked over, a tray with their drinks held in her hands. Her frown settled on Bane. "You're in my seat."

"Hello," he said, his pupils settling back to normal before sliding his attention to Eva. "You must be Kyra's friend."

"Please, don't," Kyra whispered.

"Human, right? So breakable," he continued, the

warning clear. "Tell me, would you like to join us for Kyra's appointment?"

"No!" Kyra said, making sure to make enough noise to draw the attention from the surrounding tables. "No, I'll come, I'm sorry." She reached down for her satchel, hitching it high on her shoulder.

"Wait, what's happening?" Eva settled the tray down, following them out into the street with a determination that made most men hesitate. "Who is this guy?"

Kyra held out her hand, panic seizing her throat. "Please," she begged, her voice a rough rasp. "Just... go back inside. Trust me."

"Look at the time, we're going to be late," Bane moaned with impatience. "Councilman Gallagher would be most displeased."

"I said I'm coming," Kyra said, darting her eyes between them. "Let me just call a cab, and we can get going."

"Oh, I know that you are," Bane said before returning his attention to Eva. "And so is your friend." He reached over, gripping the top of Eva's arm tightly. "You wouldn't want Kyra to be punished for not obeying, do you?"

"Please, leave her out of this," Kyra hissed. "I'll do anything you want."

"You'll do that anyway," he said, head snapping back to her. "But this way will make you more agreeable."

———

Eva pulled up on the kerb beside a flower shop, the entrance a welcoming paradise. Large green plants and seasonal flowers created an enticing arch while baskets hung from the upper floor, large enough to shadow the pavement below.

"Deadly Petal, this is the place," Bane said, opening the car door. "Come on, get out."

Kyra immediately followed, checking out the ordinary florist's shop. "Who am I meeting?"

Bane ignored her question, instead turning to knock his fist against the top of Eva's car.

"She can stay here," Kyra said. "We won't be long."

"Are we really going to do this the hard way?" Bane asked. "I'm starting to lose patience."

Eva calmly climbed out of the car, anger evident in the lines of her body. "Touch my dad's car again and I'll cut your hand off," she warned.

Bane paused, a smile slowly creeping across his face. "For such a pretty bauble, you have some fire. I wonder how long it'll last before you break?"

Kyra tugged Eva's hand, wanting her away from Bane. His gaze turned predatory as he followed them through the door. The inside of the florist's shop was just as green and colourful as outside, with every inch of the shop covered in plants, flowers, and everything related to horticulture.

The assistant at the desk glanced up from the register, eyebrow raised before he walked them towards the back of the shop. The blossoms darkened, becoming more carnivorous the further they went. Venus flytraps, monkey cups and even butterworts took over the space, along with foxgloves and monkshoods.

"Don't touch anything," Kyra whispered as Eva took an interest in a large white plant that looked suspiciously like hemlock.

"Through here," the assistant said, expression bored. "My grandmother said only one may go up." He flared his chi, a common greeting amongst witches, except Kyra suspected he wanted to feel their auras.

She met his eyes, his chi dark, as toxic as the plants they

grew. He was a practicing black witch, just not a very powerful one.

"Don't worry, my friend and I will stay downstairs," Bane said as he pressed open the door, his hand snaking out to encircle Eva's arm.

Eva turned rigid, but she walked after Bane with Kyra tight on her heels. There were more dangerous plants growing in the back room, two walls covered in pots. Oleander,

snakeroot, as well as deadly nightshade, the berries already darkened to black and collected in glass jars on the table in the centre.

An old leather sofa was pushed against the back, well used and worn with a wooden box sat beside it, full of unlabelled vials and potions.

A man at the table looked up from the vial in his palm, his smile wide enough to reveal his large, pale fangs. "Why, hello there," he purred, getting up. "Care to join me for a taste?"

"They're here for grandmother," the assistant said, closing the door behind him. "Why don't you entertain these two while I show our guest up to her room?"

"With pleasure," the vampire sniggered. "I'm sure we'll find something interesting to do."

"Go," Eva whispered when Kyra looked in her direction. "I'll be fine."

Kyra paused, stomach twisted. "I won't be long."

The stairs creaked beneath her boots, old and wooden with unfamiliar symbols carved into each step. The assistant stopped after ascending two floors, the door at the top partially open.

"My grandmother's expecting you," he said before producing a china cup. Handing it over to Kyra before he turned and descended.

She stared at the tea, the cup hot in her palms before gently pushing the door all the way open.

"Place it on this nightstand, dear," the old woman said, sitting, waiting in the pink and blue paisley armchair in the corner. "That's it, right there." She gestured beside her, a lit cigarette held between two fingers.

Kyra quickly complied, carefully stepping over the pile of rugs to settle the tea down. Candles brightened the bedroom, large candelabras lit with dancing flames that cast random shadows along the ceiling. The only furniture other than the armchair was the oversized bed, covered in luscious fabrics of every shade, and the single writing desk.

"You must be Kyra Farzan."

"Yes —"

"Well, speak up girl!" She slapped an open palm on the armrest, causing Kyra to flinch. "Frederick has asked me to speak to you regarding your recent summoning."

Kyra studied the grimoires that piled high beside the armchair. "One of the elements broke the circle, it was nothing but an accident."

"There is no such things as accidents in our world, child. That young witch was a disappointment, and deserved her punishment."

Kyra tightened her fists, meeting the gaze of the old woman. Her face was covered in a lifetime of wrinkles and liver spots, her age unclear when witches were able to live far older than a human lifespan.

Her eyes were a dark blue, once beautiful, but now contaminated with specks of black. Her left eye was partially cloudy, a cataract obscuring her vision. Her lips had thinned, barely a curve, and she had a single tooth in the centre of her upper jaw.

"Sit down!" she barked, the order automatically dropping Kyra to her knees. She settled on the rugs, clenching her hands harder to stop from shaking. "You're already broken, child," the old woman scoffed before taking a long drag on her cigarette. "How amusing."

She let out a long exhale, blowing the sour smelling smoke into Kyra's face before erupting into a chest compressing cough.

"What's the advice?" Kyra asked, wanting to get out of there quickly. The longer she kneeled, the more she felt the murk seeping up through the floorboards like a thick tar over her senses. The magic polluted her lungs, burning her throat with every breath, along with the smoke that Kyra was sure wasn't just tobacco.

The old woman continued to cough, bony body fragile. With a wheeze she spat into a tissue from her sleeve, the phlegm black. "My name's Matilda, but you may call me Grandmother."

"What's the advice?" Kyra simply repeated.

"What happens if you ingest atropa belladonna berries?" she asked, stabbing the cigarette out in her palm.

Kyra blinked, confused by the question. "Excuse me?"

"Answer, child."

"They're poisonous. Deadly nightshade can affect the nervous system and result in vomiting, confusion, breathing difficulties as well as death. Shifters are unable to digest them, resulting in paralysis and certain death if eaten in their animal form."

"And what about digitalis purpurea?"

"Why are you asking –?"

"Answer the question!" Matilda snapped with an impatient rumble.

A moment skipped by before Kyra answered, her heart a rabbit in her chest. "The whole plant is poisonous," she quietly replied. "Fox glove can cause skin irritation, nausea, and diarrhoea. Vampires seem to be extra susceptible."

"Ah, it's hard to secretly poison someone when there's skin irritation," Matilda said with a smirk, settling back into her chair. "Hemlock is the classic choice, but you already knew that, didn't you?"

Kyra stilled, not even taking a breath.

"Tell me about the conium maculatum." Matilda reached for her tea, the water sloshing as her hand trembled at the weight. "Now, child!"

The bark forced Kyra out of her stasis. "Ingestion of a small amount of hemlock can cause respiratory paralysis –"

"And death."

Kyra nodded. "And death."

"Hmmm." The teacup rattled as she set it back down. "Your knowledge is impressive, you're definitely your father's daughter."

Kyra ignored the coldness that settled in her stomach at the mention of her father. "What was the advice for the summoning? I don't have much time, and have no interest in discussing anything else."

"Be calm, child. It was a comment out of respect for your powerful lineage. Farzan isn't a name I've heard in a long time." Matilda shuffled forward in her chair, frail hands clasped together. "You may think we're different, but I can assure you we're more similar than you realise."

I highly doubt that, Kyra thought.

"You're his new pet. One on a tight leash if I go by what my grandson's said regarding your chaperone."

"What has this got to do with anything? Why has Frederick sent me here?"

"As a warning, I'm sure." Matilda grinned. "But I do still have the best knowledge in summoning."

"We used a pentagram with five concentrated points for the elements. The circle was strong. I quickened it myself." Her blood was strong, but that frustratingly didn't reflect in her magic. She was weak compared to many of the coven, and even less compared to Frederick.

She couldn't defend herself with her chi, not without making herself vulnerable. Arcane was the main offensive ability to a witch, and Kyra was unable to make anything more powerful that a ball the size of her fist. No, her abilities laid elsewhere.

"The witch who touched the shield was weak, which was why it fell. But even then I've been informed a generic summoning circle was used, which is dangerous when you haven't got the Daemon's name." Matilda seemed lost in thought. "I'm not surprised Frederick wasn't personally involved, he would have placed himself behind a protection line."

Kyra clenched her jaw, her childhood memories of her parents summoning Daemons hazy. She knew it was a risk, but everything involving Daemons was. "Then what's your suggestion?"

"You're going to have to use the ten elements." Matilda slowly reached for one of the grimoires, a page already dog-eared. "I designed this circle myself fifty years or so ago, it's strong and will withstand even an accidental rebound." She ripped the page.

Kyra accepted the paper she held out, her fingertips touching the drawing. It was more complicated than a normal circle, with five overlapping circles as well as an inverted pentagram in the centre. The elements Spirit, Fire, Earth, Water, and Air were as they should be, but in between the overlapping circles were five other elements Kyra had never used. Ice, Thunder, Light, Ore, and Shadow.

"The Daemon will be summoned into the centre pentagon, and the combined elements will trap him there until *you're* ready to send him back. It gives you back the control without their name."

Kyra carefully folded the paper, keeping it safe inside her palm.

Matilda carefully pulled herself off the chair, dropping to her knees in front of Kyra. "It wasn't just my design that Frederick sent you here for, my child. Flare your chi."

Kyra sat back on her heels, pulling her arms back. Matilda's hand had already shot out like a viper, gripping her wrist in a surprisingly strong iron grip.

"Flare your chi," she repeated, her nail pressed against the pulse on Kyra's wrist. She added a little pressure, enough to hurt, but not enough to break skin. "Do it, child."

Kyra ignored the urge to pull back again, knowing if she did the nail would pierce her skin. Flaring out her chi, she prepared herself to meet Matilda's, and was surprised when she felt... nothing.

Cold spread through her veins at the contact, her chi searching for the connection of the other witch and finding nothing but a bottomless void. Matilda had had her very spirit removed. The ability to harness her aura into a chi, and her magic stripped. It supposedly took something away from you, a punishment more cruel than death for any Breed who bore magic.

"Don't underestimate Frederick, Kyra," Matilda warned. "He's only out for himself, and you're nothing but a tool in his arsenal. Once you're no longer useful, you'll be discarded, just like I was."

CHAPTER 9
KYRA

Kyra rushed down the stairs, Matilda's chuckle resonating behind her. She needed to get out of there, the filth of the black magic seeping into her pores. Bane was nowhere to be seen as she entered the back room, while Eva sat stiffly on the old, worn sofa with the vampire beside her.

Eva immediately looked up, panic and something else pleading from her widened eyes. Blood splattered her collar, as well as the threads on her jumper. The vampire's hand rested just above her knee, his face turned towards her throat with his lips by her ear.

"What's your name?" Kyra asked, anger and frustration making her words sharp. "Fang face, I asked you a question."

The vampire hissed, but turned his attention to her. "Fuck off, bitch, I'm talking to your friend here."

Eva remained frozen beneath his palm. "Levi," she said, voice quivering. "His name's Levi."

"Shhhh," Levi whispered, "It's just me and you here, precious."

Kyra flared out her chi once more, exactly the same way

she would have if she was checking out another witch's aura. Except, this time she pushed it further, harder until it was almost a metaphysical blade puncturing into him. Silent and undetectable as her power tasted, learned.

"You died at thirty-two years old," she said, her tone deepening as she called on the darker side of her magic, the side she tried to hide, to suppress. "Undead for one-hundred and five."

Levi released his grip on Eva, turning mechanically to glare at Kyra. Eva jumped up, and before Levi could grab her she sent violent pulses through his legs, causing them to spasm.

"What are you doing to me?!"

"You're weak," she continued, "which is probably why you're assisting a black witch. Tell me, are you out on loan from your Master? Because you're not strong enough to be your own."

Levi hissed, fangs elongated until he struggled to close his jaws. "Fuck you!"

Kyra sucked in a breath, nausea bubbling. "Eva, you okay?"

Eva hovered by the door to the shop floor, arms wrapped around herself. "Fine once we get out of this shit hole." Her expression tightened, anger creasing her face.

"You wanted it, don't give me that shit!" Levi barked.

"I bet you've never met anyone like me," Kyra said, stepping forward until Eva stopped her with a hand on her shoulder. She tried to strangle this part of her power, using the syphon crystal against her arm to dampen the connection. But, if she concentrated, she could still feel the blood pump through his body. Vamps could survive without breathing for much longer than others, and their hearts did in fact beat at a very slow pace, almost silent. Kyra could make it beat so fast blood would leak from his eyes.

She couldn't explain why, or how. The power just something else she was slowly discovering about herself.

"She's just a blood whore."

Kyra couldn't help herself. Ignoring the growing queasiness, she focused on him, able to feel his blood as if it were a pulsating stream across her fingertips. Ever so slightly she increased the pressure, just enough that Levi clutched his chest in panic.

"Stop!" he gasped. "Stop! What are you doing!?"

Kyra increased the pressure just a little more, nothing that would leave him with any long-term effects. Just enough to give just a taste of what she could do. He didn't know she would never have taken it further.

"Please, I'm sorry, okay? She's been marked as a blood junkie, so I thought she was fair game."

Kyra released the pressure. "Blood junkie?"

Levi collapsed onto the sofa. "She must have been bitten recently," he choked out. "Someone old marked her with a special venom. It gives a scent, marking her as easy and willing prey."

Eva touched her throat, the bruise hidden beneath the turtleneck she wore. "How do you stop it?" she asked.

Levi heaved in a breath. "It will disappear once it's out your bloodstream, as long as the owner doesn't top it up."

Eva stormed through the shop, Kyra following quickly behind. Bane stood by the front window, looking out into the street at the passing walkers. He turned just as they arrived, head snapping to the side when Eva lifted her fist and punched him square in the jaw. Without a word she slipped into the driving seat of her car.

Bane touched his lip, blood a pearl on his fingertip.

"We're done here," Kyra said, stepping in between Bane and the car. "I have the details."

Anger radiated off him in waves, wild magic teasing her skin with little pricks of power.

Kyra choked down bile, her body repelling the Grimm from the black magic before it settled into her cells, darkening her aura. The vampire deserved it, but that didn't mean she wouldn't feel the negative affect for hours.

"Here, take it." She pushed the page against his chest. "You don't want to keep Frederick waiting, do you?"

The fresh evening air helped with the sickness, even if the wind was like being kissed with death at that height. Kyra wrapped her arms around her legs, watching the sun as it set in the distance between the towering skyscrapers. It was possible from the flat design amongst the slope of the roof it was indeed a communal garden in which she sat. Not that she'd ever asked the landlord. It didn't really matter, not when she could watch the city dance with lights whenever she pleased.

It was a shame, the space must have once been taken care of, once loved if she went by the rusty, broken garden equipment scattered around. But they were now long forgotten, the plants withered to virtually dust, and the pots cracked beyond repair.

No one else seemed to enjoy the view, the fence eroded enough she doubted it would survive much weight if tested.

It was a space to relax beneath the sky, to remind herself she was alive. No longer locked away. It was a space to be alone, to think. To cry and sulk without having to be anyone she didn't want to be. It was –

The door squeaked open, the light from the hall bleeding onto the concrete.

Kyra shot to her feet, her arm held up in warning. Her

heart raced, a thump, thump, thump in her chest that told her she wasn't alone.

"Hello? Is anyone there?"

There was no warning as she felt icy fingers wrap around her throat. She flung herself backwards, knocking against something hard, something so cold it made the air around her a blistering summer's day. She clawed at the fingers, and still there was no noise. No footsteps or breathing other than her own ragged breaths as she fought the constriction slowly tightening.

She stopped attacking the restraint, sagging in the grip, relaxing until those fingers let up just a little.

"Incenduro!" Her hand reached behind, and with the last bit of air she screamed the only aggressive spell she knew. Her small burst of arcane burned to her palm, controlled and mildly powerful as she shoved everything she could into the extension of her chi. It burned like fire, but hotter as she pressed it to whoever held her.

A high-pitched screech, the fingers releasing her completely. Kyra threw herself to the side, sucking in large gulps of air as she readied to throw another ball of arcane. She turned, seeing the flickering image of a tall, thin person cloaked in shadows. With a last pained scream it disappeared, and a single piece of paper floated from where it just stood.

PLAYTIME STARTS NOW.
YOU'RE MINE.

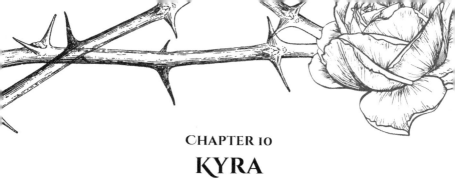

CHAPTER 10
KYRA

Blood Bar was in full swing when she passed through the doors, the small dance floor rustling with sweaty bodies moving to the live band on stage. She remembered the place before it had been taken over a few years before, the sticky floor, and worn tables full of disgruntled drunks who enjoyed the unique drink options. The fresh design was far more welcoming. High-end leather stools with chrome detailing, a small stage, and even a shiny new bar.

The new owner had kept the unique drinks spiked with blood, for which the bar was named after. He'd also created many more specialised cocktails to suit every taste.

Usually the beat of the dancers wouldn't bother her, even though she tried her best to keep away from crowds. But tonight she was on edge, her heart a heavy thump as she swallowed the panic that had been steadily growing since she first felt those phantom fingers. There was minimal bruising, but she still felt the echo of the pressure at the sides of her throat. Her attacker hadn't wanted to kill her, just frighten. A warning.

She instinctively flared her chi, ignoring the curious

glances, and disgruntled sneers of the magic bearers who felt her energy. She wasn't concealing her aura, unable to do so as she flared her chi once more, searching for the one witch who may have been able to help.

But there was nothing, the rippling awareness of everyone too much as she scanned the crowd, and found...

Eyes of ice met hers from the corner, Xander's face twisted into a scowl.

"Kyra?" a voice called from her left.

She hesitated, finding it difficult to look away from the man who despised her with such ease. Yet had also turned up to her flat for no other reason than to check on her.

Kyra finally turned, greeted by a tall, too beautiful man with short hair. "Axel," she responded, her shoulders relaxing just a little. "Is Alice here? I can't find her, and it's important."

Axel tilted his head, his smile waning as he studied her face. "You okay?"

"Is Alice here?" She repeated, praying she wouldn't cry somewhere so public.

Axel looked at something behind her. "No, I'm sorry she's not. I think she's on a case or something." He gestured to the bar behind him, at the colourful bottles that were expertly displayed. "You want to join me for a drink?"

Attention bristled, more eyes than she cared to count, watching, whispering. Kyra didn't need to turn to know they were entertaining themselves with the fact a witch like *her* was so open with her aura. Kyra concealed her chi, voice an embarrassed rasp when she said, "No, I really need to speak with her."

Alice was the only person she could trust, who knew what she was without judgement.

Concern darkened his eyes, his smile waning. "What happened?" He reached forward, but before his fingers could touch Xander appeared between them, a tall, tattooed wall that demanded her attention.

Kyra flinched, having not heard, or seen him move from his dark corner.

"What the fuck do you think you're doing flaring all over the place like that?" Xander grunted.

Kyra snapped straight at his harsh tone, her own anger sharpening, chasing away the earlier dread. He was right, she shouldn't have flared, but she'd panicked. She was sure to be reprimanded if Frederick ever found out.

"She's asking for Alice," Axel said, and Kyra had almost forgotten he was there while under Xander's cruel scrutiny.

"What the fuck would you want...?" Xander's eyes slid to her throat, rage tightening his lips. "Tell me Princess, who the fuck hurt you?" An electric current rippled beneath his voice, one that would have warmed her skin if she wasn't so distracted by the nickname.

He'd called her 'Princess' before, and both times were a mocking taunt.

Kyra let out a breath, looking away from his unapologetic glare. "I need Alice."

"Well, Alice isn't here, so you'll have to deal with me."

XANDER

"No thanks."

Xander couldn't take his eyes off the witch as she politely nodded to Axel, pointedly ignoring him. Her face was still bruised, lip split, but it was the marks on her throat that had made his blood boil. He watched her as if she were prey, not blinking until she'd disappeared into the darkened hall that led to the bathrooms.

No-fucking-thanks? That was all she could say after he offered his help?

"Xee, leave her." Axel shoved at his shoulder, lifting a dark brow. "Come on, you need a drink."

Xander didn't want a drink, he wanted to chase after Kyra and demand to know what happened, to know how she received every mark. To listen to her voice until the fear that had wobbled her tone had disappeared.

What the fuck was wrong with him?

His muscles were rigid, fists clenched by his sides when he joined his brother at the bar. A beer was already waiting for him, the bartender Sam popping the lid and placing it on a coaster before Xander had even sat down. He touched the bottle, the glass cold, and wet with condensation. It was just as cold on his tongue, even more so as it settled like a chunk of coal in his stomach.

"What the fuck was that about?" Sam asked, blonde brows drawn tight across his face. "Kyra looked –"

"Shook," Axel finished for him. "Terrified."

"How the fuck am I supposed to know?" Xander asked, taking another mouthful of beer. "She just shows up and there's drama."

"You're such an arsehole," Sam muttered, cleaning the bar. "When's the last time you got laid?" He flashed his feline grin. "You're so uptight. Maybe that's why Kyra gets you all hot and bothered."

Axel coughed, unable to disguise his grin as he choked on his drink.

"She doesn't get me hot and bothered." Xander scowled, ignoring the heavy weight on his chest. "I can't stand her."

She was everything that was wrong with magic, her very existence a mockery to the balance. It had pissed him off to see her dressed up, to go on a date like a normal person as if she didn't kill to feed her chi. She always seemed to hold herself with such superiority, in her fucking knee-high boots, and neatly braided hair like some dark, twisted, fucking princess.

Except she hadn't looked superior just then. She'd looked unsettled. Even scared.

Who the fuck had put those bruises on her throat?

Xander found himself staring towards the corridor where she'd disappeared, watching people enter and leave. Except there was no sign of the witch that dominated his thoughts.

"Xee? You there?" Axel nudged him, and Xander dragged himself away.

"Where's everyone else?" He needed to get her out of his mind. He'd only just arrived at the bar a few minutes before noticing Kyra standing lost in the crowd, unable to tear his focus away from the woman whose own eyes had widened at his harsh glare. "I thought there was poker."

"It's in the back room," Axel said, gesturing to the door beside the stairs that ascended to the overhead glass office. "Think it's Ti, Kace and Sythe. Jax decided to stay at home with the bloody cat."

Xander forced a smile, imagining the tiny black cat having a group of warrior men at his mercy. Poe had moved in along with Alice after she'd mated Riley. He'd instantly acted like he was king of the castle, demanding everything from attention, to treats and cuddles. He was a scraggly little thing, with half his ear missing, and two different colour eyes.

"He's also been sparring with Lucy," Axel added. "But we both know he prefers the company of the cat."

Lucifer was the only Daemon they hadn't killed on sight. He'd helped them in the past, and now they couldn't get rid of the fucker, even if they'd wanted to.

"Lucy needs to practice his social skills," Sam said,

crossing his arms. "He almost lost us business last time when he scared a young girl. I had to spend hours *calming* her down, if you know what I mean." A laugh, eyes glittering.

Axel stiffened beside him.

Xander hadn't been at the bar that night, but had heard Lucy's attempt at flirting was offering to flay the skin from every male who'd laid eyes on her. She'd been human, and hadn't appreciated the sentiment. Not that many modern women would have appreciated the offer, but Lucifer was still slowly adjusting to living up in the light, and not down in Hell.

Axel's bottle clunked as he settled it on the bar. "Hey, you joining us?"

Xander frowned, his attention drawn back towards the bathrooms.

"Xee?" Axel prompted. "Poker?"

Xander downed the rest of his beer, handing the empty bottle over to Sam before he stood. "Yeah, I'll meet you there." He didn't wait for Axel to ask any more questions. Unable to stop himself, he moved through the crowd until he stepped into the hall that split the bathrooms.

Where was she?

He hovered outside the women's, forcing what was supposed to be a friendly smile to the single woman staring like he was a creep.

Fuck the Fates. Although, Xander expected the three women whom his Breed revered as gods didn't care for his expletive. Which was great, because he didn't fucking believe in them anyway.

CHAPTER 11

KYRA

C hest tight, Kyra concentrated on breathing. Taking in one, long breath, she released it in a single, slow exhale. The cold water felt great against her face, diluting the tears that had escaped from the corner of her eyes.

Panic bound her lungs like a vice.

"Tell me what happened." A demand, one from the male she never expected to see in the reflection of the mirror.

"What's wrong with you?" she asked, pushing the words out. "This is the women's bathroom."

Xander's nostrils flared. "Why are you so fucking difficult?"

"Go – " *Don't you dare break.* "– Away."

"Not until you tell me what the fuck happened." Xander stepped forward, and Kyra's grip on the sink became white knuckled.

"No." She wrapped her arms around herself, as if that would keep her together. She knew she would be okay in a moment, but until then everything felt like it was falling apart.

"Honestly, Princess. Do you actually look for trouble? Or does it just find you?"

Kyra wanted to laugh. She wanted to snap back and – she couldn't breathe.

Xander's blue gaze widened, the eye contact breaking for a split second as he looked towards the door. With a quiet curse he grabbed her arm, pulling her with him into a stall and flicking the latch. Kyra barely had time to realise what had happened until she found herself straddling his lap, large arms wrapped around her tightly.

"You're okay," he said, voice dropping to a whisper against her ear. "Just breathe with me."

Kyra stiffened, wanting to wriggle herself free. But his weight was helping, her chest not so heavy.

The bathroom door opened, followed by a few, drunken voices.

"Did you see that bartender?" one of them asked. "I would put money on him being a cat."

"He's hot with a capital H!" another squealed. "Do you think I should give him my number?"

Xander shifted, pulling her closer against his chest until she felt his heart beat steadily against her cheek. She wasn't sure how long they sat there. Long enough her breathing had calmed and her tears had dried. Until the bathroom was empty once more.

The pressure had helped, which made no sense considering being constrained usually caused her to suffer a panic attack, not help.

Kyra wiggled, making Xander release his arms enough for her to scramble back. She adjusted her skirt, embarrassment burning her skin. Xander remained where he was, his large body swallowing the small space.

"Thanks," she mumbled, unable to look at him. She couldn't leave, not until he stood. She wasn't even sure how he'd managed to get them both into the stall when his knees knocked against the door.

Xander let out his own breath, leaning back to cross his arms over his chest. He looked forcibly relaxed, legs spread with his head slightly cocked, watching her. A weird heat coiled low in her stomach, one she potently ignored.

"I need to go." She gestured to the locked door, then to his knees which were clearly in the way. When he remained where he was, she flipped the lock anyway.

"We should talk about this," he said, his voice surprisingly absent of his usual attitude.

"Not with you I don't."

Xander shot to his feet. "Why the fuck not?"

Kyra finally looked at him, lips pursed as she met his eyes, so unusually pale they reminded her of the first signs of frost. "Because I don't trust you."

She pulled the stall door, only for a hand to press it closed again. Xander stood over her, shoulders hunched and coiled with tension. His eyes dipped to her lips, and Kyra felt hers parting as if an invitation.

No. Stop it.

"You hate me, remember," she whispered, pressing herself harder against the door.

Xander frowned, and Kyra couldn't help but study his square jaw, the shadow of stubble against his skin. The hair on his head was a silver as pale as his eyes, and yet his brows were as black as obsidian. She imagined his beard would be dark too, a striking contrast that only added to his handsome face.

"Riley's up in his office, Princess," Xander said, the effortless arrogance back. "I'm sure he can help you find Alice."

XANDER

He'd almost kissed her. Again. A black witch. One he couldn't stand.

'Because I don't trust you.' Her words had set fire to his blood. Why the fuck didn't she trust him? She was the one who practiced black magic, not him.

The crowd parted like water as he stormed through the bar, dancers shrinking away as he headed towards the back room where his brothers waited. The place they played poker was more like a storage closet, the walls covered in spare bottles, cleaning supplies and mops. Someone had added a small round table in the centre, probably Riley, along with four chairs. They all had to take turns to beat each other at cards, the men already shoulder to shoulder in the tight space.

It was Sythe who looked up first, a smile teasing his lips. "Royal flush," he said, settling his cards down onto the green felt.

Titus swore, slamming his hand on the table hard enough to rattle the plastic chips. "That's the third time in a row. It's bullshit." He chewed on his bottom lip, twirling the silver ring that pierced through the centre. It matched the small ring through the side of his nose. His blonde hair was tugged away from his face, knotted on the top of his head while kohl lines emphasised his almond shaped eyes.

"You up for a game?" Axel asked, looking over his shoulder. "Or you too busy with Kyra in the bathroom?"

Xander concealed his frustration. "Where's Kace?"

"Wanted to speak to Riley about something," Ti said, shuffling the cards. "Now what's this about you and Kyra?"

This time he didn't stop his growl, his fists tightening. "Blow me, arseholes." He ignored their heckles at his back, slamming the door closed behind him. He took the stairs towards Riley's office two at a time, the sense of urgency growing. He found Kace leaning against the wall in the darkened hallway, his eyes closed. His red hair swept forward when he turned to Xander.

"The boys are setting up another game of poker," Xander said, keeping his tone low. "Maybe you should go help?" He left no room for an argument.

"Or what?" Violence thickened the air between them. Out of all his brothers, it was Kace who had the most trouble controlling his beast, constant anger embedded in the lines on his face.

"You need to fight?" Xander asked, his brother relentless and utterly brutal in his rage. "Then wait for me out the back, or go to the fucking cages."

Cold calculation in Kace's green gaze. "I'm sensing some hostility brother," he said with a smirk. "Maybe it's because of a certain black witch?"

"Fuck the Fates," Xander muttered. "Get downstairs."

Kace bowed, the movement a sarcastic flourish before he straightened to his full height, an inch or so above Xander.

Xander waited until Kace had descended the stairs before he opened the office door, not bothering to knock. He knew exactly when Kyra realised he'd entered, her body stiffening before she turned her head to the side. Her cheeks flushed at his attention.

"You need me?" Xander asked, dragging his eyes away from her profile to his Sire. The office overlooked the dance-floor, the glass one-way. It allowed them to watch everyone on the floor below, while also keeping privacy.

Xander waited to be dismissed, not even sure why he'd burst into a private meeting. He wasn't Axel, or even Sythe. He'd never acted so reckless.

Riley frowned at the intrusion. *'You shouldn't be here,'* he said inside Xander's mind.

But Xander couldn't answer, not when amber eyes slid to him, irritation lighting them from within. Seemed she'd recovered from her earlier panic attack, not even a hair out of place to indicate how she'd fallen apart in his arms.

Kyra may not have telepathy, but he read her warning loud and clear. She didn't want him there, and that made it worth Riley's lecture later.

'Take your pissing contest elsewhere,' Riley muttered a frustrated grumble when he didn't reply.

'Tell me who hurt her,' Xander demanded. *'Then I'll leave.'*

Riley's upper lip twitched, caught between amusement and anger. He glanced at Kyra, who after a beat nodded once. "Kyra's been receiving threats, and this evening she was attacked."

Xander turned cold, his movements rigid as he closed the door quietly behind him. All confidence at pissing Kyra off disappeared, leaving nothing but an endless wrath.

"Why haven't you reported it?" Xander asked, unable to keep the question to himself. "What's wrong with you? Why –"

Kyra finally turned fully in her chair, eyes immediately connecting to his. "Who said I didn't?" she said with a quiet fury. "The Magicka are already aware and refuse to do anything about it. Alice is the only person who may be able to help me."

She turned to face Riley, and Xander had to stop himself from dragging her attention back to him.

"Look, I have some money, I can pay something small or we can work out a payment plan."

Riley pursed his lips, leaning back in his leather chair with the colourful lights from the bar below flashing behind him. "We don't offer these types of services. We're not mercenaries for hire."

"I know, but –"

"So we won't accept payment."

Kyra's relief was clear, her body sagging before she regained her composure. It was barely a second, and Xander caught it, unable to look at anything but her.

Riley frowned. "How long have you been receiving these threats?"

Kyra hesitated. "Six... six months."

"Six months?" Xander snarled. "You've been receiving threats for six months, and you've done what? Decorate the wall with them or some shit?"

"It wasn't serious," Kyra added quickly. "Not until tonight."

Xander took an aggressive step forward. "What's wrong with you? You should've –"

"Xee!" Riley barked. *'I would like to remind you that Kyra's a friend of the Guardians, and of my mate,'* he said, telepathically connecting them once more. *'That's enough.'* A warning. Xander's control slipping.

He was surprised he hadn't broken a tooth with how hard he clenched his jaw. *'Sire.'* He bowed, just a gentle dip of his head. Without another glance to the woman who infuriated him so easily, he walked out of the office. His anger hadn't cooled as he descended the stairs, the bar a chaos of colours and sound. He couldn't deal with his brothers, not when they saw too much. Grabbing the pack of cigarettes from his pocket, he headed towards the back alley, only stopping when he felt the welcoming wind against his face.

He hoped for once a spirit was lurking, a distraction against the fucking witch who'd opened her lips in a silent invitation that had his beast fucking begging. He *had* almost kissed her, curiosity making his chi stretch in that small, bathroom stall to lick across her aura. He'd fucked enough witches in his time to have tasted their magic, and hers was... different.

He wanted to push her until she broke apart. Until she wrapped those dark tendrils of her power around him so he could savour her fucking darkness. So he could remind himself that she was the enemy, and not a beautiful woman whom he wanted to bend over, and fuck so hard that she wouldn't dare look at another man again.

Fuck. The. Fates.

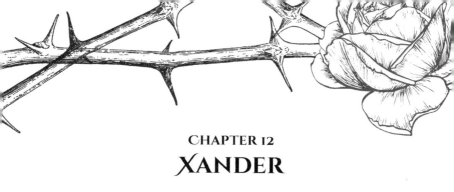

CHAPTER 12

XANDER

Xander embraced the burn, his muscles finally tiring after hours of trying. The basement gym was silent other than his own grunts, the lights off so he could work out in the peace of darkness. He couldn't sleep, unable to settle his thoughts at night. He hoped he could run himself into exhaustion, but still he couldn't relax without hearing the voices of those lost in between.

He knew when Kace joined him, the fellow Guardian waiting until he had settled the heavy weight back onto the rack.

"You look like shit," he said, folding his arms. Kace, just like the others could see well enough in the pitch black, but it felt wrong to discuss anything in the dark.

"Lights, on," Xander said as he grabbed his aviators, protecting his eyes from the sudden illumination.

Kace stood, his red hair pulled from his face, dark green brooding eyes matching the scowl that was a permanent fixture. "Titus has been getting reports from across the British Isles of missing druids."

"What do you mean missing?"

"Like fucking vanished," Kace replied. "You know, poof into thin air. What else do you think I fucking mean?"

Xander adjusted the weights. "Your attitude is really starting to piss me off. Why are you down here telling me? Go tell Riley."

Kace clenched his jaw. "I didn't want to bother him while he's still dealing with his own shit. I wanted to know if you've heard any whispers from the spirits."

"No, I haven't." Not that he'd been really listening, the voices more like a frustrating background noise. "Send Sythe." Ghosts made great spies, but Sythe was better.

"He's working on something with Riley."

"Then ask Axel. He may be able to get you some more information." He had the ability to make people talk to him, to spill their secrets. They joked it was because of his pretty face, but in reality it was Axel's easy-going personality and razor sharp intelligence.

"You mean when he isn't high or drunk?"

Xander sighed, settling the weight back down before he stood, rolling his shoulders to release the pressure. He had his own shit to deal with, like the spirits that wouldn't fuck off until they sent him crazy. "He's supposed to have cut all that out."

"And you believed him?" Kace chuckled. "He literally vanishes in the middle of a mission to get a fix, and it's me who's being punished? Do you know what, fuck you all."

"Careful," Xander warned.

Kace stepped forward, the tattoos along his left arm and neck pulsating. "Or what?"

Xander made the first swing, his fist barely connecting to Kace's cheek before he was pushed back, a kick landing heavily onto his ribs. He embraced the force, rolling with it until he was able to solidly land his second punch. Bones crunched, satisfying until a kidney shot brought him to his knees.

"Fuck!"

Xander caught Kace's fist, using his own momentum to crash him into the wall behind. The reinforced mirrors creaked, but didn't break.

"You feeling better?" Xander growled, knowing his brother needed to expel his excess rage.

Kace panted, irritation twisting his features. With a heaved sigh he nodded, wiping the blood away from his face. "I think you broke a rib," he said, voice calmer. His beast steadied.

"You deserved it." Xander's own ribs ached, but not as bad as his side that felt like it had been destroyed. "Stop being a pussy, it'll heal in a minute."

"Like I care whether it heals," Kace muttered, touching the bruise blossoming on his stomach.

Out of all The Guardians, Kace was the most unstable. Even as kids he had the least amount of control over his emotions, and it only became worse when they were cursed with their beasts. They were born druids, but now they were more. Trained killers who were forced to become monsters, so they could fight other monsters.

Xander dropped himself to the floor. "You know you're not being punished, K. Your control is –"

"Yeah, fuck you Xee." Kace flipped him his middle finger. "I'm not having this conversation. You need to go deal with your own shit rather than get involved in mine. You received another letter today, and I bet you won't even open it."

"You have no idea what you're fucking talking about." He knew he wouldn't open the letters, knowing exactly who they were from. He hadn't spoken to his mother since she abandoned him, and he had no intention of changing that anytime soon.

"Fuck you and your high horse, Xee."

Xander waited until he heard Kace's footsteps fade before he rolled onto his back, closing his eyes.

Fuck! His brother walked on the edge of sanity, and it was a countdown to see what, or who pushed him over the edge into oblivion. They were all doing everything possible not to let that happen. Kace was one of them. Reborn in blood, teeth and fractured souls.

Xander calmed his breathing, concentrating on his body repairing itself. It was one of the glyphs they tattooed, their bodies only able to withstand the enchantment because of their curse. Because of their beasts. Druids were of the earth, their magic tied to natural energies, the ley lines. Their curse wasn't of their realm, wasn't natural at all. Wounds that would normally kill mortal men were nothing but annoyances to them, their natural magic amplified through the markings on their skin.

Xander heard the new footsteps approaching.

"The cushioned floor we got installed was worth it I see," Riley chuckled. "As were those reinforced mirrors."

Xander felt the floor shift beside him, opening his eyes to stare up at his friend.

"I was going to invite you to spar, but I see you've already taken a beating." Riley held out a hand.

Xander copied the same gesture as Kace before he gripped the open palm, but instead of climbing to his feet he pulled Riley down with him. "You need to put Kace back on rotation, he's becoming unbearable."

Riley sighed, settling himself as Xander sat up. "His control's still questionable. He nearly killed a civilian last time."

"He's been going into the cages at the club. His control is better, and that progress should be acknowledged."

Riley raised a brow. "He shifted and tried to eat Lucy yesterday."

"Lucy's a Daemon, so you can't really blame him. Besides, the key word there is *tried*." Xander lifted his shirt, checking the bruise that was already turning purple on his ribs. "I don't think keeping him home's helping. We're overwhelmed with activity, and the Order are fucking useless as usual."

"Since when were you the voice of reason?"

Xander dropped his shirt. "Since Kace just split my liver because of his pent up frustration."

"Fine," Riley said. "You can take him with you."

Xander turned to his friend, whose lips quirked in amusement. "Don't say it –"

"Kyra needs protection."

Fuck.

"That's nice, maybe she can get a dog or something." Xander groaned, climbing to his feet. He moved back to the weights when Riley reappeared in his vision. "You know why I can't."

He was created to help and protect.

She was born to sacrifice innocents.

"Shouldn't. Not can't." Riley crossed his arms. "She asked for Alice –"

"Then send Alice," Xander barked. "She's more than capable of protecting Kyra, and they're friends. It's a win-win situation."

"Alice is currently hunting down a serial killer with Spook Squad, and opening another division in Manchester."

Xander contained his growl. "Don't worry, I'll make

sure she knows she's a shit friend, with even shitter priorities."

"Careful Xee," Riley warned.

"You know my history." Xander added weight to the bar, setting himself back down on the bench. "Not to mention we'll probably end up killing each other. It won't work, ask someone else."

"I'm sure you can control yourself long enough not to –"

"Why are you even asking me?" Xander went to lift when Riley suddenly gripped the bar, his fingers leaving dents in the metal. "Fuck sake." He released the weight, and slipped off the bench. "Ti can babysit the witch. I have more important things to do, like wash my hair."

"Stop being an arsehole. I've chosen you, as my *second*, because you're the most stable of us all."

"Then un-choose me." Kyra was this suspiciously composed energy that his beast was drawn to. She was the calm before a storm. He hated that she made him crave someone he didn't trust.

"I've already decided." Riley smirked, the smile pissing him off even more. "Remember to take Kace with you."

Fates, kill me now.

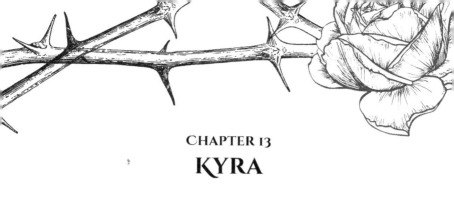

CHAPTER 13
KYRA

"Double check it," Frederick said. "We don't want to make the same mistake again."

Adeline nodded, clapping her hands together with a loud slap. "Kyra, check the lines against the drawing while everyone else gets into position. Make sure all the candles are properly lit, and there's enough wick to last."

"Yes, High Priestess."

The new summoning circle was impressive. It was much larger than the previous design, taking up the entire room. Just as before, there was an inverted pentagram within the centre. The top two points were the flow points, but the new design had the circles covering the spike of the pentagram's star rather than just connecting to the tip. Their own bubbles that overlapped one another, creating a floral design. A dangerous flower with five petals.

It was within the overlaps where the singular candles were placed, each representing the newer elements.

Kyra stepped into the centre, slowly spinning to make sure each carefully created line was correct. Salt granules had been teased onto the strokes, adding an extra protection that they all needed. In the overlapped circle between Spirit and Earth stood the first lone candle, one that represented Shadow.

Cassandra stood for the first anchor, Earth. She held her candle, the wick already lit as she stood and waited with surprising patience. Directly beside her was the element Ore, the candle's flame dancing strong.

Water was the first flow element, and with no Faye, Frederick stepped up into the circle. His candle was dark, but with a quick flick of his wrist and a pompous smirk it burst into life. Beside him in the circles' overlap, stood the candle for Ice.

"How's it looking?" Adeline asked as she stepped into Air, the second flow element. Her candle too was unlit, until she quickly clicked her fingers. Thunder stood to her left, the element that was the blend of both Fire and Air.

Fire was next, and the last anchor. Saul watched with quiet determination as Kyra checked his lines. Beside him, in the final overlap, stood the candle for Light.

"Kyra?" Adeline asked again. "Answer me."

Lastly there was Spirit, the element Kyra represented. Reaching over to Shadow she lit her candle, stepping inside the safety of her little circle. "We're ready," she said, ignoring the sense of dread that had only grown since she'd first set eyes on the design.

"Then quicken the flame," Frederick commanded. "And let's do this."

Bane stepped forward with a sharp blade, his expression empty when he reached over to slice the tip of her finger. The blood pooled quickly, but he stopped her from closing the circle.

"Sacrifice, and toss it into the centre," Frederick said. "Maybe this Daemon would appreciate a fresher kill."

Bane nodded, so deep it was almost a bow. He produced

a bird, small and delicate with beautiful pale feathers. Using the same blade he sliced open the innocent bird's chest. With a few flaps of its wings it collapsed, landing in the centre with a sickening rustle when Bane tossed it.

Kyra closed her eyes, trying to ignore the sounds as the bird died. She concentrated on the wax that burned her skin, savouring the pain.

"Kyra!" Adeline barked. "Hurry up!"

Kyra kept her eyes closed until she felt Bane step out of her circle, and as soon as he was gone she allowed a single drop of her blood to fall into the flame of her candle.

The connection was immediate, stronger than she'd ever felt when the dome enclosed around them all. Within a few beats a second dome materialised, surrounding the inner pentagram.

Frederick laughed, but everyone else remained eerily quiet as each flame began to flicker in turn. A heartbeat, one that mimicked her own. Kyra knew she should've collapsed, her body unable to process so much black magic in such a short time. But somehow she stood, her legs anchored in place.

"Can anyone else not move?" Cassandra asked, voice slightly alarmed.

Saul grunted, shaking his head.

"Don't panic," Adeline said, "It's perfectly normal." They would have believed her if her gaze hadn't flicked over to Frederick with concern.

His returning smile was anything but comforting. "Do it."

Adeline started the spell, and as before the words flowed through Kyra's head like water. Pain radiated inside her skull, the agony enough to cause black spots across her vision. Copper coated her tongue, and Kyra knew if she cut herself then her blood would be black.

She didn't actually know what would happen after so much exposure. Most black witches took the resulting effluence, whether it was dispersed inside their aura, or taken out in their body by way of blood and flesh. Many sacrificed their fingers, eyesight, or worse. All until their bodies could no longer deal with the dark force ravaging their very soul, and at that point their minds were devastated beyond repair.

Every spell required a sacrifice to various levels of severity, black witches gambled with the greatest sacrifice of all.

"Ah, so what he said was true," a voice laughed. A flash of white light, a large man appearing inside the inner dome. Armour covered parts of his dark skin, the edges harsh and sharp. Wings tried to snap to their full length, but they caught on the circle with a spark and a hiss.

"I'm sorry," Frederick said with his calmest voice, "who said it was true?"

The Daemon turned, his teeth sharp and pointy when he smiled. "Clever, but you know I would never share his name." It gave Kyra the view of his profile, his wings slowly sliding themselves away into slits parallel to his spine. It left his back bare, the armour not covering the tattooed swirls that seemed to decorate his powerful shoulders. Horns pierced though his hair, the sharp tips facing behind him, rather than front.

"What would you like me to call you?" Frederick asked. "And I'm not asking for your true name."

Names held power. You could cast a death curse with just a name. With Daemons it was more, their true names anchored to their magic. Knowing their name gave the summoner control, which was why Daemons protected them by any means necessary.

The Daemon laughed, shoulders shaking with exaggeration. "You can call me Dirk."

Frederick bowed. "I am Councilman Frederick Gallagher, voice to the witches, and Supreme of The Magi –."

"That's a lot of pretty titles, Fred," Dirk chuckled, slowly turning to check out each witch. He stopped at Kyra, his eye contact unwavering. "You," he said, stepping forward until the inner circle burst into sparkles. He pressed his hand forward, the dome shaping around his palm, but not breaking. "You're not afraid, and yet this room stinks of fear and shit."

"What happened to our witch?" Kyra asked, the question just appearing on her tongue. "Is she safe?" She felt everyone's eyes turn to her, but she refused to look away. To breath the contact.

It was true, she wasn't afraid. She should have been, anyone sane would have, but it seemed the overwhelming murk coating her aura like a bad taste was affecting her judgement.

"Safe?" Dirk laughed, the sound a harsh bark. "She's gone, dead. A fitting gift, don't you think?"

Kyra recoiled at the word 'dead,' rage burning through her veins. "She was only a kid."

"Now you're just making me laugh. Just because she was young, doesn't make her innocent. You should all understand that better than most."

Frederick cleared his throat. "It was I who called you, not Kyra, or any of the coven."

"Fred of the many useless titles, tell me why I've been called?" Dirk turned, giving Kyra his back once again. "I was surprised when I was told of a coven of black witches being able to summon us without a name, and even more surprised once I felt the power of this circle."

"I'm the strongest amongst my Breed, and it is I who wishes to make a deal with you."

"We both know that's a lie, you are not the strongest of your Breed." Dirk licked his lips, his tongue grey. "I can taste your chi, and I doubt you'd ever be able to control death magic without shitting yourself."

The coven looked between one another, but remained silent.

Frederick's smile tightened, the curve of his lips shaped to be professional. Trustworthy. That same smile had sentenced many people to death.

Kyra gagged, the sound loud against the silence. Her stomach twisted, nausea rising. *No. No. No. Please don't puke!*

"What are you offering, Fred?" Dirk continued, red eyes sliding back to Kyra. "A feast of your coven?"

"I'm offering you true freedom."

Dirk's brow knitted. "The gate that kept my kind bound to the Nether has already been broken. It allows us to move freely between the realms. We're no longer prisoners to the darkness below, therefore free."

"But you're still tied to your names like a chain," Frederick continued. "Forced to obey those that call it, summoning you like obedient dogs. You shouldn't be punished for choosing power. Let me break it for you."

Dirk froze, hands curling into claws. "You know how?"

Frederick paused, smile deepening. "We have the power, and with your resources we will. You have my vow."

"Pretty words," Dirk drawled. "And what would you want in exchange for this empty promise?"

"Your knowledge. Teach us the old magic. Dark arts that my kind are too fearful to appreciate."

Dirk chuckled, the horns on his head disappearing into his hairline. "How can I trust that you're sincere?"

"I'll add that if I betray you, you'll have the reassurance of a... collateral."

"A collateral?" Dirk asked. "Hmmm. A witch, of my choice?"

"Agreed," Frederick replied without hesitation.

Dirk paused, tilting his head. Without his horns and wings he looked like a generic man, just one with red irises and skin tinged with grey. "Drop the shield. Let us agree to this blood oath."

Frederick nodded, his palm pressing into his dome.

It didn't fall.

"Adeline!" Frederick said, composure dropping for a split second. "Drop the shield so we can properly welcome our guest."

Adeline paused, her fingers held tight to her chest. "Of course," she finally said, reaching forward with her own palm. One by one the others followed, until it was only Kyra who remained.

"Kyra?" Frederick said, his smile strained.

Kyra gripped her candle tighter, but leant forward until her skin touched the circle. The dome fell, their auras rebounding with a painful snap. It left them vulnerable, and the tension along the witches was palpable.

Dirk sniggered, his fingers pressing forward in reassurance that the circle was no longer there. "Interesting coven you have here." He spun slowly, meeting everyone's gaze, one by one. When he reached Cassandra he stepped forward, waiting until she looked up before moving back to Frederick. "You and your coven will help us break the summoning law, giving back total freedom. In return I'll share my knowledge." With a long, pointy nail he sliced across his palm before holding it out.

Frederick watched the nail, his smirk tipped at the corners. "Myself, the coven, and my personal black witch will help you break the summoning law, but you'll share all your knowledge in the dark arts in advance rather than as payment. We are equals, after all."

"Equals," Dirk echoed.

Bane appeared with a fresh blade, and Frederick sliced his palm the same length as Dirk had.

"A blood oath to seal our new relationship," he said, clasping hands.

Dirk grinned, yanking Frederick closer until their chests touched. "It's done, but understand that if my summoning name's abused or shared with anyone, I'll cause you so much pain you'll beg for death."

"I would expect nothing else." Frederick pulled his hand free. "And If you think about betraying me, I will show you exactly what it's truly like to be a slave to your name."

"This seems to be a worthy joining," Dirk said with a crooked smile. "Before I give you my true name, I wish to mark my collateral."

Frederick wiped his hand down his cloak. "You may mark, but that's all. You only gain them if I betray you, which I don't plan to do."

Dirk had already stepped away. "You." He stopped in front of Kyra, moving until his face was only an inch or so from hers. "You still don't stink of fear, why?"

"I'm terrified," she lied. She'd witnessed summonings since before she could walk. Had bathed in blood before she could speak, but she should've still felt fear.

His hands moved faster than her eyes could track, his palms gripping the side of her head. "The others, they bathe in disappointment and dread, yet you taste different, raw. It's interesting. I have yet to meet a witch whose power tastes quite like yours." His breath was cold, as were his lips when he pressed them against hers. She tried to pull back, panic gripping her chest as his hands squeezed, his tongue stroking against hers with a quick flick.

His hold released, and Kyra fell to the floor. An intense chill settled against her tongue, pins and needles choking her throat. She wasn't sure how long she sat there trying to control the alien sensation in her mouth, but when she looked up everyone had left.

Kyra settled herself on all fours, her weight on her palms as she took in a few unsteady breaths. Her eyes settled on the bird in the centre, the weak creature forgotten amongst the commotion. Reaching forward she cradled its body in her palms, feeling the weight of the life lost.

Her palms warmed and her fingertips sparkled as she closed her eyes, pushing just a little bit of her chi into the bird. *"In morte vita,"* she whispered, imagining the cut along its chest knitting together, and then its heart beating. She imagined blood pumping, healing, and breath filling its little lungs.

A sharp pain started high on her thigh, blood seeping into her skirt as it echoed the same length and size as the cut that had sliced the bird's chest. She knew without opening her eyes that the bird was whole once more, a replicate wound now echoed in her own flesh. She didn't understand that part of her magic, because it was of death, and yet she could bring life for the right cost.

"What a waste," Frederick tutted beside her.

Kyra opened her eyes just as the bird was snatched from her palms. It chirped, wings flapping as it tried to escape.

"Please, don't!" she said, climbing unsteadily to her feet. She hadn't heard him approach, thinking she was alone.

Frederick raised a brow. "Our new friend's gone to prepare some grimoires, I'm sure we'll be hearing from him soon enough." He raised the bird to his face, the creature struggling in his grip. "I do love a successful outcome."

"You've agreed to help him, but you know their magic doesn't work with ours."

"I'm aware, but clearly Dirk doesn't." Frederick smirked. "We may not be able to do their magic, but I'm sure we can adapt it to benefit us." He met Kyra's eyes. "Daemons have access to unlimited power through the ley lines. If we could just tap into that, we could expand our chis beyond their natural ability. Could you imagine how powerful I could be if I wasn't so restricted?"

"You're crazy," Kyra whispered. "You would trick a Daemon, for what? An idea of unlimited power? You don't even know if that's possible."

Frederick dropped his attention to the bird, holding it out to her. As she went to grab it he flicked his wrist and broke the bird's neck. He allowed it to fall lifeless into her outstretched hands. "Life and death are two opposing forces, and yet here you are. Nothing is impossible, you've shown me that."

She cradled the bird to her chest, Fredrick reaching forward to stroke a finger against her cheek.

"Be very careful Kyra," he said, his voice strangely soft. "You've shown me yet again you cannot be trusted. Maybe you would be better suited like Saul."

Kyra knew he needed her voice for spells, but she couldn't control the fear that shot through her like a poisonous dart.

"You're on your final warning. If you stand out of line again, your license will be revoked and you'll be sentenced before The Magicka. Don't test my patience," he said, stroking the head of the bird. "I wouldn't want you to end up like this little guy here."

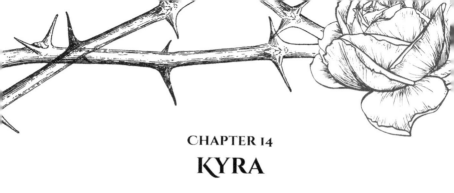

CHAPTER 14
KYRA

Kyra finally reached her floor, her legs weak, but no longer shaking. A vile taste had settled in her mouth, and she couldn't even blame the vomit. After emptying the contents of her stomach twice, the taste that coated her tongue from the kiss had only grown stronger.

Blood crusted her skirt and tights, but as it was already black, it blended into the weaves without drawing too much attention. A couple of shifters on her way home had looked at her with a peculiar expression, and she'd dared not look at the Vamp who'd sat a few seats beside her on the tube.

She needed her own car, but the money she could have used to buy one had been stolen along with her duffel bag. She'd never intended to stay so long in the city, knowing London was popular amongst Breed. Yet she was still there.

She may have no longer been inside a cage, but she was trapped just the same.

The wound on her leg was sticking to the fabric as she walked, uncomfortable as she made her way down the corridor to her flat. It would scar, but her thighs were already a history of such spells and sacrifices. Some of them she'd been willing to bear, but many of them she hadn't.

The lights were off, and the dread that she'd barely controlled earlier rose with vengeance. With sweaty palms she reached for the switch, knowing full well she'd never turned it off.

With a click the single light that illuminated the living room and adjoining kitchen wheezed into life. She hadn't screamed in years, knowing that type of sound only pleased the people who'd hurt her. But she screamed then. It only lasted a second, and the embarrassment that burned her cheeks strangled the lasting remnants of panic.

Xander sat on her sofa, head resting back, legs stretched and ankles crossed as if he was ready to nap. He said nothing as she collected herself in the threshold, his expression hidden behind the sunglasses he wore.

"How... how did you get in?" she asked, her voice husky as she checked the wards at her feet. "I've only just had the locks changed."

"They were shit," Xander said with a shrug, his nostrils flaring. "You stink of death."

"Thanks, it's natural," she replied, her voice only slightly stronger than before. "What are you doing here?"

Xander slowly climbed to his feet, his boots thumping on her carpet as if he'd landed them with extra force.

"Xee, what's with the scream?" a voice asked from the corridor.

Kyra hadn't sensed the other Guardian, barely able to step out the way as the one with beautiful red hair appeared in the doorway. He frowned, eyes scanning the small space quickly. His mouth opened as if to speak, but whatever he said was drowned out by the clang of a wok against his head.

"Back the fuck away!" Eva shouted, her hands clasped around the end of her makeshift weapon.

"Kace," Xander warned. "Don't."

The red head growled, turning to face Eva with his scowl.

"Back off," Eva said, the wok still held out in front of her. "I'll hit you again, I don't care."

"Will you, now?" he all but purred. Moving forward until he backed her against the wall, his hands planted on each side of her head. "Don't worry, I like a little pain."

"Kace," Xander barked. "Go stand guard outside."

"What am I, your fucking dog?" he snapped back.

"Kyra?" Eva called past Kace, annoyed by the proximity of the Guardian. "You okay?"

Kyra began to reply, and then her stomach recoiled for the third time that night. Heaving forward she gagged, spitting black vomit onto her clean floor. Hands pulled gently at her hair, moving it away from her face.

"Thanks," she said, expecting Eva. Except it had been Xander who'd helped, and Eva stood beside her with her face creased in concern. Her friend glared at Xander, then settled back on her.

"Everyone out!" Eva shouted. "Now!"

Xander stood straighter. "What happened?" he asked, ignoring Eva as she threatened him with her wok.

Kyra sucked in a breath, the nausea easing. "Oh you know, my life."

Xander nodded to Kace, who excused himself into the corridor.

"Eva," Kyra said quietly, shooting Xander a scowl. "Give me five minutes, please."

Eva shot daggers at Xander, but followed Kace out the door. "I'll be just out here, okay?"

"Tell me everything," Xander demanded as soon as they were alone. "You're... different."

"Different," Kyra laughed, the sound on the edge of hysteria. "Now that's something I've always been. What do you want, Xander? I'm not really in the mood."

He seemed to bristle at her tone. "I've been asked to protect you until whoever's behind those threats is caught, or worse."

"You?" Kyra blinked. "Why you?"

"Trust me, it wasn't my idea," he grumbled. "Now pack your shit, you can't stay here."

Kyra looked at the dark stain she'd made, knowing it'll take her forever to clean the stain. "I can't leave, if *he* finds out... I can't risk it."

"Whoever *he* is, can go fuck himself. Pack for a few days, we'll figure everything else out later." Xander reached for the bag strapped to her shoulder.

Kyra stepped back. "No."

"No?" He pulled off his sunglasses. "You asked for help, and now you don't want it? Make up your fucking mind, Princess. We're not some community service protecting damsels in distress."

"Screw you!" she said, unable to meet his hard gaze. "I don't know what to do, I need time to think."

To figure out a plan.

Xander stepped closer, but froze when Kyra winced. "I felt your wards, and anyone can step over them as long as they don't intend to harm you until they're inside. You'll only be gone a few days, just while Kace and Ti secure the place."

Kyra blew out a breath, frustrated at her own reaction. She was overwhelmed, the urge to run growing with every passing second. "One night," she said, knowing that even with such little time she risked Frederick's anger. But her home wasn't safe. "And then I come back."

"That's not how this works."

She wasn't taking no for an answer. "One night."

"Fine," Xander growled in agreement. "Whatever, it's your funeral."

"Fine." She only needed a change of clothes, owning nothing of sentimental value. She was ready with her small bag within a few minutes.

Xander barely acknowledged her as he made his way out into the corridor to speak to Kace. "I'm taking her back to mine, update Riley and contact me if anything changes."

Kace nodded in acknowledgment, his attention remaining on Eva. He'd placed himself against the opposite wall, with Eva hovering in the threshold of her own front door. She turned to Kyra when she appeared, her hands still clenched around the wok as she shot out questions far faster than Kyra could answer. "Are you okay? Was the murk bad? What happened with Bane?"

"Who the fuck is Bane?" Xander rumbled. "Was that your date?"

Kyra clutched the bag to her chest, ignoring him. "I'm just going to be gone for a day. Please don't worry, I'll call you when I can."

"Seriously? With these guys?" Eva looked between them suspiciously.

"I don't have time to explain. Stay safe, and stay away from Bane."

Eva lifted her weapon, pointing it towards Xander. "Hurt her, and I'll shove this up where the sun doesn't shine." She turned to Kace. "You too arsehole."

Kace suddenly barked a cough, his face twisted into what looked like a smile. "Noted."

Kyra sat on the edge, the bed comfortable enough but oddly impersonal. Sterile almost. Xander's place was a decent size, in a well sought after area in the city with a stunning view of skyscrapers and glittering lights. Except it had no character. The sheets were a dark blue, relatively decent cotton, but basic. The wooden panel detailing on the wall was generic, with no personalisation at all. The two nightstands were empty other than the lamps, which were ablaze as soon as she'd been shown the room.

Xander hadn't exactly said she couldn't leave, but the extra loud slam of the door gave her the assumption she wasn't welcome to explore. He'd muttered that he only had the one bedroom, and that he would stay on the sofa. *"Out of your way."*

Translation: *Stay out of my way, and I'll stay out of yours.*

Great. In any other situation she would've protested, but the murk that was making its way out her system had taken its toll. Exhaustion beat heavily against her. Exhaustion that wouldn't improve with sleep. Not that she could sleep in such an unwelcoming environment, where all she could think of was the male who didn't want her there. Not to mention her mouth still tasted vile, and no amount of scrubbing seemed to work.

So she settled for snooping, because Xander had no TV in the bedroom and she wasn't feeling up to his holier-than-though attitude if she decided to explore anyway.

A bookshelf was the only other freestanding furniture, three tiers with one holding a single book. The other two were empty, which really took the minimalistic decor to another level.

He was either a man who needed very little, or he rarely stayed there.

The wardrobe was built into the wall, concealed apart from the dent of the handle. It held a few outfits as well as three sets of boots, which made it almost as stark as her own. She hadn't found any underwear in the wardrobe or the drawers, and the idea of Xander preferring to go commando was knowledge she didn't need in her life.

Climbing to her feet, she felt a warmth drip down her leg, the cut on her thigh re-opening. The pain was dull, but the heat spread as she carefully opened the door, peeking into the hallway. Empty, and after a second she slipped out, keeping to the wall. The hall was dark, but not enough for her to worry as the light from the kitchen seeped through. The bathroom, on the other hand, was encased in shadows further down. The door was silent when she opened it, her heart thundering in her chest as she frantically searched for the switch.

"Lux mea," she whispered after struggling, a small ball of light appearing by her outstretched hand. It illuminated enough for her to find the pull, and with a click the overhead light glowed. "That's bet –" Kyra's eyes immediately landed on the very much naked man in the shower.

Her mouth dropped open, but she was unable to look away from the tattoos that accentuated Xander's strong shoulders and back. They sloped down his sides, the left dipping down to curve perfectly onto his cheek. His right leg was covered, the designs wrapping around while his other was bare. He faced away, one hand planted on the tile and the other relaxed by his side. The shower was off, the air cool, but his skin was still glistening from the water beads.

"I'm... I'm so sorry!"

His head turned slightly, voice a deep rumble. "Can I help you?"

"Erm..."

Xander twisted fully, his hand coming up to push his pale hair away from his face.

Kyra dropped her eyes to the floor tiles, hoping he didn't notice the embarrassment burning her cheeks. "I'm so sorry."

"You've already said that," he replied.

"I was looking for a med kit, or maybe some bandages."

"It's in here somewhere," he said, stepping out of the shower. "I'll grab it."

"Thanks," she muttered, keeping her eyes on the floor. "I didn't realise you would be in here. You know, naked."

"Naked? In the shower? Now that's a surprise." He reached for a towel, wrapping it low around his waist. "I wouldn't have taken you for a prude. Don't all black witches dance naked in the moonlight?"

Kyra's eyes snapped to his, wondering if her face looked as bright as it felt. "Bandages?" she reminded him when he just stared.

Xander paused, brow raised before he stepped forward until they were toe to toe. Heat radiated from his bare chest, close enough Kyra stilled, tension an electrical storm beneath her skin. She tilted her chin, and Xander's upper lip curved, blue eyes glinting with challenge. Oxygen expelled from her lungs when he leaned closer, only to reach over her shoulder and grab a small, green tin from somewhere behind.

"You smell like blood," he whispered intimately into her ear, and Kyra's heart beat faster. "Show me, and I'll wrap it."

It took a second to understand his words, the embarrassment renewing. "I can do it." She reached for the tin, but he quickly lifted his arm and pulled it out of reach.

"Where's the wound?" he asked. "I don't want you bleeding out on my floor. It'll look bad on me."

"Xander," she croaked. "I can do it."

He only lifted the tin higher.

The embarrassment made her tone sharp. "What are you, a child?"

Xander frowned, brows knitting together. He handed her the tin, a white cross painted across the top before stalking out.

Kyra placed the medical kit onto the counter beside the sink, her head falling forward as she tried to relieve some of the stiffness from her back and shoulders. She clamped her hands down on the counter, anchoring herself with the cool texture.

How did she get herself into that position? In the home of a man that hated her.

Maybe I'm just a glutton for punishment, she thought as she looked up at the mirror, the dark bags beneath her eyes heavy. The cut on her lip looked as well as it could, only slightly bruised with little to no swelling.

Frederick wanted her to be the perfect subordinate. To not question his decisions while he used her for his dubious spellcasting. If she stayed, she was confident she would become a shell of herself. But if she ran, she risked worse.

Letting out a settled breath she lifted her skirt to check the cut though her black, opaque tights. The fabric stuck to both the old and new blood, the tights intact apart from the ladder along her knee. The cut beneath looked nasty, wider than she remembered and seeping.

"Take off your skirt."

Kyra jumped, having not heard Xander re-enter the bathroom. He wore a pair of jeans, the button undone to show the deep V of his hips. Her eyes dipped lower, immediately jumping back to his face.

No underwear. Great.

"You're bleeding. Take off your skirt," Xander repeated, thankfully not looking at her face as he opened the medical tin. When she remained exactly where she was, he growled, "You want to do this the easy way, or the hard way?"

"Excuse me?"

Xander leaned forward, but Kyra refused to retreat. "You can either willingly take it off, or I'll rip it off. Your choice, Princess."

Kyra glowered, but exhaustion was growing with every passing second. "You're an arsehole."

"So I've been told," he drawled. "But at least I don't pretend to be anyone I'm not."

"What the hell's that supposed to mean?"

"It means stop arguing, and take the fucking skirt off like a good girl so I can treat your leg."

Kyra bristled at the 'good girl' comment, a curse at the end of her tongue. Shooting him a baleful glare, she pulled at the waist of her skirt. Xander's brow raised as he waited, the fabric barely hitting the floor before she felt his hands on her hips.

"Hey!" she squeaked, struggling against his hold as he placed her like a doll on the counter. "What do you think you're doing?"

Xander looked up, his eyes such a pale blue she couldn't help but study them. He kept the eye contact as he reached forward, and ripped the tights clean from her leg.

"Xander!"

"What happened?" he asked in a cold, detached voice. The complete opposite of the full body flush that had started in her cheeks, and now reached her toes. "Kyra?"

"It's a self-sacrifice," she said, struggling to swallow as he carefully traced his fingers along the scars that decorated both her thighs. The light above made them glow against her skin. "It's better me, than something else."

"Ah yes, a blood sacrifice," he said with a curled lip. "How noble."

Kyra tried to ignore the sarcasm that dripped from his words. "Don't judge a whole Breed because of your ignorance."

"I'm not ignorant. I'm aware witches require some sort of sacrifice, the severity depending on the spell. I just don't understand why you would choose magic that requires death."

Kyra hissed as he pressed something against the wound. "Do you think I chose this?" She gestured to her scars. "Do you think I chose to have the whole magical community hate me on sight?"

"You could have chosen another specialisation –"

"No!" she snapped. "I couldn't."

His hand paused, touch featherlight.

"Any witch with a large enough chi can try black magic, but unless they have the natural power the spells will fail, or cause irreversible damage to the caster. You have to be born with the ability to practice black magic properly. Our chi's different, a mutation that makes our magic stronger, but toxic." Her voice cracked. "If we don't practice some sort of black magic our chi could become overcharged, and that can be fatal for more than just us. So no, I couldn't choose another specialisation."

"Whatever you say," he grumbled, his touch surprisingly gentle. "Should we be concerned that some of your blood is black?" Xander reached into the tin for a salve, the medicine cold against her fevered skin. "It looks infected."

The scent of clove oil and chamomile drifted softly, the ointment having an anaesthetic effect. "It's not infected, it's just my body rejecting the effluence."

He gripped her knee, keeping her in place. "Stop moving."

"You know nothing of black magic," she said, her voice dropping to a whisper. "A black witch is someone who uses their ability to manipulate blood and death for their own gain. They embrace and savour the mortality, because in return it gives them power. Then there are dark witches, those who use their natural born ability to manipulate blood and death for good."

"For good?" Xander smirked, securing a bandage around her thigh. "Sure, Princess."

Kyra lifted her leg, kicking him back with a frustrated cry. "Screw you."

Xander shot her a heated look, his hand curling around her foot to hold against his bare chest. "Only in your dreams."

Kyra let out a sound of frustration. "Black magic is stronger, and has more possibilities, but dark witches don't embrace the death. We find ways around it."

Xander lifted her leg before she could pull it back. "So you're telling me –" With a gentle pull she slipped to the edge of the counter, her legs automatically parting for him to step in between. "– You're not a black witch, but a dark one?" His thumbs absently brushing over her scars, his lips near hers.

She tried to scoot back, but was met with resistance. "My magic is simply a coincidence of birth." She pushed against his chest, needing space between them before she combusted at his touch. How could a man who openly hated her, cause such a reaction?

Xander's eyes blazed, his irises shifting into liquid silver.

"You hate me, remember?" The words came out husky, not like the accusation it was meant to be.

Xander smirked, his thumb stroking down on her thigh as if he knew her internal struggle.

Bastard.

"I need to finish wrapping your leg," he said with a rumble that sent a vibration to places that didn't need attention.

Kyra was unable to look at him, her heart beating violently in her chest. Closing her eyes she tried to calm her pulse, but it only made her achingly aware of the hands that brushed her inner thighs.

She was going to hyperventilate if she didn't calm down.

"You're done," he said after a while. "You're welcome, by the way."

She would have thanked him despite the sarcasm, but she couldn't trust her voice right then. It was a while later, when her breathing had calmed did she reopen her eyes to find herself alone.

CHAPTER 15

KYRA

"This is a waste of time," Xander grunted, arms crossed as they stood outside the Supernatural Intelligence Bureau's head office at first light. "We need to discuss those threats, not run some fucking errands."

"This isn't an errand, and I need to keep everything as normal as possible," she said, looking up at him. His face was furrowed with impatience, but at least his eyes were back to ice. Well, before he'd hidden them behind his sunglasses. "I have a meeting with the Commissioner."

"That tosser, why?"

She decided not to answer, instead scratching at her thigh. The wound was healing much faster than usual, her muscle strong. She didn't want to admit it, but Xander had done a great job in wrapping it. The bandage not too tight beneath her jeans.

"S.I don't hire dark witches," Xander continued after a pregnant pause. "What could you possibly do for them?"

She noticed he'd called her dark, and not black.

"I'm specially licensed," she said, lips pursed. "Also things cost money, like food and rent."

She'd been commissioned by S.I, and more recently been asked to support cases with Spook Squad, The Metropolitan Police's Breed team. She actually enjoyed it, especially as Alice was a member of Spook Squad. But she was still contracted with S.I, and the commissioner had started to offer her out for certain services without her permission. It blurred the line on what she was allowed to practice, but she wasn't given much choice. If she didn't do it she risked being dropped, and then the ways she could legitimately earn money were... limited.

"You seem to be fine for Ravyns."

Kyra tightened her smile. She'd rather not earn money through the market. "We both know I can't spend Ravyns down my local corner shop."

Xander frowned, staring up at the black skyscraper commonly named the Tower. "What can you even do?"

Kyra paused, debating what to tell him. It wasn't like he could judge her even more. "I work with the dead."

Xander visibly cringed, his upper lip curled. "Of course you do."

She'd met many people who'd taken an instant dislike to her because of what she was, but she'd never had anyone been so open with it. Xander seemed to take it to the next level, as if her very existence disgusted him.

You disgust me.

"You can wait here," she said after they entered the atrium. "I shouldn't be long."

"How am I supposed to protect you if I'm down here?" His impatient rumble forced her to stop.

She turned to glare at him. "I'm not a defenceless –"

"Kyra?"

Kyra froze at her name, surprised to see Winston at the security desk.

"What are you doing here?" he asked, darting his eyes up to Xander. "Who's this?

"I'm here to see Commissioner Brooks," she replied, despite Winston ignoring her entirely to frown at the man at her back. "You told me you were covering the Liverpool department." He was the one who'd cancelled their date at the last minute. He'd told her that there had been an emergency in another city, and wouldn't be back for a while. Clearly a lie.

Winston blinked, as if remembering she was there. "I... I was." He cleared his throat, red seeping up his neck. "I can rebook the restaurant."

Kyra rustled in her bag, finding her pass and signing herself in.

Winston went to reach for her, but stopped at Xander's deep voice.

"Don't touch her."

Winston sneered. "And who exactly are you, arsehole?"

"Winst, man? Everything okay?" Another security guard approached the desk, darting his eyes between all three of them.

"Everything's fine, Stan," Winston said, tension along his jaw. "Kyra, I'll call you."

"No thanks." Before Kyra could add anymore, Xander had grabbed her hand and pulled her towards the lift. She yanked herself from his grip, crossing her arms as they waited for the doors to open.

Xander turned to the side, nonchalantly leaning against the wall. "He's a bit skinny for you, don't you think?"

Kyra ignored him, carefully watching the counter descend the floors.

"What kind of name is Winston, anyway?"

Kyra closed her eyes, praying to whoever'd listen for the lift to hurry up.

"Bet he's a shit fuck."

Kyra finally looked at him, but he was too busy smirking at Winston over her shoulder. "Stop it."

Her stomach clenched when he directed that smirk at her. "Or what, Princess?"

The lift dinged, doors opening as she stepped to the side, allowing everyone to exit. "Stay here. I can't risk losing this job."

"Not gonna happen." Xander stepped in beside her, waiting until she clicked the number for the correct floor before continuing. "I'm here as protection, not to arrange your funeral."

"It's a building full of Paladins, people literally trained to protect people. I'm sure I'll be okay." Kyra couldn't help her frown, knowing she would never have a funeral. No, her body would be burned beyond even ash, forgotten in both life, and death. "Besides, all you've done so far is piss off the security."

Xander chuckled, but thankfully remained silent.

It took only minutes to get to the forty-second floor, the main operation for the whole Paladin London Division. The lift opened out onto a labyrinth of grey cubicles, and even though she'd concealed her chi, she was unsurprised by the hostile and curious stares as she made her way towards the office of Commissioner Brooks.

"I told you to stay back," she angrily whispered, feeling Xander as a shadow behind her.

"Oh, you made it then," Barbara, the receptionist said when Kyra approached. "I didn't think you would turn up." She pursed her brightly painted lips, long exaggerated lashes fluttering as she greeted Xander. "Oh, hello there."

He winked. "Why, hello to you too."

"So, shall I take a seat?" Kyra asked.

Barbara flicked her hand absently. "Yeah, sit wherever.

I'll let Commissioner Brooks know that you've made it this time." She pushed her breasts together, leaning forward.

Kyra took a seat, Xander taking the one beside her, no doubt watching Barbara showcase herself. She'd met the Commissioner a few times to discuss the possibility of work, and each time she'd bitten her tongue. He used to be a Paladin for the very division he now controlled, the best according to himself. Kyra wasn't sure how he'd gained the job, his chi relatively weak compared to even Barbara, whose faint scent of clean ozone with an undertone of musky wood highlighted her ability with earthen spells.

No, she doubted he truly controlled Supernatural Intelligence. Likely a puppet for someone else.

Barbara loudly chewed gum, popping a bubble every twenty seconds or so. She openly stared, nose wrinkled. "What's it like to practice black magic?"

Kyra rested her palms on her knees, her attention on the door. "Will Commissioner Brooks be much longer?"

Pop.

"You don't look evil," she said with a high-pitched giggle. "I never know what to really expect when I see a black witch. Aren't you all damned or something?"

Pop.

"I don't know, it depends if we make a deal with the devil or not," Kyra replied tartly, ignoring Xander's smirk. "Gift him our first-born child."

Barbara's jaw dropped open with a dramatic gasp, eyes widening. "The devil's real?"

Before Kyra could respond a light brightened at the edge of her desk, followed by a loud buzz.

"Barb, baby," a whiney voice began when she clicked a button on the intercom. *"I need you to run to the pharmacy to get that ointment for my —"*

"Miss Farzan's here," Barbara interrupted with a squeak. "That black witch you hired."

Silence stretched.

"Ugh, send her in."

Kyra pursed her lips. "Stay here," she whispered to Xander, not giving him time to respond. "Please."

The large oak door opened silently, the rustic design odd compared to the surrounding office space. Commissioner Brooks sat in a tall leather chair, the silhouette of London a powerful backdrop from the large window behind. He watched her as she closed the door behind, a slim man with greasy red hair dressed in a suit several sizes too big.

The room was reasonably large for an office, with a sleek black glass desk that was covered in dirty fingerprints. Two chairs were placed in front of it, identical to the one he sat in, but on a smaller scale. To the right was a floor to ceiling bookshelf covered in picture frames and random trinkets, with only one space dedicated to actual books. The photographs were all of himself in various poses, some alone with a brooding expression, and others awkwardly taken with celebrities and politicians.

In the centre, with its own dedicated spotlight was a wand.

"Thank you for meeting me," Kyra said when he held out his hand, his smile a little on the condescending side. "I appreciate you're busy."

"Of course," he said, his hand slick with sweat when he squeezed harder than necessary. "Please, take a seat."

He pulled his arm back, his elbow knocking the single frame on his desk. It clattered over, revealing a photograph of Barbara seductively posing in luminous pink lingerie. Her lipstick even matched the underwear. Brooks quickly replaced the frame, setting it beside the chrome lamp with a flustered snigger.

"So," he began, reclining in his leather chair. "Tell me why you didn't turn up to the meeting I worked so hard to get for you?"

"I'm sorry, I was –"

"Actually," he said, smacking his lips. "I don't care." He adjusted the lapels of his jacket, resting further back in his chair until it almost tipped. "You've embarrassed yourself by not turning up to meet the client. It made you look unprofessional. I very much doubt you'll be able to find legit work in the entire city after this."

"I was called on an emergency –"

Brooks dismissed her with a flick of his hand. "Enough, I don't want to hear it. I knew I shouldn't have trusted black witches."

"An emergency for Councilman Gallagher," she continued as his smile faltered. "Maybe you could confirm with him yourself?" She knew he wouldn't call Frederick, otherwise she wouldn't have said it. "Or maybe I'll just..." She let her words drift off.

"No, no," he said quickly. "There's no need to contact anyone from the Council."

She couldn't blame his slight panic. Other than Frederick, she'd never met anyone else who held a seat on the Council, the people who reigned over all Breed. If they were anything like Frederick, she hoped she never had to deal with them.

Brooks paused, pale skin glistening. His smile seemed forced, lips stretched so wide she could make out every single tooth. "Aren't you lucky I was able to do you this favour?"

Kyra waited.

"I defused the situation with the client, and they've

agreed to give you another chance. You're very lucky, because it took a lot of convincing."

"I'm sure it did," she said, the words harsher than intended. "What exactly am I supposed to be doing for this client? You know my restrictions under the law."

"Oh," he grinned, hands rubbing together. "Nothing you haven't done before, I'm sure."

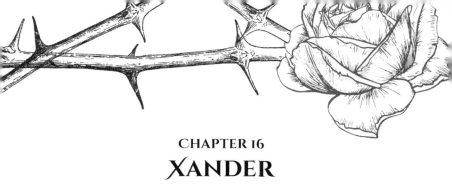

CHAPTER 16
XANDER

The air was bitter, the sky pale and threatening snow.

Xander disregarded the curious glances from the two siblings, their attention strained between watching Kyra tease salt around the grave, and him. They bickered – as siblings frequently did – but with an extra venom entwined with hatred. He wanted to blame grief, considering they were both standing above their recently deceased father's grave. But from their frequent peeks at their watches, he assumed they were likely just soulless arseholes.

"Is this going to take much longer?" the man said, checking his expensive gold watch for the fifth time in the last thirty-minutes. "I have a meeting to get to."

"And it's cold!" his sister added, tightening her designer scarf. "This should have been resolved days ago."

"Indya, I'm dealing with it," the man said, his smile fake when he turned back to Kyra. "Now, can you answer my question?"

She looked up from the position on her knees, the salt

laid in a circular pattern, pale against the freshly turned soil. "Not too much longer," she replied in her soft voice.

"Then get on with it," the woman said, her tone sharp. "Aren't we paying for your necromancy services by the hour?"

Xander hadn't realised he scowled until the woman glanced at him, and clearly took a step back behind her brother. Her reaction didn't bother him, not when it was something he was accustomed to. He didn't have the friendliest of faces, not when his hair was so pale it was almost silver which was a great contrast to the black of his brows. And then there were his eyes. He'd always gotten attention for his eyes. *Striking*, they'd been called when he was growing up, but cold. Pale blue irises that seemed to startle people, but to him they were just eyes, ones that saw things others couldn't.

"Hey, hey you!" a voice called beside him, followed by a partially transparent hand fluttering in his eyeline. "I know you can hear me."

Xander leaned heavier against the headstone, folding his arms. Cemeteries, the one place he purposely stayed clear of. She'd said she was a dark witch because she didn't embrace death, and yet there she was, calling the fucking dead.

It had taken years of patience to learn to ignore the spirits who screamed for his attention. To pretend he couldn't hear or see them. They were a pain in his arse, always demanding things like explanations, or forgiveness. It wasn't his fault they'd died... usually.

"Hey, I know you can hear me!" A face appeared this time, partially blocking Xander's view as Kyra finalised the lines in the salt. "Hey, you prick, you could at least acknowledge me!"

The spirit flickered, his face disappearing altogether

126

before reappearing. He was relatively weak, pulling power from somewhere close. Possibly the newly dead to generate his somewhat transparent form. Xander remained relaxed, careful to not respond. He concentrated on Kyra's soothing voice, so damn soft and calming that it pissed him off. Surely someone who worked with the dead shouldn't sound so warm and comforting?

Her voice and face should reflect her magic. Ugly and coarse, with crooked teeth, wrinkles and warts. Except, as he already knew, her skin was soft, a dark bronze that hinted at sunshine and warmer climates. Her face, frustratingly not unpleasant, was a mixture of heritages, with dark amber eyes that were slightly upturned and emphasised with cat-like eyeliner.

"Yeah," the spirit grumbled, "well, fuck you too." He lifted a fist, knuckles passing through Xander's nose as if he was just a slight breeze. When Xander didn't flinch he sighed, shoulders drooping as he wandered off further into the cemetery.

Bored, he pulled a pack of cigarettes out of his pocket, lighting one quickly between his lips. He ignored the woman's cutting stare, instead breathing out a steady smoke. He blinked, realising the smudges in his peripheral were more ghosts slowly moving towards him. Some were practically solid, the fresher ones' faces always twisted with confusion and dread. Others were barely visible, just glints in the light. But they all still pestered, pulled to his aura in a way he didn't understand or care to learn.

It was why he stayed away from places where they would accumulate in great numbers. He sure as hell didn't want any to follow him home. He had enough issues with his brothers arguing in his ear, he didn't need dead people too.

A brush on his shoulder, a hesitant hand.

Xander didn't need to turn to know it was the father who stood by his side. A stream of light still tethered him to the grave, stopping him from passing over to whatever was next.

"Stop it," the father said, "It's uncomfortable to be this close, and yet I feel you pulling me."

Trust me, Xander thought. *It's not on purpose.*

He wanted to shake the hand off his shoulder, but knew he couldn't without having to acknowledge it, and that gave the spirit power. Kyra met his eyes then, a crease appearing between her delicate brows. He forced himself to nod, to acknowledge her concern. He wanted her done so they could leave, not pause to see whether he was freaking the fuck out or not.

"Get on with it," he vocalised, the words laced with a growl.

The siblings stepped further back, closer to Kyra.

"It's ready," she said, pulling a short knife from some-where in her bag.

The hand left his shoulder. The father's whole body solidified enough Xander could make out his cruelly pinched features, identical to that of the son. He saw the daughter in his eyes, soft but beady. His shirt was untucked, the suit jacket straining against a large stomach. That was another thing, ghosts wore the same clothes, or lack of, from when they died, not the pretty outfit friends and families buried them in. Ghosts were bad, but naked ghosts were worse.

"Why does my chest hurt so much?" the father asked. "Is that how I died?"

"It will be over soon," Xander whispered beneath his breath, deciding to acknowledge him after all. "Then you can rest."

"Rest?" he parroted, glowering at his children. "How

can I rest when all they want to know about is their inheritance. They've always cared about my money more than me. Their mother would be ashamed."

The beast, usually dormant, rushed to the front of Xander's mind. It took him a second to figure out why, the scent of fresh blood fragrant. Kyra had cut down her arm, the slice thin, but blood pooled at the wound none the less. Anger pulsed through his veins, and he was thankful he'd worn his glasses to hide the change in his irises.

The siblings were already slightly skittish, if they saw the beast through his gaze they would probably piss themselves.

The father must have felt a change, his ghostly sorrow and anger turning to fear. "How does this work? Does it hurt?"

Xander couldn't answer even if he knew, his instincts screaming as magic, thick and dark oozed out of the surrounding dirt. Kyra's lips moved, her words lost to the gentle hum that increased in pitch with every drop of her blood onto the grave. The soil blackened, the blood moving, merging until a shadow of the body was echoed.

The earth sunk, and the sister squealed.

"What's happening!" she cried. "I don't want to see him all dead, you know! I was told there wouldn't be a zombie!"

Xander would have snorted if his beast wasn't so prominent.

"Oh, now she cries," the father muttered beside him. He began to walk to his grave, his body becoming corporeal once he stepped over the salt.

The father stared at his children, tears like glitter glistening down his opaque cheeks when he turned to Xander. "They can't see me, can they?"

It was Kyra who answered. "No, they can't see you, Mr Harrison."

"He's here?" the girl asked. "Daddy, are you here?"

"I'm here Indya, I'm here." He reached forward, his hand disappearing until it was barely visible once it passed the salt threshold. He still brushed his ghostly fingertips along her cheek before repeating the gesture on his son.

Indya sucked in a breath, her palm moving to touch her face with trembling fingers.

"Dad," the son began, "this is really important. We need to know where you've hidden your will. I called the family solicitor and they knew nothing about it."

"See," the father said, shoulders drooping. "That's all they care about."

Kyra flicked her eyes towards Xander, but didn't repeat the words.

"Daddy, all your assets have been frozen. My allowance has stopped," Indya said with a stamp of her foot. "Just tell us where you've hidden the will, please."

"Witch, what is he saying? Where is the will?" the son asked with an edge of impatience. "Tell me!"

The father sighed. "This is all my fault, for bringing up two ungrateful brats. I was always too busy with work after their mother died. I threw money at them, instead I should've been there."

"Daddy, we're entitled to our inheritance," Indya cried, dabbing forced tears with the edge of her scarf.

The father, turning to Kyra nodded. "Tell them, tell them to look behind the Montgomery painting, they will know which one. The code is their mother's birthday."

It didn't take long for the siblings to leave, not even a goodbye to their father who watched them go. As soon as Kyra broke the salt he immediately lost his shape, his body flickering as the power that kept him there weakened.

He was free.

Kyra, dropping to her knees carefully moved the soil

with her bare hands, covering the salt with delicate and controlled movements.

"Tears?" the father said, crouching beside her. "For me?"

Kyra didn't look up from what she was doing, unable to hear him once more.

"Mr Harrison," Xander said quietly. "It's time for you to go."

Kyra turned to him, her face wet, and eyes red. Her makeup had smeared, the smoky look somehow suiting her.

The father reached forward, but didn't touch her. "My children didn't shed a single tear when I died, and yet this stranger honours me with hers." A crooked smile, followed with a flash of white light.

Kyra said nothing as she finished what she was doing, and Xander offered her no words of comfort. It was a while later, the sky starting to darken and the grave back to normal when he finally broke the silence.

"Could you have called his body?" he asked when she climbed to her feet, brushing the remaining dirt from her knees. He'd heard of black magic that could control the dead in such a way, the thought sickening.

Kyra looked at the cigarette he held between his fingers, the end a bright orange. "They will kill you, you know," she replied instead.

Xander laughed, the sound offensive against their surroundings. "Answer the question."

Kyra's cheeks coloured, and he wasn't sure if it was because of the way he demanded, or that she didn't want to answer his question. "Why? So you can judge me? No thanks."

"Is anything easy with you?" Xander took a long drag from his cigarette, breathing the smoke out through his nose. "It's a simple question, Princess."

"I'm not your Princess," she growled, and Xander couldn't help but smile.

She was always so controlled, calm. He enjoyed riling her up, seeing her true nature.

"If you must know, yes I can call the dead. It works best within twenty-four hours, I refused to do it after that."

He eyed her curiously, pressing her harder. "Why?"

"Even with the magic repairing the natural breakdown of the body... it's not worth the trauma," she said with a voice like liquid fucking velvet.

"So you're a Necromancer?" Not really a question, more like a venom coated verification. "I didn't think Paladins were hired for this type of work."

"Paladins are agents trained and hired by Supernatural Intelligence. I'm not a Paladin."

He scowled, the ghosts staggered behind him forgotten as she held his full attention. "Since when was Supernatural Intelligence forcing the dead?"

"How am I supposed to know?" she replied with a quiet, but sharp snap. "I was asked to do this, so I did. Supernatural Intelligence offers more services than your Neanderthal mind can clearly comprehend."

"Do you really do everything you're told?" he bit back, the tendons at his nape rigid.

Kyra flinched, eyes widening as tears still wet her skin. Her mouth opened, her next words drowned out against the loud rumble of the earth. Heavy vibration beneath their feet. Xander reaching out as Kyra staggered.

"Fuck!" Alarm as the ground opened up with a crack, splitting between them with an impressive force. Kyra threw herself back, her boots scrambling back as rock and dirt fell into the growing hole.

Xander's chest turned to ice as bony claws speared

through the darkness, hooking themselves onto the edge only inches from Kyra's feet.

"Don't move," he whispered through clenched teeth. He steadied his gaze on the Shadow-Veyn that crawled from the earth, flesh covered fur scraped away to reveal a shock of pale skull. A hellhound, it's snout longer than a wolves and too-thin teeth dripping with venom. He was small, classification B if he went by its lack of sharp bones that were usually an extension of its spine. Dark vapour drifted out of the holes of his nostrils, the smoke floating around to the exposed ribs at its side.

From the scent of panic coming from Kyra, he knew the hound wasn't concealed in a glamour. The Shadow-Veyn hunted openly, without fear of repercussion.

Fuck.

Red eyes, too small for the hollow sockets rolled freely until they settled on her.

Double fuck.

"Run!" Xander barked, jumping over the hole and launching himself onto the hound's back. His arm encircled its throat as he tried to stifle its foul breath, full of dead carrion and rot. "Run!" he repeated as he was thrown, knocked against a headstone so hard it crumbled against his back. The hellhound turned with a snarl, putrid lip peeling back to reveal three sets of sharp teeth.

Xander felt his tattoos blaze, the glyphs permanently marked on his skin glowing as arcane coated his fingertips. He cast a concentrated ball, the power ripping through the hound's fur to leave even more exposed bone. The hound rolled, barely give him a second glance before bounding after Kyra.

Xander charged after them both, heavy boots covering the distance almost as fast as the hound. He called to the other part of his soul, to his beast who always watched from behind his eyes. He welcomed the sweet pain as his body shifted, his arms changing to monstrous pure white paws with large serrated claws. He collided with the hound in a tangle of muffled snarls and sharp teeth, blackened blood coating his tongue within seconds.

The hound cried out, rolling them both as Xander's teeth ripped flesh clean from bones. A sharp pain, nails scoring down his flank.

He ignored the burn as teeth dug into his shoulder and venom pulsed through his blood. Green immediately began to weep from the wound, his body designed to repel any type of toxin that the Shadow-Veyn secreted. A venom that would kill anyone else in one bite.

This was what they were made to do, their sole purpose.

His beast analysed every angle to get his own strike. A linear mind that knew only violence, hunger and sex.

Kyra cried out, and his beast roared in response. He bared his teeth, a warning to the hound who turned towards the sound. The Shadow-Veyn panted, head low as the smoke that drifted through its ribs began to solidify, crawling along its for in an attempt to heal the damage.

Xander steadied his weight for a final strike, the earth wet beneath his monstrous paws.

Do it.

The command shot through his mind, his beast forcing their muscles forward in a push of pure strength. It only took a split-second, his fangs slicing through the hound's throat with little effort. Blood tinged his fur pink, his lips lifted into a wolfish grin as the Shadow-Veyn collapsed dead.

The ground trembled once more, the body suddenly swallowed by the very earth it had desecrated.

An angry shout, one that had him searching for Kyra with a bite of panic. He felt her magic first, prickling across his senses like angry wasps. She was caught against a solid stone wall, too tall for her to climb. She stood, palm encased in her own deep purple arcane with licks of sparkling white.

A second hound tensed before her, ready to leap as she waited with features settled into a resolute expression. She was going to fight it. Which either made her crazy, or stupid.

Where the fuck did this mutt come from?

Xander had never moved so fast, his body like lightning as he shot across the cemetery. The hound's head turned, and he didn't give it a chance to attack. He leapt, landing between them with a growl of warning. His tail unfurled into seven distinctive whips, the tips sharp with a single barb. The hound tested his patience, stepping forward until three of the tails thrashed forward to cut and slice. With a howl the hound jumped over the wall, and it went against every instinct for Xander not to follow, to kill.

Arcane burned against his back, his tail screaming with pain when he turned and found Kyra. Her eyes were wide, her blood fragrant in his nose.

Do it.

Xander frowned to himself, not understanding his beast's thought.

Take her.

Xander shifted back, pushing his beast back within the confines of his mind. An angry roar echoed between his ears, followed by a frustrated snarl.

His voice was deeper when he grumbled, his throat raw. "Were you bitten?"

She blinked at him, her body still rigid as arcane cracked like flames in her right palm. "What was that?" she asked, her voice just as strained.

"Hellhounds," he replied, carefully raising his hands to show he meant no harm. Sweat was a sheen across his bare skin, the cool air reminding him that the remnants of his clothes were long gone. "Young, just pups."

"Pups?" she parroted, more of a squeak. She staggered forward, her legs unsteady as he caught her.

"Were you bitten?" he asked once again, lifting her into his arms. "Kyra?"

Colour drained from her face, and then he noticed the three distinct marks on her collarbone.

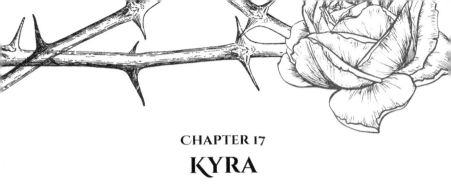

CHAPTER 17

KYRA

Kyra sucked in a pained breath, her shoulder screaming as Xander stormed into the bathroom with her gripped tightly in his arms. The light remained off, the darkness enclosing except for the burst of brightness from the hallway. She didn't struggle when he gently dropped her into the shower, only for the warm water began to cascade over.

She did however protest when she felt cold male flesh step beneath the spray too.

"Xander!" She could just make out his profile, his features cast in shadow.

Rough hands pulled at her top, the fabric ripping with little effort. Water hit her open wounds, and Xander growled at her cry. He moved until his large body blocked the spray.

She stood for a moment, panting past the pain. The metal cuff she wore on her upper arm seemed to absorb the surrounding cold, the crystal dormant. Xander reached up, as if to take it off.

"Don't!" she said, his fingers brushing the crystal that was set between the two overlapping bands. It was the only syphon she had left. The only crystal that was capable of absorbing her excess, volatile magic. "Don't touch it."

He dropped his hands to her jeans instead, the fabric caked in mud. Pushing him away she turned to face the white tile, the button loud when it popped open. She carefully yanked at the wet denim, Xander a heavy presence at her back.

Her shoulder ached, and she ignored it as she almost fell, ungraceful as she pulled and yanked until her legs and feet were free.

"Ready?" he asked before he slowly allowed more and more water to hit her skin. She bit her lip, stopping herself from crying out. His hands were soft, hesitant when he gently moved her braid and touched the edges of the wounds. The claw marks started from the back of her shoulder, moving along her collarbone to end on the top curve of her left breast. Kyra remained still, not stopping him as he began to remove the strap of her bra, but left it fastened.

It was only a few minutes, just enough for the warm water to melt away some of the tension from her muscles when it was cut off, and she became achingly aware of him behind her.

She had never been thankful for the darkness, but right then she was.

Kyra almost whimpered as the cold air assaulted her wet skin, and something stretched taut between them. Xander was silent, his movements invisible as he closed the distance. She froze at the contact.

His breath was a burst of heat, his slightly stubbled cheek brushing across hers before his nose touched her collarbone. Ten seconds. Twenty. She wasn't sure how long he stayed there before she began to shake, trying to not think about the solid muscle pressed against her in a comforting warmth.

"It's clean," he said, finally stepping back. "You'll be okay."

Kyra just nodded, struggling to swallow.

"We need to get it wrapped up."

Again she nodded, just a gentle acknowledgment that didn't really confirm whether she heard the words or not.

"Kyra?" Fingers gripped her chin, turning her head, and that was when she lost it.

The full-blown panic came from nothing, her heart thundering in her chest as she closed her eyes and then quickly snapped them open. If she wasn't already wet she would have been drenched in sweat, her hands shaking as she reached around in the dark until they landed on hard, naked male chest. She should have shoved, screamed for him to leave so she could deal with her reaction alone. Instead her nails dug into his skin, pulling him closer as the tattoos she couldn't see burst into life beneath her palms.

She concentrated on the intricate lines and swirls, the tattoos brightening the bathroom to the point she could just make out the outline of his strong jaw. The light reflected in his eyes, revealing they'd shifted to the liquid silver that had fascinated her. Except with a blink they were gone.

Her breathing calmed, her chest no longer aching when she pulled her hands back. "Sorry," she whispered, feeling her cheeks heat. As soon as her touch stopped, the glowing faded and she was enclosed in the darkness once more. But this time she was calmer, more prepared.

Xander grunted, stepping back out of the shower. "Lights, on. Low," he said, and the light above burst to life, just enough to make out the familiar bathroom.

Kyra kept her eyes directly at his face. She knew he wasn't naked, having somehow pulled on a pair of jeans between the cemetery and his place. But that didn't mean the water hadn't stuck the denim to him like a second skin.

Her face burned hotter, especially when she was sure she could see the clear outline of his...

"We need to get it wrapped up," he repeated slowly, dark brow raised when she just stood there like an idiot.

"Yeah... yeah, okay." She cleared her throat, moving to stand in front of the counter beside the sink. She pulled herself up, the movement causing one of the cuts to open and blood to trickle. Xander was there to meet it with a clean cloth, the tin and bandages already beside him.

She watched him as he carefully applied the salve, the scent now familiar, relaxing. He worked in silence, his face schooled into an almost militant boredom as eyes of ice remained solely on the task at hand. It was easier to watch him when he wasn't looking at her. Wasn't openly judging.

Just as he started to cut the bandages she decided she couldn't stand the silence, or the tension any longer. "So, you turn into a white wolf lion thing with lots of tails?" She tried to make it sound casual, but it came out more of a question. "That's interesting. Can you all do that?"

What was he? Some type of hybrid druid shifter?

Xander moved his eyes up, holding hers for only a second before they skirted back down. "You're going to scar," he said instead of answering. "But you're lucky it was only a scratch. Hounds are venomous, their bite deadly. Your arm looks fine," he added, gesturing to the thin cut she'd made at the grave.

"Lucky me," she laughed, the sound hollow. "What was that thing? Why haven't I seen one of them before?"

"Shadow-Veyn," he said, meeting her eyes once more. "Monsters created in the Nether. They were once trapped down along with the Daemons, and now they've been released to roam and hunt freely up here."

Kyra couldn't drop the eye contact, which was almost a challenge in itself.

"Now, why were not one, but two hellhounds hunting you?" He gripped the counter on each side of her thighs.

She lifted her chin with a frown. "How do you know they were hunting me?"

Xander's grip tightened, the counter groaning. "Because if I hadn't attacked first, they would have ignored me completely." His eyes finally dropped back to her shoulder, and she released a ragged breath. "They were hunting you. Why?"

"How am I supposed to know?"

His nostrils flared, and the counter cracked. He swore in a language she'd never heard, the words beautiful, but harsh.

"Kyra," he said her name like it was a warning. "Shadow-Veyn, especially hounds run on pure animal instinct. Unless they're commanded by their masters. Why was a Daemon's dog hunting you?"

She looked away, seeking the stronger light in the hall. "This was stupid, I have to go back." She went to jump off the counter when Xander stood closer, boxing her in. She felt magic tingle her fingertips, ready. "Xander, back off." She made sure her words were strong, void of any emotion that threatened to ruin her.

"What happened?"

"You have no idea what I have to do to just survive. The stuff I'm made to do." Her fingertips sparked, so she pulled them closer to her chest. "This was a mistake, I have to go back."

"Like fuck you do," he snarled. "Tell me what the fuck is going on? What sort of trouble have you gotten yourself into?"

"I've... I've..." She struggled to push the words out. "I've been given to a Daemon as insurance."

You disgust me.

The memory of his words rebounded. She almost wanted him to say them to her again, to remind her that the choices she'd made to survive were aberrant. Instead his face twisted to the exact expression he had over a year ago. She wasn't sure why it bothered her so much, but her heart still ached anyway.

"You agreed?"

No. She hadn't technically agreed, but she hadn't fought hard enough either. She'd been *given* to a Daemon. Creatures of pure horror. Breed with no morals, and who regularly feast on the witches stupid enough to summon them.

She'd been *given* like an unwanted pet.

"Why didn't you mention this before?" he demanded. "This is pretty fucking important information, Kyra."

"Because it had nothing to do with those threats." She felt his rage, the heat a pulse against her exhausted senses. "My life is what it is," she added quietly. "There's nothing I can do about it."

"Who promised you to a Daemon?"

Kyra wanted to close her eyes. To hide. "I can't say."

His anger was still apparent. "Can't, or won't?"

A moment passed, and then another. She thought he would have broken his jaw from the way he gritted his teeth so hard, but the silence stretched to the point she flinched when he finally broke the stillness. "Tell me everything."

Her voice cracked. "I can't."

CHAPTER 18

XANDER

Xander slammed the front door, a physical crack splitting the wood. The sight of it immediately calmed his temper to a simmer when the break continued until the window shattered.

Shit.

"So, it went well then?" Alice asked, unamused.

"Where's your mate?" he replied instead, hoping his tone wasn't as irate as he felt. Apparently it was if he went by her expression.

"What happened, Xee?" Riley called, entering from the kitchen. "Where's Kyra?"

"She wanted to go back."

"What do you mean back? What about those threats?" Sparks brightened Alice's fingertips. They matched the blue green of her fractured eyes, her magic erratic. Xander thought she was weak when he'd first met her, not understanding Riley's interest in pursuing a witch with such uncontrollable power. But Alice had proven herself more than once. Even risking herself to help one of his brothers.

Kyra, on the other hand, was nothing but a destructive storm that looked to tear them apart.

"You can't help someone who doesn't want to be helped. Both Kace and Ti said her place was clean, and there was no trace of anyone but her on that roof garden." He turned towards the stairs, wanting to go to his room. To be alone in the dark. He kept up the rent for the other place out of convenience and privacy. But this was his true home, surrounded by his brothers. His family.

"Who's she gone back to?" Alice asked, stopping him as he took a step. "Xee it's important. She might be in some serious trouble. More than she's –"

Xander interrupted with a frustrated growl. "She's a black witch. She's made lying a fucking art."

"Watch your tone," Riley snarled.

Xander rubbed across his face. "Look, how am I supposed to know? You're her friend Alice, you try and scrape that information from her because she's not telling me shit." He slipped past her, ignoring the audience that was growing from the hall.

"Xee, wait!" Riley called after him.

Xander paused on the stairs, not bothering to look back over his shoulder. "Is that an order, *Sire*?" He'd used the word on purpose, his anger at Kyra's blatant stupidity enough to break him.

They weren't shifters, but they still had a similar enough hierarchy when it came to their beasts. Riley had always been the alpha, the leader. He was both the strongest and the fasted, but he hated enforcing it. To him they were all equal, making decisions as a team. It worked for them all, but when it came down to it all the Guardians would drop to their knees for Riley without hesitation.

Riley swore, and something thudded behind him. "Everyone out of here, now!" Grunts and curses, and even Alice protested until Riley barked another demand. Xander felt his brother beside him a second later.

"She makes you angry. Irrational. I understand more than you understand, but you're supposed to be the most stable of the guys. I need you to chill the fuck out before you force them to shift."

Xander was rigid, his breathing barely controlled. "I don't know why she gets this reaction from me."

Riley's bark of laughter surprised him enough that he turned, and saw his friend grinning.

Xander closed his eyes, soothing the rage from his beast. "She's in some deep shit, and won't let me help. She won't even give me the details."

"That's females for you. Always thinking they know best." Riley's smile disappeared when he sighed. "Do you know where she went?"

"I couldn't seem to let her go, so I followed her until she got into a chauffeured black car. After that," he growled, "I have no idea."

KYRA

Kyra made herself small beside Bane, silent.

"You didn't stay at your place last night?" he asked quietly, brow raised as he turned in his seat. "Or the previous night. Is there a reason?"

"I stayed in a hotel," she lied, hoping he couldn't sense her increased heartbeat.

Bane only nodded. "I've made Frederick aware of the stress those threats have caused you. He was displeased to find out you'd left without letting us know. You know you must update me of extended disappearances." He let out a sigh. "Don't worry, I'll calm him down."

She knew he expected a thanks, so she forced a smile

before turning towards the window. The road blurred, the car rumbling beneath her as they headed outside of the city limits. Bane had been outside when she'd returned home, stern as he opened the car door and gestured inside.

"We going to the coven?" she asked, trying to keep the conversation light, and off what she was doing the day before. "Has Dirk been in contact?"

Bane only stared, head tilted as he appraised the slightly yellowing marks on her throat, and then the edge of her bandages on her shoulder. "What hotel did you stay at?"

"The one around the corner," she replied quickly, slanting her eyes back to him. "I wasn't aware I couldn't stay at a hotel?" She kept her voice soft, but there was steel behind the forced calm.

Bane smirked. "We're headed straight to the bastion. He's requested your attendance at all meetings. I came by to pick you up last night, but clearly you weren't available." His attention skimmed the bandages once more before turning to his own window.

It took everything in her to keep that smile in place. The three head witches of the Magicka were required to stay within the castle, with Frederick living within the bastion, and the two others possessing a tower each.

What exactly did Frederick have planned if he was willing to invite a Daemon so close to the grounds of the Magicka?

The car drove through large iron gates, the metal teased into a beautiful motif of roses and razor-sharp thorns. The bastion was exactly like she expected, with old brick and stairs leading to a flat roof and turrets. It had been adapted into living quarters, cut off from the main castle to allow for some privacy. Enchantments had been carved into every brick, protection spells that seemed to burn like embers in

146

her peripheral, but were dark as coal when stared at directly.

She was escorted through the large oak doors, also enchanted, and down the hall to where Frederick relaxed back in a velvet armchair. He didn't smile when she appeared, or even look up from the newspaper he was reading. He lifted a single hand, dismissing Bane who closed the door behind him with a click.

"Councilman," she greeted politely, taking in the room with one quick sweep. "I'm sorry If I'm late."

The walls inside were the same stone, but paintings and tapestries full of colour had been hung to chase away the cold. An oversized hearth burned behind Frederick, the fire spluttering.

"I see you are well," he said as he carefully folded the newspaper, settling it onto his lap. "You gave us quite a scare when Bane found your flat empty."

Kyra waited for him to finish.

"He's made it quite clear that those threats have upset you greatly. To show my concern for your welfare I would like to offer you a room here until we can find another suitable replacement to your flat."

"You... you want me to move in here?"

The newspaper disappeared with a click of his finger. "Of course, I wouldn't want harm to come to my favourite witch, would I?" A snigger.

"No, thank you. You were right, they were nothing to fear."

Frederick patted down his ruffled shirt, more at home on the front cover of a pirate romance novel than a powerful witch. "You turn down my hospitality? After everything I do for you?"

Kyra heard the underlying threat, knew not to speak

back even as panic formed words on her tongue. "I appreciate the offer, but no thank you."

Frederick climbed to his feet, sweeping forward until he was only a step away. "Your change of attitude worries me. Should I be worried, Kyra?"

"No... of course not."

"I forget how delicate women can be. So breakable," he mused. "You understand that I couldn't tell him no when he chose you? It should be an honour to be picked out amongst the cattle of the others."

Kyra froze, and when he reached forward to touch her bandaged shoulder she sucked in a pained breath. His thumb pressed down until she felt her skin break, blood darkening the white of the dressing. She caught her cry, not wanting to give him the satisfaction.

"Do not embarrass me, Kyra. Dirk is our ally, and he cannot witness any weakness between us."

Kyra took a second to make sure her response was strong, her voice void of pain. "Of course."

Frederick's smile was cruel when he lifted his hand from her shoulder. He clicked, the room around them changing. The walls that were once stone became a clean white paint with walnut panelling. The floor was the same shiny wood, a red rug rolling beneath their feet like a large bloodstain.

"Glamour," he explained when Kyra looked around. "I grow bored of my surroundings, so I like to change them up every now and then. It's a trick learned from the Fae, the one thing that is marginally useful from them."

A wand appeared in his hand, the end tinged black as if burnt. He pressed it against the hearth, the only thing in the room that hadn't changed. Runes appeared in the stone, swirls she didn't recognise that moved like thick vines, carving their way through until the stone was barely recognisable.

"The walls of my bastion are enchanted. Only those I choose can pass into these walls. What we do, and say here will remain between these walls." He held her gaze, a final warning. "No one would ever suspect anything in the home of the Supreme."

The fire flickered, turning green as Dirk stepped out between the dancing flames with a grin splitting his face.

"Welcome," Frederick said with a sweep of his arms. He gestured to the new table by the armchairs where fresh tea had been poured. "I believe it would be a suitable place to strengthen our business arrangement further."

Dirk prowled out, leather clothes morphing into identical imitations of Fredericks. It somehow suited him better with his harsher cheekbones, shoulder-length hair, and crimson eyes. Those same eyes settled on Kyra, his appraisal taking his time before he finally took a seat beside the flames, hooking his leg over one knee. "I've brought you a parchment," he said to Frederick, rolling his shoulders as if he missed the weight of his wings.

Smoke appeared in his hand, and as it dissipated it showed a single piece of paper no larger than his palm.

Frederick barely concealed his annoyance. "That doesn't look like much? What happened to a grimoire?"

"My knowledge is vast, and mostly locked away behind over a thousand years of memories. We'll start with the parchment, and work our way from there. *If* our arrangement works," he added. "It will open up many possibilities between our Breeds."

"Excellent." Frederick forced a smile. "Then why don't I reintroduce you to Kyra, the black witch you chose as insurance."

Red eyes settled back on her, and she locked her knees to stop from running.

"You made an interesting choice with this one," Frederick continued. "She's more than just a black witch. Her chi's able to hold more power without suffering the consequences. Although, her arcane and aggressive magic is weak, so you're unlikely to have any resistance. At least not magically." Frederick sniggered. "She'll be the one who practices the spells you share."

"So why bother with you when I've already been given this witch?" Dirk unfurled from the chair.

"She needs my power behind her, do not mistake that," Frederick warned, his tone harsh as he pinged his eyes between them. "Kyra's mine. She will only do what *I* say."

"I thought she was mine to play with?" Dirk chuckled over his shoulder. "I like to be *very* hands on with these spells."

"Only with my permission," Frederick added, trying to keep some sort of dominance in the conversation.

Kyra swallowed, but remained a statue when Dirk stalked over, circling her as if she were a prized horse.

"Little Black Witch," Dirk greeted her. "I can still taste your delicious aura. Can you still taste mine?" His hand brushed against hers, and she couldn't stop her recoil.

Frederick barked a laugh. "It looks like she needs a little more training."

"Indeed," Dirk said with a smirk. "But I guess it's half the fun to break them in." His attention settled on the blood on her shoulder. "My hounds were a little excited to scent their master on you, however one of them didn't return."

Kyra looked at Frederick, who only raised a brow.

Dirk pressed closer. "You wouldn't know what happened to my hound, would you?"

"I'm sorry," she replied, tipping her head back slightly. "I don't know."

Dirk's smile turned cold, his next words whispered for her alone. "Such secrets. I wonder if your own master's aware of the deceit in your eyes?"

She held her breath.

"Kyra, why don't you go prepare yourself," Frederick said, the door clicking open at her back. "Bane will show you to your quarters. We'll meet when the moon is high to begin working on the parchment."

"I need to get my stuff," she said as Bane entered at her side. "From my home."

Frederick's features tightened. "Bane will do that, now if you could –"

"No," she replied, ignoring the sharp nails as Bane grabbed onto her wrist. "I'd like to do it myself If I'm to stay here for an extended period of time."

"Do as you say?" Dirk sniggered. "I hope the sacrifices you've prepared are far more obedient."

"Sacrifices?" Kyra echoed, her blood turning cold.

Frederick's face glowed, his lips twisted. "Go." He dismissed her with a flick of the wrist. "Don't take long. We have a lot of work to do."

Kyra didn't need to be told twice. She remained silent as Bane shoved her into the waiting car, and then slid in beside her. She ignored his glare, her energy erratic as she tried to control the spike caused by her nerves.

She only had the one chance. She had to make it count.

Kyra very slowly dislodged the cuff on her upper arm, loosening the crystal against her skin. Her senses awakened, the essence she tried so hard to ignore appearing in delicate, glistening threads. The streaks attached to each individual person's heart, the magic tethering them to life. Bane's thread was strong beside her, his essence steady but dark. Almost a shadow.

She had to wait, just a little longer as he slipped out the car first, holding his hand out to her. Kyra smiled, her fingers touching his when she yanked that thread. He let out a pained scream, and with all her strength she pushed him to the pavement. She felt his essence slip away from her mental grasp, but she was already moving, running down the street. She couldn't have torn his soul from his body even if she'd tried, his aura too strong. But it was enough as she ran with as much speed as she could gather through the streets and alleys.

She paused by the river Thames, lungs burning, and before she threw her phone into the water she made a last call to the one man who despised her.

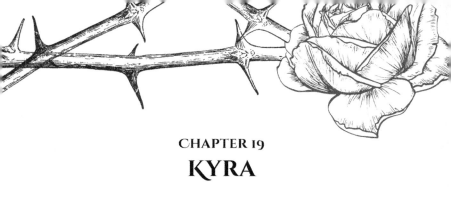

CHAPTER 19

KYRA

K yra tried to make herself appear as relaxed as possible, her hands restless in her lap beneath the large table. She was on one end, opposite Riley, with three men on either side. Their attention crawled all over her skin, silent accusations of betrayal sharp enough to cut.

Why the audience? she thought, but unable to vocalise. The men were all different, and yet their dominant presence was if they were a single entity. They were the Guardians.

Xander sat directly beside Riley, his attention too intense as she looked anywhere but him. Alice paced behind her, muttering profanities beneath her breath as she listened to Kyra recall the Daemon summoning in detail, twice, and then the meeting with Frederick and Dirk. But only after they agreed to look out for Eva.

"I know the Magicka are always looking to innovate and learn," Alice said, her chi electric as it expanded. "But I didn't think Frederick would be so fucking stupid to partner with a Daemon."

Riley sat cool and composed, black hair swept gently

across his brow, longer at the top than the sides. He watched her with slightly narrowed steel-grey eyes, lips pressed into a thin line.

Alice stopped beside Kyra, blue and green flames burning up to her elbows. She frowned, and the magic disappeared into her palms. "He's already dangerous, and if he figured out a way to use Daemonic magic too..."

"What Councillor Gallagher does has nothing to do with us," one of the men on the left said. His hair was obsidian, spiked in all different directions. It was a beautiful contrast to his warm caramel eyes.

"That was before he partnered with Daemons," the red head beside him grumbled, Kace, if she remembered correctly.

"Shouldn't the Council deal with this?" Axel added. He smiled at Kyra when she looked over, his eyes a little unfocused.

"You think the Council will do anything?" Alice snorted, placing her palms flat against the table.

"That's enough," Riley said when everyone began to bicker. "Kyra, can Frederick summon any more Daemons without your assistance?"

Kyra hesitated when everyone's scrutiny settled back on her. "It's possible with the help of the coven."

"What are the risks if you went back and pretended nothing happened?"

Alice slammed her hand on the table. "She was attacked by a fucking hellhound!"

Riley ignored her outburst, his brow raised as he waited.

"I'm not going back," she said with a quiet intensity. "I knew the risks in coming here, but I can't stand by while he sacrifices innocents for power."

"Daemon and witch magic are very different," Xander finally said, his voice flat. "His chi alone wouldn't be able to manipulate it without risking a great deal of damage to himself." His face was smoothed into an emotionless mask, cold and uninterested as he discussed everything like it was simply the weather.

Kyra licked her dry lips, her hands continuing to twist and turn in her lap. "I would be able to do it."

"Of course you couldn't," one of the men said, she wasn't sure which one. "That type of magic would kill you without glyphs."

Kyra scanned across them until she found the owner of the voice. "I would be able to do it," she simply repeated to Kace.

"Frederick has broken numerous laws by summoning a Daemon," Alice continued. "Laws he helped write. Why didn't you go straight to the Magicka?"

"Because Frederick controls it all. I couldn't risk it."

"What do you suggest?" the male beside Xander asked, expression obscured by his honey brown hair. "He's a councilmember, and we have no evidence that he did anything that's being described. Who would trust the word of a black witch?"

Xander growled, the sound vibrating across the table.

"What?" the man snarled back. "It's the truth. You don't go against a councilmember without a death wish." He settled further back in his chair, face shifting into a scowl. He pushed back his hair, dyed if she went by his much darker roots. It revealed an old, but angry red scar that sliced down his left eye, ending on his upper lip.

"Then we get evidence, don't we Jax?" Alice said back.

"Jax is right," Riley said calmly. "We need evidence, but not at the risk to Kyra." His next words were directed at her. "You need to go under the radar for now, until we figure out what he's up to. You don't chance that type of power without a plan."

Kyra felt Alice's chi stretch, a gentle brush of comfort. It was powerful, like little bursts of lightning along her aura. She wondered what hers felt like in comparison? Was it as reassuring? Or was it painful? Contaminated.

"You're having a party, and didn't invite me?" a deep voice purred from the hall behind.

"Not now Lucy," Alice groaned. "I thought you were out with Sam?"

Kyra turned to watch Lucifer strolling in like he owned the place, flashing her a wink. Her initial reaction should have been fear considering he was the same Breed she was trying to run from, but instead she was relieved to have another friendly face in a room of scowls.

She must be going mad, because not once did she think she'd be relieved to see a Daemon.

Lucifer clicked his tongue, bracing himself on the back of Kyra's chair. "Rude." His broad shoulders stretched the fabric of his shirt, strategically ripped to show the skin beneath. "I've asked you many time to tell me when the orgy starts. Now, who's top and who's bottom in this room full of testosterone?"

Kyra turned in her chair, and Lucy smirked at her before moving to the spare seat. His smile was crooked, his black hair slicked back using pink clips with little kittens on. It would have looked ridiculous on any of the powerful men, but he seemed to make it his own style.

"Guardian business," Kace grunted. "And you're not a Guardian."

Lucifer softly planted his palms face down on the table, and leaned forward to mimic Alice's pose. His nails were painted the same shade of pink as his hair clips. "You've all made it very fucking clear I'm not a crappy Guardian. I just stay here for the shits and giggles." His head swivelled to her, crimson eyes narrowing. "They think I'm some sort of sexy pet. Now, if I could only get one of them to stroke me..."

Kyra felt her lips tug while someone else groaned.

Alice rolled her eyes. "Lucy, how could a hellhound track Kyra?"

Lucy clicked his tongue. "I don't know, did it piss on you or something?" he asked Kyra, reaching forward until his finger brushed against her arm. He leapt back with a snarl, chair toppling over as his irises glowed. "Fucking, ow." Horns pierced through his hair, curling down to his jaw.

Xander had shot to his feet at the same time, but he made no move forward.

Kyra remained exactly where she was, unable to look away from the horns, or the kitten clip that had broken and was about to fall. Daemons were masters of glamour, able to change their appearance with a single thought to make themselves seem more approachable.

Lucy hadn't lived beneath the sun for very long, but she noticed the change since she first met him over a year ago. His skin was no longer a sickly ashen shade, but a tanned bronze that wasn't too much lighter from her own.

He was capable of the glamour, but other than to hide his horns and wings he seemed to be adapting naturally. Except for his red eyes which he preferred to keep as they were, he could pass as any of the other Guardians.

"You've been a naughty girl," he chuckled. "Naughty indeed."

Kyra's stomach recoiled, nausea tickling her throat. "Is there a way to block it?"

"Block what?" Xander asked, his body a thing of granite.

Lucy ignored the question. "Who?"

Kyra swallowed hard. "Dirk."

The smile slipped off Lucy's face, only for a split

second, just enough to see the panic before his lips tightened into a shadow of his previous smirk.

She wasn't the only one who'd noticed the change.

"So she's being tracked?" Xander asked.

Lucy cocked his head. "Not directly, but there's definitely something there. Not many of my kind can command hounds to scent down a possession charm. Not that there are many of my kind left." His eyes slitted to Riley before sweeping across the others. "You guys took care of that."

"Is there a way to block it?" Kyra asked once again, her voice surprisingly strong compared to the storm inside her chest.

"Maybe..." he mumbled. "I would need to read up on it."

"How can you not know?" Xander rumbled.

Lucy spun, which showed the back of his shirt was just as shredded as the front. "I'm sorry, you try be over a thousand years old and remembering every little thing."

"You're over a thousand years old?" Alice asked.

"How am I supposed to know? Why would I count?" Lucy rolled his eyes. "Rest assured, I'll figure it out. I just need access to the library."

"You don't have access to the library," Riley muttered. "You haven't even returned the book you stole the last time."

"Not the boring fucking British library. I'm talking about the *secret* library, the one where you've hidden the good stuff."

"The abbey? That's impossible."

Lucy shrugged. "Well, what a shame, and I really liked you too, Kyra. Good luck though, I hope Dirk doesn't make you –"

"What type of book?" Xander asked.

Lucy grinned. "Black grimoire, grade three."

Riley knocked his knuckles against the table in thought. "I doubt we'll be able to get Lucy past the sentinels at the door, and that grade of grimoire won't be able to leave."

"Which means we'll have to get him inside the chamber without him passing the threshold," Xander added. "Lucy, you able to pinpoint me on a drift?"

Lucy's grin widened. "Of course not, but If you were to give me an image of the library I can use that."

"Hmmm," Riley grumbled. "Xee you'll have to go in and turn off the anti-drift security measures, then Lucy should be able to get in. Until then Kyra can stay here."

"No, she's coming with me." Xander's tone left no room for argument.

Riley frowned. "And face the possibility of a Shadow-Veyn tracking her to the abbey?"

"She's coming with me," Xander repeated. "Sire." A gentle bow of the head, but his eyes were hard, face tight.

Riley stiffened, and after Alice settled her hand on his shoulder he nodded. "Fine, but Kyra, are you ready for this?"

His change of tone drew her attention.

"Once the charm has been broken there's a large possibility that the Daemon will know, and that means –"

"Don't worry," she interrupted, anxiety wrapping itself tightly around her lungs. "Frederick already knows I'm gone."

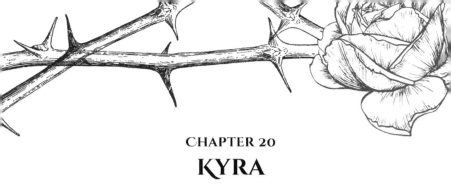

CHAPTER 20

KYRA

Kyra trailed a step behind Xander, the beautiful white marble a distraction. The walls glittered as if silver had somehow been woven within the bricks, the light leaking through the open slits creating bursts of colour across the stone.

She'd never seen an abbey, never mind walk through the labyrinth of entwined corridors and halls. Xander had barely spoken, his sunglasses securely in place as he stormed down each pathway with purpose.

Energy seemed to pulsate, a gentle and comforting vibration as she ran her fingertips along the wall as she scrambled to keep up behind. They passed rooms, some empty and as pale as the ones on the outside, while others looked like classrooms and studies. Through one of the slits in the outer wall there was a square courtyard, the greenery vibrant even from the distance. Druids passed them, all male, both young and old muttering beneath their breaths as they passed. A few approached, but were quickly dismissed with a cutting glare from Xander. Most kept a wide berth as they went about their day, their expressions a mixture of anger, fear, and curiosity.

Xander stopped when the corridor split into two, head angled as if he were listening. A room was stationed opposite, and before she could have a peek inside a man appeared and quickly shut the door. More whispering. More prickly stares.

"Why an abbey?" she asked quietly, wanting to speak over the inaudible murmurs. "Are there monks here?"

Xander remained silent for a few more seconds before he made a sharp right, not looking back to see whether she was following behind. "Before the Great war, but no more. Druidism is a recognised religion, although it isn't widely practiced even amongst my Breed."

She had noticed some of the older men in white robes, red and black embroidery around their cuffs. The designs were similar to the ones the younger males had tattooed around their wrists, or that Xander had across his body. Designs that Dirk also had.

She knew little about the druids, other than they were born only male. Her parents hadn't thought she needed to know about other Breeds, believing it would distract her from her duties. When she'd finally broken free from them, she'd immediately thrown herself into research, not wanting to be ignorant as she carefully created her new life.

Out of all her studies there was very little literature on druids, and even less on Daemons. It seemed strange to her knowing that Daemons existed, yet the majority around her believed they were simply tales told to sinners and naughty children. She'd been studying their languages and runes since a babe.

"Can you tell me about the markings?" she asked, gesturing to the man in the robe who'd decided to follow them down the last two corridors at a distance.

"You ask for knowledge that isn't freely given," he said without turning to her.

Kyra bit her lip. Knowledge was power, she knew that. It was why she tried to learn as much as she could when she was free. Her knowledge could possibly save her life. Or it could be her downfall.

"Dirk had markings similar across his back, tattoos like –" She didn't even see Xander stop before she was suddenly pressed against the wall with an angry male grumbling down at her.

They were nose to nose, his chest close enough she could feel the vibration of his growl. "How've you seen his glyphs?" His arms remained at his sides, fists clenched.

Kyra blinked up at him, her own temper bubbling just beneath her skin. "Excuse me?"

"How've you seen his glyphs?" he repeated, slower, his gaze burning even through the aviators he preferred to wear. It infuriated her more that she couldn't see his eyes, only her own reflected in the mirrored glass. "In what position were you in, when you saw his bare flesh?"

It took a second for Kyra to realise what he'd asked, embarrassment making her anger burn hotter. Her palm tingled, her hand lifting to slap. A second before it connected to his face he caught it.

A muscle in his cheek twitched, his grip tight on her wrist.

"Am I interrupting?" a velvety voice sniggered.

Xander stepped away, but turned to block her from view. "Edwards," he grumbled in some sort of greeting.

Kyra stepped out from behind him, but Xander moved to block her once more.

"It's Councilman," the man replied sharply. "And who do we have here?"

Xander crossed his arms, so Kyra remained silent as she spotted other druids moving a step closer.

A Councilman? Shit. That's all she needed. *What if he calls Frederick?*

"I'll ask again," Councilman Edwards said with a touch of impatience, the other druids closing in like wolves. "Why are you here, and with an outsider?"

"You want to try and remove me?" Xander tilted his head, the gesture animalistic. "Try it."

Kyra could just see the councilman, a tall, slim man with dark hair peppered with salt. His face was traditionally handsome but his lips were cruel, twisted.

"You have all made it perfectly clear you're no longer Guardians of the Order, so why are you here?" He held up his hand, and the druids all departed. "You've broken our first rule by inviting a *woman* into our sacred place."

Kyra bristled, and Xander must have sensed it because he stepped back, pressing her against the wall. He kept a slight cushion of air, enough for her to move if she needed.

She understood his silent warning. *Stay out of it.*

She concentrated on the tight fabric flush against his back, and not the growing panic at being trapped. But she wasn't trapped, not really. Light glittered everywhere, reminding her she wasn't in the dark or alone. She reached forward, her fingers touching Xander's strong shoulder, using his warmth to anchor her anxiety. If he could feel her, he didn't react.

She was aware of her reactions, had been trying to control them even as her memories ravaged her personal shield brick by brick. She would build it up again, reminding herself that she was no longer a defenceless child. Years she hadn't suffered a panic attack, and yet there she was trying to stifle another one in just under a week. She had no idea how she'd faced down both Frederick and Dirk, but a little lack of space was what was splintering her control.

"So..." Edwards drawled, his words aimed at her. "What sort of witch, are you?"

"She's under my protection," Xander said before she could answer.

"Interesting." Edwards sniggered. "I wonder whether you're one of Frederick's personal ones. He was more pissy this morning than usual."

Xander's muscles were steel beneath her fingertips.

"Tell Riley I need to speak with him," Edwards continued. "It's important. Now go on, but don't be long. You clearly believe you have the right to be here because of your birth, but I may decide to remove your privilege anyway."

Kyra listened as his footsteps retreated, and then waited until Xander stepped forward before releasing her shaky breath. They were alone, the large corridor empty.

"At least you're an arsehole to other people too," she muttered, more to herself.

Xander looked over his shoulder, lips set into a thin line.

"I thought you *were* a Guardian? So why did he say you're no longer Guardians of the Order?"

She didn't expect an answer.

"The old Archdruid was corrupt and did things to his own people that's been removed from our history, like a dirty secret. As a group, we decided we no longer wanted to be a part of it. We're still druids, so we're able to use the resources here, so it makes sense to keep things... civil with Edwards."

"That was civil?"

Those lips lifted into a small smile. "Come on, the library is only through there. We won't have long once someone sees us entering. So we need to make this fast."

She didn't need to know more, the urgency to get the charm removed almost a physical force beneath her skin.

Xander explained anyway. "Outsiders aren't allowed in here. Or the abbey in general."

"Then why bring me?" she asked. "You insisted that I came."

Xander decided then to return to his silence, waiting until the druid that passed by had disappeared down another corridor before slipping inside the room.

"Stay against the door and don't move. Once I initiate the spell we must stay there until it's complete."

Kyra pressed herself against the wood, peeking over Xander's shoulder at the room. The library was large, the walls the same pale marble as everything else she'd seen in the abbey. The entire room was dimmed, the temperature controlled for the books that lined the eight separate floor to ceiling bookshelves. In the centre and the only source of light was a glass box, just large enough for one person to sit comfortably inside. It was empty, the glass door closed despite a book being carefully pinned open on the small desk.

"We don't have long," he said, stepping towards her and planting both his hands flat beside her head. Kyra breathed in his scent, turning her head as patterns appeared from beneath his palms, the curves moving until the entire door looked as if it had been scorched. "Remember, don't move from the wood."

The patterns continued to spiral, past the door to climb against the walls in beautiful swirls and whirls, and with them, her panic.

"Take the picture."

Kyra lifted on her toes, trying to see past Xander's body to watch the patterns burn and pulsate. They moved across the shelves as fast as her heartbeat raced, her mind believing she was trapped.

"Kyra," Xander rumbled, drawing her attention to him. "Front pocket. Picture."

His hands were rigid around her, his body hot as she looked up at him.

Right. Phone. Picture.

She was unable to look down with him pressed so closely against her. Her hand skimmed down his stomach, his muscles stiffening as she carefully searched for his pocket.

"Take your time, Princess," he growled.

Kyra palmed his phone, flicking on the camera and taking a picture of the library over his shoulder. Her arms began to shake, dread beginning to slowly uncoil. "Do you have a range of growls?" she asked, trying to distract herself.

Xander frowned, his eyes obscured by the stupid sunglasses.

"Or just that one growl in particular?" She removed his shades, his body as solid as oak and unable to stop her. His eyes were hard when she met them, but glittered with such carnal expectation that she felt her thighs clench together in anticipation even as her breathing quickened.

Stop it.

"Send the picture." Another growl, one that would have sent shivers along her skin and heat pooling between her legs if she wasn't concentrating on not passing out.

Kyra glared up at him, her grip tight on the phone as she pulled her attention away to tap at the screen. She didn't have to ask who to send the image to, not when *'Batboy'* was the last contact opened.

Chest tight, her body shaking entirely as she gulped in great –.

She couldn't breathe.

"I wonder if your pussy's as sweet as I think it is, Princess."

Kyra's head jerked up, his words seeming to shake her free of the panic. His eyes were on her lips, and that clearly pissed him off if she went by the stony set of his jaw.

"I bet if I had use of my hands," he continued, a voice a low grumble. "I could make you come against this door."

Kyra tried to reply, her lungs aching and chest still tight.

"Or would you prefer my tongue, Princess?"

"I doubt you have the talent." Her voice was husky when she finally spoke, the dread constricting the cords.

Challenged brightening his eyes, his head dipping towards –

The door clicked. Xander broke the tension between them as he stepped back with a sudden movement, causing her to flinch. The runes glowed gently when he released his hands, as if they continued to burn even without his contact.

"You were about to have a panic attack," he said in explanation. "I wanted to distract you."

Kyra kept herself against the door, her heart aching inside her chest. "I don't like to feel trapped," she blurted, needing to explain. "It makes me... I don't like to feel trapped."

"Why..." Xander shook his head, turning away but not before anger darkened his features. "The markings, the ones you asked about before are reflections of their tattoos." He turned back to face her, his emotions under control. "Young druids would tattoo glyphs on their wrists, and sometimes if they're strong enough they'd also tattoo their throats. The glyphs are designed to help balance their arcane without the magic destroying them."

If they're strong enough.

"You have most of your body covered," she said, a half question considering she had seen a large portion of his body already. "Then why does Dirk –"

The air shifted, and before she could finish her question Lucifer appeared in a burst of smoke.

"Oh, are we telling secrets now, Xee?" he said with an ear-splitting grin. "Please, tell your beautiful Dark Priestess why Daemons have similar glyphs tattooed on their bodies as druids?"

Xander cut him a sharp glare, head cocked as if he was listening through the thick wood. "Hurry up, we don't have long. You can't be found here."

Lucy pouted. "Neither can she." He gestured with his chin. "Tell me, were they flabbergasted to see a *woman* walking their precious halls? As if the mere idea of someone with ovaries could sully their precious abbey."

Kyra would have commented at the 'Dark Priestess' comment if she wasn't so fascinated with Lucy's entrance. She'd read about drifting and had tried to understand how someone could transport themselves from one place to another with a single thought.

She could never learn that ability, witches' powers restricted to the law of elements.

"Honestly," Lucy continued as he scanned along the edges of the bookshelves. "I'm surprised their shrivelled dicks didn't combust at the sight of a pair of breasts."

"Lucifer," said Xander in a chiding tone.

"Yes, yes, of course," he said with a dramatic bow. "Right away me lord. I hope you don't growl at your mother like you do me."

Xander froze, eyes hardening. "What did you say about my mother?"

Lucifer had reached for a grimoire, the leather thick and worn. "Your mother called," he drawled. "You know, the creature that somehow birthed your gigantic head? She sounded like a real fucking matriarch when she demanded you return home *immediately*." He tried to make his voice more feminine, but failed.

Xander remained rigid. "Did she give you a reason?"

Lucy raised an eyebrow. "Is love for your mother not enough?"

Xander growled.

"Fine," Lucy grunted, picking up two more books and holding them to his chest. "No, she gave no reason. Just said that it was urgent. Also, I'm saying this because I'm your friend, and also because I'm an arsehole, but your mother is a right cold bitch."

Xander pressed his palm to the locked door, eyes closed for a second before he stepped back. The glow intensified for a few seconds, orange sparks breaking off from the corners. "We have less than five minutes, do you have what you need?"

Lucy gestured to the five books that he now had in his arms.

"They can't leave the library," Xander said through clenched teeth. "If you try you'll call the –"

Lucifer's image seemed to shimmer, and then he dropped the books with a sharp shout. A woman appeared, translucent as if washed out. She wasn't exactly a woman, but she wasn't exactly a ghost either.

"Whisp," Xander finished. "Shit."

Thief! Several voices resonated inside her head, a chorus of sounds that were like shrills. Kyra stepped forward, wanting to get closer to the woman, who wasn't really a woman. It seemed to sense her presence, her head snapping to the side. The woman's features were beautiful, but without shadow. She was two-dimensional as if she were a drawing, or maybe a cartoon. She was all one colour, a soft dove grey that was like cloudy glass. She wore a robe similar to the elder druids had in the halls, but no embroidery decorated the sleeves. The entire garment simple.

You shouldn't be here, the multiple voices in both male and female said inside her mind. *Leave.*

Lucifer took step back, hands held up in surrender. "A warning would have been nice!"

"You knew the books couldn't leave," Xander snapped back as he touched the wood of the door again. "Fuck, they know the Whisp's out."

You taste like death, the Whisp said to her. *But not as in mortality. As in rebirth. Healer. Creator.* The Whisp floated forward, her bare feet dragging across the floor before she stopped an inch before Kyra. *You taste of Chaos.*

"What are you?" Kyra asked, wanting to reach forward, to see whether she felt something solid or just air.

We are Whisp. We are the keepers of knowledge long forgotten. We protect.

"Kyra?!" Lucifer barked at her, his fingers flipping through several pages of the closest grimoire. "Tell me what happened with Dirk before he marked you." From his tone, he'd asked more than once.

Kyra licked at her lips. "He kissed –"

The door rumbled, heavy fists beating against it.

Lucifer reached for another book, paper blurring as he searched for the right page.

"Time's up!" Xander shouted. "Lucy, plan B."

Hands wrapped around her waist, and before she could utter a sound her surroundings changed with a static pop.

Kyra's legs buckled as soon as Lucy's hands released. She fought the nausea and dizziness, breathing heavily as she slowly turned her head.

"Congratulations for not puking on your first drift. For that you get a gold star." Lucy grinned, holding a thumbs up. "Don't worry, the sickness will pass once your molecules all merge back together. Or they won't, and you'll forever be missing some bits. Who knows." He shrugged.

Kyra groaned, shakily climbing to her feet. The nausea had already passed, but the sudden bright light wasn't helping the dizziness.

"Did you know those druids have more than one restricted library?" He clicked his tongue. "Sneaky bastards, keeping all that knowledge locked away."

"Where's Xander?" she asked, her throat surprisingly raw considering she hadn't actually puked.

"Err, probably dealing with some pissed of druids right about now. He'll be fine, he's a big boy." His features cooled, eyes darkening. "We don't have long before Dirk comes. He would have sensed you drift."

"He can find me?" She didn't need a mirror to know the colour had drained from her face, or any colour that was left after the drift.

"I have no idea, but you should have thought of that before you sucked face with him," Lucy said as he rocked back on his heel. "What were you thinking? Dirk is... dangerous."

"You seem to think I had a choice?"

"I'm not joking Kyra, he's old, one of the originals. He's feared even amongst my kind."

The cold wind whipped at her hair, the strands escaping from her braid. "How can I stop him tracking me?"

"Whatever he spelled you with is traceable, it's how the hounds..." Lucy's head shot to the side, surveying their surroundings. "Explain to me exactly what happened."

Kyra had to think, her thoughts scrambled as she tried to remember the kiss, his tongue, and the taste.

"It's a basic possession charm," Lucy said, eyes still wide with alarm. "It can be removed the same way it was administered."

"With a kiss?" she asked. "Then get it out."

Lucy took a large step back, arms raised. "No way, I'm not risking my head."

"What?"

"You want Xee to eat me? Hell no, he can deal with it."

Kyra was about to snap back her reply, but the ground trembled beneath her feet. She twisted, looking for a crack in the earth. The hairs at the back of her neck tingled, arcane burning her fingertips as she searched for whatever made the ground rumble.

Lucy snarled, reaching for her wrist and drifting them with a static pop. Her surroundings changed, not that she really had paid attention to where they'd just been. This time however she recognised the road, and the empty bus shelter that was only a few minutes from the abbey.

Her feet settled solidly onto the concrete, her heart a rabbit in her chest as she searched for any hellhounds that may have followed. The shelter was made entirely of glass, one wall open to the elements.

"Fucking nasty vile creatures," Lucy muttered, tugging at his torn t-shirt.

Frustration made her voice sharp. "Lucy, please help me get rid of it before we're both eaten."

His eyes narrowed, nostrils flaring. "Look, I'm a Daemon living with seven men who were literally created to kill and hunt my kind. They're arseholes, but they're not bad. Most of them had fucked up childhoods, which I think we can both relate to."

"You had a bad childhood?"

"I count up to three-hundred my childhood," he

snorted. "There are a few of us whose transition wasn't by choice. I just embrace the hand I was dealt."

Her face softened. "Lucy –"

"Don't look at me like I'm a victim. I've done some horrible things. Wanted to do them even. But I'm still not helping with that charm. It's a complicated relationship already with the Guardians, I'm not going to mess that up even if –"

"Mess what up, exactly?" Xander asked as he stepped into the shelter. He looked between them, forehead furrowed. Red marked his right cheekbone, his sunglasses nowhere to be seen.

Lucy held up his hands in submission. "Ah, the funny thing is –"

Kyra didn't hear the rest of the sentence, knowing she had no choice with a hound hunting. Reaching for Xander she ignored his surprise as she pulled his face towards hers. He was granite beneath her fingertips, frozen until she licked her tongue against the seam of his lips, needing him to open for her. Silently pleading with her mouth.

A vibration, maybe a moan before his hands were around her waist. He tugged her closer until his hard body was flush against hers, his tongue sweeping in to brush and tease. The taste of the charm grew, wiggling inside her mouth. He grumbled, his tongue poking at the spell before words tumbled from his throat, muffled even if she could understand the language. The charm loosened. The taste lessening before Xander sucked, and then suddenly it was gone.

It was like an elastic band, a sharp pain of the rebound as Xander spat to the side.

"Than –"

His lips were hard against hers, his tongue exploring her mouth with little flicks that had her fighting a moan. His

173

fingers stroked along her jaw, angling her better for his kiss while her whole body thrummed with need.

I bet I could make you come against this door.

This time she did moan, unable to stop the sound as he dominated their kiss as if he wanted to devour every inch. Her hands reached up to his hair, wrapping them in the silky strands to easier keep him against her. The air thickened, the tension stung taut...

Lucifer cleared his throat, and the sound was like ice water across them both.

She would have stumbled back, but Xander still gripped her waist.

"Dirk will know his mark's been removed," Lucifer said casually, as if he hasn't just witnessed whatever *that* was between them. "So I suggest fucking off for a few days until the trace has dissipated."

Xander lifted his head, his expression empty, cold despite his fingers stroking along her hip. He turned toward Lucy, but Kyra couldn't bring herself to look anywhere but Xander's smooth skin, his strong jaw freshly shaven. She was hyperaware of his hand, and it would have been calming if her blood wasn't on fire.

"Can she be tracked?" Xander asked, his voice deeper, but void of emotion.

How could he act so callous while she was struggling not to combust? She pulled at his hand, needing space. His fingers gripped her harder, pulling until she sucked in a panicked breath. His release was immediate, so fast she staggered back and almost crashing into the glass of the shelter.

She dropped her eyes to the floor, trying and failing to calm herself. There was a blackened mark on the concrete, a liquid that sizzled like acid.

"I don't know," Lucifer said with a shrug. "But I would get a few hundred miles away, just in case."

"Then we will leave for the north. We can be there before nightfall."

The air shifted, Kyra's chi rippling as Lucifer disappeared into a drift. She dared look up. To study Xander's glacial expression.

He grunted, but didn't approach. "How much of a leash does he have around you?"

Kyra straightened, anger cutting through her embarrassment. She met his eyes of pure ice. Hoped he could see the fire that burned in her own. "I had to make choices to survive."

Xander stepped forward with a deliberate step, and her pulse raced when he slowly reached forward to touch her cheek. She felt no panic, no vulnerability at his hands so close to her throat. She hadn't felt a sense of panic at the kiss either, not when he gripped her jaw or when he pressed her close.

She wasn't sure if it was because of the crackling awareness that seemed strung between them, or that she'd learned subconsciously to trust him.

"I can't pretend to understand your choices," he said quietly and so damn controlled. "But right now I have to go to the Borderlands, and I can't leave you behind."

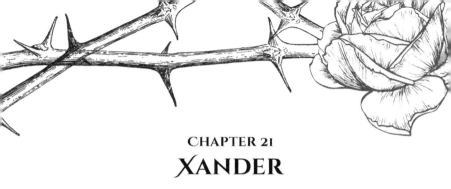

CHAPTER 21
XANDER

They had driven straight through, conscious that there could be hounds hunting. Xander could still taste the charm, charcoal and carrion at the back of his palate. He wasn't familiar with the magic. He didn't know its limits or restrictions, but every mile he drove away from the city he felt himself relax just a little bit more.

He risked a glance to his left, Kyra still soft with sleep and curled in her seat. He had expected questions, to catch her staring at him then watch colour bleed into her cheeks before those large cat-like eyes skirted quickly away. But she had been strung so tight beside him, her chi sharp and electric as if she was subconsciously protecting herself.

She was always asking questions, so curious. He'd wanted her to ask, to snap at him with such controlled anger his beast wanted to poke and press her just so they could watch her reaction. But instead she had sat in silence. For hours she'd been a statue he didn't dare to tease in case she shattered. It had taken three hours before she'd spoken a single word, and that was only to comment about the rolling hills of the countryside before they went back onto another motorway. It took a another two hours until she unwrapped her arms from around herself and relaxed against the door with her eyes closed.

Her pulse had slowed with sleep, so Xander had sat in silence and listened to her quiet, and steady breathing. Every now and then he would simply look over, noticing the crescent shadows that her lashes cast against her skin. Look at the way the strands of hair that had escaped her braid had curled.

He hadn't expected her kiss, and definitely hadn't expected his own reaction. He'd had many lovers over the years, but nothing compared to the burn he felt when she set her lips on his. How blood had rushed after a single touch, and when he'd heard her moan he'd became hard as fucking steel.

All from a single kiss. A kiss that had nothing to do with passion, or sex, but was a way to get rid of the Daemon's charm. A kiss that left him wanting more, craving more of the one woman he couldn't stand.

How fucking pathetic.

The steering wheel creaked until he released it.

It angered him that she'd had no choice. That she was put in such a vulnerable position. But that didn't matter, not when he had to keep himself distant. His brothers were working on the threats, stalking her place until they found the scum that had left her those notes while he kept her away. And then she would go back, practicing the magic he'd grown up hating, fearing. He couldn't help but judge her life, her choices even if they were for survival.

A small noise, a whimper.

Xander reached over, careful to not scare her. "Kyra," he said quietly.

The whimpering intensified.

"Kyra!"

She shot up in her seat, the cry caught in her throat as she flinched away from his touch.

"You were having a nightmare," he explained when she looked over, eyes wide.

She blinked, fingers immediately touching the loose strands of hair, tucking them behind her ear. "How long was I asleep?" she asked, her voice hoarse.

"Not long, we're about twenty minutes away."

Kyra blinked, frowning out the window at the quickly darkening sky. "It's snowing."

He'd pulled off the motorway, the open busy road changing to dirt tracks and towering trees. He knew in the spring the surrounding area would be covered in thick grassy knolls and beautiful meadows. The place he grew up was a slice of paradise in the Borderlands, but ever since he was given over to the Archdruid like some sort of prize as a young boy he'd never wanted to come back. Twenty-two years later, and he still wasn't sure why he'd returned, having never spared a thought to the mother who'd turned her back on her only child.

And then she'd called. The community forbade the use of electrical devices, believing they corrupted their gifts and yet she'd gone against her own rule and called him.

"If you look in the distance," he said to distract her, and maybe himself, "you'll see the mountains."

Kyra smiled, the silhouette of the high peaks shadowed against the pink and purple sky. "I've never been this far north. It's beautiful."

"It's cold and wet," he said as the tyres slipped in the snowy sludge. "But in the summer it's beautiful." He turned down a darkened passage, the distant spirits greeting him with caution.

He'd asked a spirit once how he'd found himself there, his name lost in memory but his image somehow still vivid.

He'd been old, died naturally in his sleep surrounded by friends and family. His face had been wrinkled with a lifetime of laughter, and his eyes had glittered as he'd told a quiet four-year-old about those he loved. He hadn't been ready to pass into the light, to take the step into whatever was next. Instead he felt a tug, and he'd followed it until he found his way to the community.

He hadn't understood the difference between life and death when he was young, not understanding that not everyone could see those that had passed. It was a gift, unique to the Aes-Si Seer and something that was coveted by many black magic users.

"We're here," he said as he pulled up outside the main manor, the spirits that usually protected the entrance vanishing as they approached. The pale brick visible beneath the foliage was still tarnished, scars of the battle he'd witnessed as a child. "Conceal your chi. Please," he added softly when she recoiled.

Black witches had attacked the grounds, wanting to somehow absorb their gifts and use it to control the dead. They'd slaughtered all that had fought, destroying everything in their wake until there was nothing left but corpses and pain.

With the ground still wet with blood he was sent away, abandoned with memories of the screams. He'd cried until his voice had broken and nothing but distressed sobs remained. And still his mother had turned away, never once calling out to her son.

Xander hadn't realised he'd gone rigid, not until Kyra's warm palm settled on his shoulder. He tried to relax, to forget what had happened, but old rage burned through his veins. He was only a child, and he'd been tossed aside like he meant nothing.

She didn't ask any questions, not when he was wound

so tight. He was thankful for that as he slipped out the car, anchoring himself to the soft earth beneath his feet and to the cold wind that lashed out like icy whips.

He thought he would feel pain when he looked upon his mother, but he felt nothing as the tall, willowy woman walked out of the double doors. Her face had aged but was still beautiful when she brightened at him, her smile genuine until it settled on Kyra.

"Sienna," he greeted, unable to call her mother when she wasn't that to him.

"They warned me of an uninvited guest," she said in an icy tone not that different from his own. "I had to see with my own eyes the reason the spirits have all hidden. Witches are not welcome on these grounds Xander. Remove her at once."

Awareness rippled down Xander's chi, but there was no witch he could sense. Kyra was there, her aura dimmed. Concealed to the point she felt almost human. He wondered if it hurt to strangle her power until it was next to nothing. As a druid his magic wasn't reflected in his aura, or his chi, so had never seen the point to conceal himself. He was of the earth, of natural magic.

A witch was different.

Black witch auras in particular were like layers of deceptive shade, with an acidic edge that caused pins and needles if brushed against. Kyra was different, her energy gentle but powerful. Like the calm before the storm.

The spirits had whispered to the Seers of Kyra's magic. The community in which the Seers all lived surrounded by the dead, both fresh and not. They glistened in the encroaching darkness, sentinels who saw and heard everything. Yet they kept their distance.

Interesting.

"Then I cannot stay."

His mother gave him a pointed look. "The spirits are afraid."

"Then let them be cowards. You called me here, not the other way around." Kyra pressed closer to him, and he had to swallow the pleased growl that wanted to escape his throat. At that point he wasn't sure if it was himself, or his beast.

His mother slid her harsh gaze to Kyra, smile tightening. "She may only enter if her magic is bound, our community would not see her inside otherwise."

He was about to refuse, but Kyra nodded. "How would you bind my magic?" she asked tentatively.

"You would willingly wear a specialised choker, one designed to block your access to your chi."

"No." Kyra's response was immediate. "I'm sorry, but not a choker. I would have nothing around my neck."

"Then a manacle, locked around your wrist until you leave."

Xander noticed Kyra look down, her nod of agreement a taut jerk. He reached back to touch Kyra's hand in reassurance, but his question was aimed at the woman who birthed him. "What do you want after all these years?"

"Not now. Not after your long journey. A room has been set up in the main manor. Why don't you and your... guest go freshen up before we call for dinner." She turned, dismissing them as a man stepped outside. "Andre will take your belongings."

Andre reached out for Kyra's bag, and then for Xander's. With a click he attached a thick metal manacle to Kyra's wrist. "Your room is on the first floor, third from the right," he said directly to Kyra, not acknowledging Xander.

Kyra blinked up at him, nodding her thanks when he disappeared into the house. She moved closer to Xander, silent as she took in the place he grew up.

She wrapped her arms around herself as she checked out the manor, the bricks old and covered in various shades of ivy. A baroque balcony jutted from the largest window to the left, a woman braced against the iron railing, watching them.

Xander hesitated, taking a second to fill his lungs with the fresh air before stepping inside. It was just as he remembered, and he couldn't decide if that was a good thing or not. Candles lined the walls, lights flickering to cast shadows and shades.

"Are you okay?" he asked when he caught Kyra staring into the darkened corners. He noticed the manacle on her wrist, her fingertips playing across it.

She looked up, eyes wide before she dropped her arm to her side. "The spirits are scared of me?" she asked instead as they slowly made their way down the hall, towards the double staircase in the centre of the foyer. The large room was glistening with colour, the beautiful tapestries, rugs, and ornaments a welcoming contrast against the stark brick. A few Seers stood on the gallery above, stony faced as they descended the stairs. They didn't approach, their lips turning up in disgust as they plastered themselves against the wall as if simply being close was enough to taint themselves.

"I think you repel the spirits," Xander explained, keeping his voice carefully neutral. "Because of your aura." He was interested in the theory about the spirits, and even happier that their conversations wouldn't be overheard by the curious spooks.

The halls of the manor and surrounding buildings would have been wall to wall with ghosts, and with Kyra there he could prowl around without worry. He hadn't noticed their adversity toward her at the cemetery because they'd hovered so close to him, but it made sense.

"Repel?" she repeated, voice high-pitched. "Of course I do." She brushed her hand on the walls as she walked, the manacle clinking as she moved. She paused, fingertips touching a darkened scar. She stopped completely, both hands now pressed against the brick. "What happened?"

Three people hovered, a silent threat as they stepped towards Kyra and ignored him completely. "You shouldn't be here," the one on the left hissed.

"You have sullied these halls with your filthy touch," another jeered. "Touch it again and I'll slice that hand clean off, witch."

Xander slid his eyes to the three men, a snarl on the edge of his lips.

Kyra noticed, closing the space between them. "Come on, our room's only there." She tugged at his hand, her warm fingers wrapping in his when he remained firm. "Xee?"

His head turned to her. She'd never called him Xee before. It was something only his brothers and friends called him.

"Come on," he said, allowing her to guide him down the hall that he used to run around as a babe.

The room was open when she found the correct door, the bed made up in various shades of purple and the candles lit and flickering. His attention remained on Kyra, her shoulders tightening slightly when she spotted the single bed. She didn't comment as she sat down on the edge, her eyes scanning the delicate details in the wall until she found another dark stain just left of the dresser.

It wasn't as big of a scar as the one in the hall, but it remained there as a memory and as a warning of all that had happened. He wasn't sure if his mother had chosen this room on purpose, or if there were more scars throughout the other bedrooms.

A line appeared between her brows, and then she carefully slipped off the bed to her knees. "It holds an echo," she said, her voice holding a slight rasp as she reached forward until she was able to touch her fingertips to it.

"You can still feel it?" he asked, gesturing to the manacle.

Kyra glanced down. "It's muffled, but I can still feel my magic. I could probably call to it if I tried, but I don't want to give them any more reason to hate me."

"They have no magic of their own and detest everyone who can use it. I'm surprised they trusted a merchant who sold such goods."

"It works, just not to the extent they were probably led to believe." She looked up, dark amber eyes holding sorrow and unshed tears. Her fingers pressed harder against the scar. "What happened?"

"Their culture is to honour the dead, to help spirits find their way into the light with their inherited gifts. There was a coven of black witches that wanted to use those gifts for their own, selfish needs. They wanted to control the dead, use them as a source of power."

Kyra sucked in a breath, a single tear escaping down her cheek. "And they didn't take no for an answer?" she whispered. "How many?"

He knew what she'd asked, found himself reluctant to answer. "They murdered thirty-two, including children."

Her smile was sad, her voice tight when she spoke. "I understand why you hate me."

Pain twisted his stomach, his hand itching to wipe away that tear that glistened on her cheek. "I don't hate you," he said, realising as soon as the words left his lips that it was the truth. "You didn't do this."

"No, but others like me did." She pulled her hand back, cradling it against her chest. "I'm sorry."

"There's no one else like you." Her eyes moved to his, an emotion he couldn't pinpoint flashing across those beautiful irises.

"We should shower," she said, climbing to her feet. "Before they call us for dinner."

He couldn't miss the chance to tease her. "Like our last shower?"

A blush burned, drying her eyes. She wasn't sure how to take the comment, and her uncertainty made him laugh.

"I don't know if you've noticed, but they live a much simpler life here. There's no electricity whatsoever, and only the most basic plumbing."

Kyra spared a panicked glance to the adjoining bathroom.

Xander grinned. "Don't worry, I'll show you how I used to bathe as a boy."

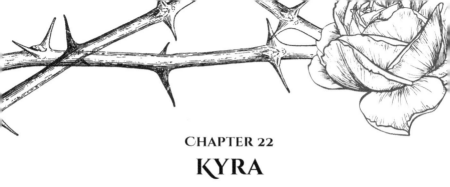

CHAPTER 22
KYRA

Kyra wasn't sure what she expected, but this certainty wasn't it. Xander had guided her through the frozen gardens, towards a large open building just at the edge of the surrounding woodland. Rose and lavender drifted up from the milky water, the heat stinging her cold skin.

"A communal bath?"

Xander chuckled, probably because of her horrified expression. They'd passed several people on their way, and not one had acknowledged either of them. Even now, the eight or so who were already enjoying the water immediately turned their backs, and then quickly left to leave them alone.

Xander's face was smooth as stone, relaxed while she struggled to control her pulse.

"The water's created by the rivers and lakes that are fed by the mountain springs. The water's pure, but they've added a few homeopathy herbs and minerals."

Kyra bit her lip, dropping down to touch the water. It was hot, the texture somehow smooth and glistening on her skin. The bath seemed to have been carved from rocks, the cold air from the open front creating goosebumps across her skin with the only illumination from the hundreds of candles flickering.

"How is it –" She turned to face him, her eyes dropping to the hard planes of his stomach as he pulled at his shirt. Muscles rippled with each tug of the fabric, her eyes dropping to his abs, and that tattoos that decorated them. When he hooked his thumbs into his jeans she looked away, moving to face the black sky, the stars glittering. She'd never seen the stars so bright, the lights in London obscuring them too much. They would have stolen her breath if she wasn't so hyperaware of that man at her back.

"Heated?" he finished for her, and she swore she heard laughter in that husky voice. "You're overthinking this, just enjoy the water."

She waited, but heard nothing. She was about to call out to him when there was a gentle splash.

"It's safe," he said. "There's nothing else, unless you want to go to bed sweaty. Give me a warning though, I'll make sure the window's open, otherwise you'll stink the place out."

He was definitely laughing at her.

The water truly looked majestic, like crushed opals, and milk against Xander's fair skin. Except the word fair was far too tame for what it was, he glowed, a warm golden undertone that begged to be stroked. Not that Xander was a man who allowed such easy touch.

"I'm not going to eat you," he mumbled, relaxing back until the water pooled around his shoulders. "Unless you ask nicely."

She wasn't sure she was ready for this humorous Xander, not when she struggled to swallow while he looked so utterly calm. He watched her, a smile teasing his lips. The candles that illuminated the room hit him in such a way it accentuated his hard lines, and he seemed to move to better angle that light.

"You have no shame," she said when he raised an eyebrow at her hesitation.

He stood straighter, the water now pooling low on his waist. Droplets dripped down his chest, his hand coming to wipe across a thick pec. "Is there anything I should be ashamed of?"

Oh, bloody hell.

"Look away," she said, hoping her voice didn't wobble.

He stared, a slow smile curving his lips in challenge.

"Look away!"

His smile grew, brightening his face. She blinked and it was gone, his usual military cool expression returning as he closed his eyes.

Well, he technically had looked away.

Pulling at her shirt before she lost the nerve, she quickly removed all her clothing. Her pulse was rapid as she slipped out of her underwear and carefully stepped into the steaming water. It was deliciously warm, heating her bones from the inside out as she sank her head beneath. She wanted to stay there, to let the cleansing water wash away everything until she was clean. Until she was new.

A tug on her braid, only gentle, but it was enough for panic to spark. She flinched when she came up, Xander standing so close her arm brushed across his chest. He held the end of her hair in his hand, his eyes direct when she met them.

"Sorry," he said, the apology empty. "Do you ever undo your braid?" It remained in his hand, his fingers gripping tightly.

Such an innocent question, but her throat still closed when she answered. "Sometimes."

"Why so tight?"

"It stops stray hairs," she said. "Spells, charms, and curses. I don't trust anyone not to use it against me."

"You don't like your hair to be touched." It wasn't a question.

She shook her head.

"Why?" He carefully tugged the braid again, and when she didn't protest he pulled the hair tie from the end. The hair immediately began to curl, finally releasing it from its constraints. Her hair wasn't naturally that curly, more of a wild wave when she allowed it be free. He still didn't let go, stepping slowly around her until he was at her back, his hands carefully releasing the strands.

Kyra concealed the fear, reminding herself that it was Xander, and despite his attitude he wouldn't intentionally hurt her. She tried to slow her breathing, her chest aching as his fingers moved softly, stroking through until they reached her scalp.

"They're called the Aes-Si Seer, completely human with no special powers other than the ability to hear and speak to the dead."

His fingers continued to stroke, his thumb moving to brush against her shoulder. He knew what he was doing. His words distracting, his strokes soothing.

"Druids are always born male, something my mother didn't realise when she chose a male to take to her bed. When I was born she realised her mistake, and even though I have the same ability as all the other Aes-Si Seers, the community were disappointed. They have no magic, nothing to attune their auras to the earth like I could. I was different, my genes soiled because I was not just a Seer, but a druid."

"Is that why you left?" she asked, turning her head slightly. She froze when he added pressure, his fingers changing to brush her throat, across the top of her shoulder then back again in slow, lazy sweeps. There was no panic, not when all she could concentrate on was his touch, his finger leaving a blaze of heat in its wake.

His hand would hesitate at the cuff she wore high on her upper arm, but he didn't touch the crystal that lay flat against her skin.

"I was removed from the community when I was eight, given to the Archdruid that ruled at the time."

"Removed?" She wanted see his expression, but he pressed her closer, his chest now flush against her spine. She was thankful for the murkiness of the water, her body sensitive as he continued his painfully slow strokes.

"Hmmm," he grumbled, sending vibrations along her skin in such a way she suppressed a moan. "They blamed me when the black witches attacked, thought it was because of my magic that they found the community."

"What? But you were a child." Anger darkened her tone, and she swore she felt lips against the side of her neck. She hitched in a breath, not daring to move as those same lips brushed against the shell of her ear. Not a kiss, but it still made her pussy ache, her breasts heavy as the water teased in gentle ripples against her oversensitive flesh.

She clenched her fists, her hands wanting to stroke him in return and replace those dark memories. But she wasn't only a witch, she was a witch who practiced the same magic that had destroyed his childhood. "Why have you come back?"

They fell into silence, her own heartbeat a roar inside her head as he continued to stroke along her sensitive skin. She'd never been so intimate with another person, never having allowed herself close enough when fear would coat her tongue. She'd had sex, a carnal joining of the most basic instinct, but that was nothing compared to the desire that throbbed just then. How her breath caught at every innocent caress, her stomach tightening with anticipation.

Kyra couldn't stop the shiver that rattled down her spine, didn't stop Xander when he placed his left hand on her hip and those talented fingers began circling there too.

"Open your third eye," he whispered, and it took her a second to realise it wasn't just the whistling of the wind. "If the manacle lets you."

She obeyed, concentrating on opening her mind to see beyond the mundane world, her third eye opening to see perceptions beyond ordinary sight.

Her resulting gasp made him chuckle, his thumb moving to brush her thigh, suspiciously close to between her legs.

Colours burst across her vision, as if she sat in the centre of a rainbow. She wiggled, Xander releasing her so she could spin, hand lifting out the water to reach for the sparkles. "What is it?" she asked, her smile genuine.

"It's called a ley line, a natural energy. They seem to connect ancient sacred sites around the world, undetectable to everyone who wasn't attuned to the earth. As a witch, you wouldn't be able to sense them, but you can see if you concentrate."

She knew what it was, but had never realised they could be so beautiful.

"Hmmm. This ley line runs straight through, but it's attracted to the crystals imbedded into the surrounding rocks. They couldn't understand why I loved being in here so much, saying I must've been a mermaid."

Kyra's resulting laugh seemed to make him smile, just a slight tip of his lips. "Thank you," she said, meeting his eyes of frost.

"For what?"

"For sharing them with me. The ley line, and your

past." She let her third eye slip, unable to hold it any longer as the manacle on her wrist burned. His face was cool, but not completely expressionless as his eyes dripped to her lips, and her own parted. He moved closer until her hands pressed flat against his chest, his heart strong beneath her palms, skin hotter than the water.

The air thickened, suffocating as steam rose around them and the night sky became a beautiful backdrop of glittering stars. Slowly, as if not to startle her, his hands caressed her hips, brushing beneath the water until they hooked beneath her thighs and pulled her close enough she felt his heavy cock between her legs.

Xander's eyes darkened, pupils swallowing the icy blue of his irises. "Tell me to stop."

Stop? She couldn't think of anything worse. Instead she let out a little gasp, his fingers exploring the sensitive skin. At her silence his thumb dipped, just a single brush against her aching clit. This time she let out an encouraging moan, her body rolling against his, wanting more.

"You drive me fucking crazy."

Kyra reached up to tug on his hair, using it to pull her further onto his lap. "Only you."

His cock accidently nudged her entrance, and Xander went preternaturally still, his body rigid as if he fought control. "See," he pushed out between clenched teeth, spare hand reaching up to pinch her nipple. "Driving me fucking crazy, Princess."

Another brush of his thumb, a single finger teasing her...

Xander's head whipped to the side, his growl bouncing off the rocks. "Fuck off."

Kyra froze, pushing off Xander as she spotted the man standing at the edge of the water. His eyes skimmed off Xander as if he wasn't there, landing on her with a dismissive grunt.

"Dinner's in an hour," he said, hatred etched across his entire face. Without waiting for a reply he turned on his heel, leaving them alone in the bath.

Xander pulled back, dragging a hand down his face while Kyra sunk lower in the water. What was she thinking?

"I'm sorry," she said, not understanding why she felt the need to apologise.

Xander frowned, his fingers brushing under her jaw until he'd tipped her head back to better look at him. "Trust me, if we weren't interrupted it would be me who'd need to apologise. I can't seem to control myself around you."

Kyra felt the need to apologise again.

"Fuck." His lips were far gentler than she expected when he pressed them to hers. The kiss was over quickly, the pressure leaving her wanting more when he pulled back, only to lay his forehead against hers.

"You asked why I came back," he said, a dark current rippling beneath his voice. "I came back because it was the first time in over twenty years that my mother's reached out to me. That the community acknowledged my existence. At dinner we'll find out why."

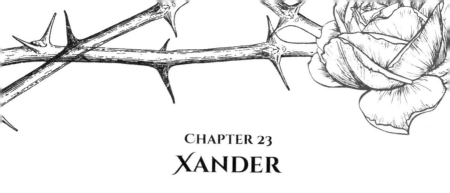

CHAPTER 23
XANDER

Xander couldn't stop staring at Kyra, the attention making her squirm. At this point her blush seemed to be a permanent tint across her cheeks. He found he enjoyed making her uncomfortable, his beast infatuated as she shot him a look of pure fire while they walked towards the dining hall. A silent fuck off that made him want to smile.

He'd had no intention of doing anything other than bathe, but her skin had looked so soft. An invitation that he couldn't ignore. He'd wanted to see what she would do if he distracted himself while his mind was ravaged with images of blood and death. Memories of the past that were quickly dowsed by simply the presence of her.

He'd expected a fight. Had wanted a fight with this witch that had such unexpected compassion in a magic bearer trained in death. And instead she'd softened beneath him despite his cutting words. With every squirm and moan his beast had rumbled across his mind, pushing, wanting more. So he pushed her more knowing that if he went too far he would feel her sharp anger, her inner strength fascinating to him. She'd made his cock so painfully hard he was ready to beg her for relief.

He needed to know exactly why she sometimes recoiled at touch, or why her eyes would widen in panic before she quickly hid them behind thick lashes. He'd find out the story behind every flinch and nervous reaction because he'd decided that he wasn't going to keep his distance at all. Not until this... hunger was diminished. This need.

She'd given permission to touch, whether she'd realised it or not. Her body had welcomed his caress, pressing back against him with every stroke. When she had shifted in that water just an inch, exposing the delicate slope of her neck he couldn't help but brush his lips across that bit of sensitive skin and savouring her pulse race at his touch.

"You're scowling," she said, her own frown pinching her brows. "You're going to scare them. Stop it."

Xander lowered his lashes, allowing his expression to turn cold, empty. He wasn't sure how he felt when Kyra paused, taken back at the mask he wore. She'd redressed in her own armour, her dress black with her hair bound in its usual thick braid. Her legs were bare, boots hitting her at the knee with a ridiculously high heel.

She looked like a witch, a power barely contained beneath her fingertips. He couldn't help but be amused when the Seers who waited in the dining room all turned silent at their approach.

They glared, full of hatred and ignorance. They ignored him completely, eyes widening and then skirting away to return their full attention to the small witch at his side. Instead of crumbling she lifted her chin, meeting every angered glare with a cool and collected one of her own. His beast gave a pleased growl, and from the way she turned to face him he suspected he'd accidentally vocalised the rumble.

Five guards hovered, guns strapped open on their hips with their hands relaxed on the grip. His mother stood at the head of the table, her smile wide as she gestured for them to take the two open seats at the far end. The Seers, thirty or so began to talk amongst themselves, quietly at first but the volume building until he had to concentrate to distinguish between the different conversations.

The spirits that would usually linger were gone, scared off. That was the main subject between the Seers, their concern for the dead. No one spoke to either of them, which was preferred as they both quietly ate the broth served.

The aggressive glances continued, the muttering and the insults. Kyra gave no indication that she'd heard, her attention on the bread roll that she pulled gently apart. One Seer was brave enough to speak louder, calling her a *vile vixen*. When he didn't get the reaction he wanted he said it louder, his chair scraping as he stood.

"Why does that sordid witch dine with us?"

Kyra continued with her roll, not bothering to look up as they all murmured in agreement.

"She needs to be burned for what she's done."

His mother Sienna stood, but before she could speak Kyra finally responded.

"Tell me, What exactly have I done?" she asked, her voice calm as she moved her gaze across the five men with guns, then back to the speaker.

The man stuttered, looking between the others. "You're a witch. Your very presence here has terrified the dead."

"And for that reason I deserve to be burned at the stake?" she added. "I don't know why I'm surprised, you're the same people that ostracised a child because he was different to you."

The man flushed, his face burning when he took an

aggressive step forward. "You know nothing you little bitch."

Xander was between them in a blink, savouring the scent of fear as he let his mask slip to reveal the calm but lethal predator beneath.

"Look!" the man cried, his eyes skirting away to look anywhere else. "She has *him* under her spell!"

"I think that's enough," Sienna declared. "Thomas, please sit down. We all know why I've called for this dinner and why it's important."

Thomas paused, hands fisted at his side.

"Actually, not everyone," Xander said. "Tell me, why am I here when I'm still not welcome?"

His mother was the only person to look at him, to smile. But it wasn't of maternal love or even familiarity. "We want you to come home, to be with your people."

"I very much doubt the '*we*' in that statement." Xander's laugh was dark. "I'm not one of you, you made that perfectly clear to me as a boy."

"Our numbers are dwindling," she continued. "Our gift is no longer being passed onto our children."

Xander remained where he stood. "And how exactly is that my problem?"

Sienna's smile turned to the other Seers. "Look at how you've grown, so big and strong. We were wrong to cast you aside because of your magic. *I* was wrong."

Displeased murmurs, faces twisted in irritation and anger.

Her arm elegantly waved towards the far door and two women appeared in the threshold. He recognised the one on the left, the woman who'd watched them from the balcony as they'd arrived.

Sienna gestured to the newcomers. "Your children will

have the gift, and so I call upon your duty as an Aes-Si Seer to spread your seed."

The two new women wore sheer robes, their bodies oiled and naked beneath. They were beautiful, faces carefully made up to highlight their thick lips and large eyes. Jewellery draped between heavy breasts, drawing the eye.

They walked in short, slow steps. Hips swinging sensually as they reached forward as if to touch him. He growled a warning, the sound harsh as they snapped their hands back as if burned. The men with guns closed in, ready for their order.

"That's enough!" Sienna said. "You're my son, you will do your duty for your people."

"I'm not your son," Xander said, stepping back when the two women went to touch him again. He saw Kyra tense in his peripheral, her fingers gripping the table tight. "You lost that privilege when you handed me over like an offering. Do you even know what was done to me? What I had to go through?"

Her eyes shimmered, the truth that she knew apparent in the subtle tension along every line of her body.

Xander smiled with teeth, noting the edge of fear. "I was beaten until close to death. Broken apart and pieced together like some sort of experiment. They made me into a monster. *You* made me into a monster."

His mother's lips tightened. "You were always a monster, it's why we lost so many of us when those witches attacked. Drawn to you."

"That's bullshit!" Kyra cried, her chair toppling over behind her. "How can you even say that to him knowing he was a defenceless child?"

"You don't need evidence, just look at his eyes!" Sienna barked, her tone so acerbic it could cut. "The old gods gave him those eyes of death, a penance for what he would do.

But all will be forgiven once he gives us more Seers to carry on our legacy. Children who will have the gift as well as magic. They'll be able to defend themselves against *your* kind."

"Xander isn't the monster here, you are," Kyra said, voice quivering.

Sienna cocked her head, expression desolate. "Maybe, but you didn't witness when those three witches came strolling in with darkness burning from their fingertips. They slaughtered my friends and family without hesitation, and they'd laughed the whole time." A quiet sob, a single tear glistening down her face. "Blood had coated the floor, so thick there wasn't anywhere left untouched."

Power hummed, and he was sure he noticed something pass behind Kyra's eyes. "You put all that blame onto an innocent child."

His mother tensed, eyes narrowing. "Canticum pro defunctis, that's why the spirits have disappeared."

Kyra paled, but it didn't cut through her anger.

"Sienna this should never have passed the vote," the man beside his mother said. "*He* brought a black witch into our community knowing our history. Who says their combined chi wouldn't attract more of her kind again?"

"We need to breed stronger children," Sienna hissed. "That was why the vote passed, and that's why we had all agreed to invite Xander back to join us." She clicked her fingers, and the two women purred, pulling at their sheer robes until they dropped to the floor. They ignored his warning snarl this time, their hands tentatively brushing across his chest, their fingers dancing. Teasing at the edge of his shirt.

What did they want? For him to fuck them right there on the table?

"Take her away."

Their palms were on his skin, beneath his shirt.

Kyra let out a shout, a guard reaching out to grab her manacled wrist. "Get off me!" The guard was twice her size, and he easily lifted her over his shoulder, heading towards the doorway.

Pain ripped through his body, his beast bursting through his skin without even a warning. A roar echoed from his throat, his eyes set on the one guard who held Kyra tightly. Cheekbones were bright with colour, but it was her fury that he scented as she twisted and fought. She hadn't even realised he'd shifted, not until the guard suddenly dropped her to the floor.

And then the screaming began.

He ignored them all. Flattening his ears to his skull as he hunched down, his lips peeling back to reveal large canines. The guard pulled his gun from his hip, hand shaking.

He didn't care about the weapons, didn't care as the Seers frantically panicked with some escaping into the hall while others pressed themselves against the back wall. His growl vibrated his chest, his nails cracking the tiles beneath his paws as Kyra turned and stepped toward him without fear or panic. A tail whipped out, curling gently around her waist. He urged her closer, into his side.

Mine.

Everyone cowered. Everyone cried. Except for Kyra, who gently brushed through the pale white hair at his nape, her fingers tracing the darkened lines that were an echo of the tattoos on the man. He couldn't hear her words over the screams, not when he was slowly curving his body to protect her from the guns that were pointed in their direction.

It was his mother who recovered first.

"Xander?" she asked, her once powerful voice trembling. "What have you become?" She held up a hand, and the gunmen hesitated.

Xander pushed past the beast, shifting back into the man. Kyra had been released once his tail had vanished, but she still moved to stand with him. The Seers that remained stood frozen, their faces familiar from his childhood. He shouldn't have shifted. Riley had been right, he was the steadiest out of them all. The least likely to lose control, and yet he had shifted without even thinking it through.

Fuck.

"We'll leave," he said, his voice more of a rumble.

His mother straightened her spine, tears dripping down her cheek. "No, I invited you here, so tonight you're our guests. Tomorrow you're to leave and never return."

It was a final dismissal by the woman who'd raised him until he was eight.

A tightness clogged his throat, his heart a solid block of ice in his chest.

"After tomorrow," she continued, turning her back for the final time. "You are nothing."

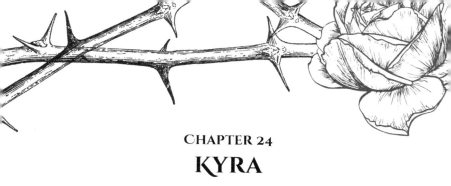

CHAPTER 24
KYRA

Xander paced, the tattoos at his back flickering beneath the candlelight. Back and forth, his powerful strides only taking three steps across the room. He'd said nothing, not in the ten minutes they'd been back in the bedroom or in the time it took to walk through the halls.

They were shunned, ignored as if they too were ghosts.

"I'm sorry," Kyra whispered, not sure why she offered an apology but did so anyway. His shoulders tensed, but he didn't slow his continuous pacing. His anger tense beneath his skin. "I never thought I would find another parent as shitty as mine, and here we are," she laughed, the sound forced.

Xander said nothing in response, which was okay because she felt like talking. Distracting.

"I was conceived on purpose," she continued, her voice soft. "Which sounds lovely, doesn't it? That I was wanted enough that I was planned. But a baby was not what my parents sought. No they actually wanted a living vessel. Power requires a great sacrifice, and death is the highest offering. It was even better if that offering was directly blood-related to the casters."

A slight pause, Xander's turning to face her before he continued his pace, fury evident in every stride. "They conceived you specifically to kill you?"

"At first, yes. But they realised shortly after my birth that I wasn't simply a black witch. Black magic requires sacrifice of the soul and mind, slowly polluting the caster until there's nothing left but a hollow shell. Even hours old my chi held no ill effects from the magic they tested on me, my chi able to repel the effluence and withstand the stronger magic for far longer than they could combined."

"Canticum pro defunctis," he said, his tone a low timbre that was laced with acid. "What does it mean?"

Kyra paused, his anger igniting her own. Guess they were no longer on friendly terms. "Exactly what it translates to. A song for the dead."

This time he did stop his pacing, face carved in horror. "You're a soul witch." He flung the name like an insult.

Her hands clenched, arcane tingling her fingertips even with the restriction of the manacle. She'd never reacted in such a way, always being able to suppress her irritation, to protect herself from others. And yet with Xander she felt it bubbling, ready to blow.

"A soul witch. A rare designation born from two powerful black witches on the eve of a blood moon. Death is nothing but an essence. They look like threads that tether your consciousness to the realm, and I'm able to manipulate or sing it to my will." She laughed without humour, her eyes burning from unshed tears. "My father used to tell me I was neither living nor dead, but a conduit in between both worlds."

"A witch with a secret," he sniggered. "What a fucking surprise."

Kyra jumped to her feet, and Xander faced her, eyes smouldering as if he too were on the edge. Which she understood, but that didn't stop her.

"I had to keep it a secret," she snapped out at him like bullets, knowing his persona of ice had melted, and if she wasn't careful she was going to get burned. "Because if being hated on sight just because of my magic isn't enough, I would be hunted for my abilities, and not many people would ask nicely. According to Magicka law, I should have never made it past my first birthday."

"Frederick knows, doesn't he?" A snarl more than a question. "That's what he has on you. That's why you do everything he asks like a little fucking dog. Your power is repulsive," Xander continued ominously. "To control the dead is –"

"You may believe I'm this horrible person, but I have no interest in harming others." Her voice was more of a screech, but there was steel behind the words. "I feel it, every slice and every cut. I feel the death of the animals as if my own soul's being ripped out."

"You would say that, wouldn't you." He closed their distance, a predator behind icy irises. "That doesn't change the fact your magic is pure death, powered by others' misfortune."

"Don't you dare tell me what my magic is!" She pushed at his chest, unable to have him so close with his teeth bared in hatred. "I never asked for this magic. I never wanted to be able to taste your very essence."

Xander's reply was obscured by his snarl.

"I never wanted this," she replied, her voice quieter, but no less angry. "I was kept in a cage my entire life, a room trapped in an endless darkness with no source of light. I was allowed out only to assist with spells. To be used as a conduit over and over."

Her voice strained against the hurricane of emotions.

She swore she'd never tell anyone of her past, but as usual Xander pushed and pushed.

Exasperated, she let the tears finally falling. "I've never known a life where I haven't been used because of my unique chi. A *pet* as you so delicately called me. Don't you dare judge me when I'm trying to break the cycle."

There was a pregnant pause, Xander so close all she saw was him. His skin. His tattoos. His stupid bloody judgmental face.

"Are they dead?" he asked, his voice dangerously quiet. "You parents, are they dead?"

Kyra's chest tightened. "I killed them."

She'd never admitted it, not even to Frederick who suspected what she'd done. But he didn't really know what had happened. What she was truly capable of.

"I poisoned them with nightshade. Just a little, enough for paralysis." They'd been trapped inside their minds, eyes wide with fear. "They hadn't suspected anything, not until I let them see exactly how powerful I was." Another hot tear burned down her cheek. "I removed their souls from their bodies while they were still alive."

It wasn't supposed to be possible, and she'd had no intention of hurting them beyond the temporary paralysis. But she'd been so angry. She'd felt a tug, a thread of sensation that she instinctively pulled. Their souls had ripped free from their flesh before she could stop it, their harrowing screams something she'd never forget.

"I didn't mean to," she added, swallowing hard. "I just wanted to get away. But it proves that I'm exactly what you believe I am." She touched the cuff on her upper arm. "It's why I wear the crystal. It's a syphon, it breaks the connections I feel to souls. Without it I... I can't control it."

She held her flinch when his face became cold fury, his

eyes like rapid lightning.

Xander let out a strangled noise from the back of his throat. "I can't be here, not right now."

Kyra wiped across her wet face. "Wait, you're leaving me here?" Her hand brushed his arm when he headed towards the door. "Xander, pleas –"

His lips found hers, her back knocking heavily against the wall behind. He held her there with a strength she craved, her whole body alight with sensation. She savoured the anger in his kiss, the passion and pressure of the connection. Slipping her fingers into his hair she pulled him closer, until her tongue fought for dominance she had no chance of winning.

Kyra felt her moan vibrate between them, desperate in her need. Her hands explored the expanse of his chest, the tattoos brightening everywhere she stroked. She needed more, his chi electric against her own even as his body remained rigid above her.

She wanted him to touch her just as he had in the bath, but instead his fists created cracks in the walls at which he held back.

"Please," she whispered. Pressing harder with her nails she stroked down, his abs tense as she moved even lower. Xander had pulled jeans on haphazardly after his shift, the zipper down so she easily slipped beneath the denim, wrapping her hand around the hardness of his cock.

"Kyra!" he growled, pulling back just enough he could curse out her name.

He stiffened in her grip, growing impossibly thicker as her thumb brushed across the velvety head, already leaking for her. His next groan ended in her mouth, his hands slipping beneath her thighs to lift her closer. She felt him heavy between her legs, with only a sliver of fabric separating them. The movement pulled her hand away, but she didn't

206

mind. Not when he began to move his hips against hers, the need to have him inside her growing.

"Please." She pretty much begged, leaning down for the next kiss and using his mouth to help her forget. Every stroke of his tongue, nip of her lips and roll of his cock just something else she could concentrate on. To lose herself in.

His fingers stroked up her bare thighs, his thumbs finding the edge of the soaking wet lace with a pleased groan. There was no hesitation when he moved aside the underwear, his fingers spearing through slick folds with a determined caress that tore a moan from her throat. When he pressed the pad of his thumb against her throbbing clit she cried out, already knowing how wet she was as his fingers set a steady rhythm that had her seeing stars.

"That's it, Princess," he growled. "Scream for me."

He added a second, thick finger. Curling them inside to brush against the spot that had her clenching, whimpering for a release. An orgasm coiled low in her stomach, growing with every brush against her clit and every thrust of those talented fingers.

"Please," she moaned, needing more. She needed him to stretch her. To chase away the nightmares for them both.

His face was carved with carnal desire, his movement desperate as he tugged her hands above her head with one of his locked around her wrists.

Kyra stilled, fighting the fear at being restrained, at being –

She couldn't breathe.

Xander released her just as quickly, concern slicing through any desire. "Kyra?" He carefully released her. "Fuck."

Kyra closed her eyes, body trembling while fear coated her tongue like acid. Xander's arms wrapped around her waist, her head placed against his heart, the steady beat something familiar. Comforting. She inhaled his scent, already feeling her pulse settled down to something that wouldn't cause her to pass out. Only when she looked up did he pull back, his shoulders blocking most of the light.

"Wait," she begged, not wanting to be alone. She was always so alone.

His hand tightened on her waist, and this time she couldn't stop the flinch as her mind fought her body.

He let out a strangled groan, his movement frantic as he stepped away. "I need to go."

"Please, don't go. I'm sorry I –"

"Don't you dare fucking apologise for something you can't control."

Kyra licked at her lips, and Xander traced the movement.

"If I stay," he growled, "I'm going to fuck you up against that wall."

Kyra's thighs clenched, pulse racing for an entirely different reason.

"I'm going to fuck you until you scream my name. Until those nightmares that darken your eyes are replaced with nothing but me." Xander closed the space once more, his larger body curving over hers. "Is that what you really want?" he whispered. "To be fucked like that? Because I can't do gentle right now, not with the beast riding me."

Kyra swallowed, her body aching. All she had to do was close the gap, to take his lips again and lose herself in his body. All she needed to do...

Fear strangled her words.

"Go to sleep, Kyra." He moved to the bedroom door, the wood groaning beneath his grip. "You'll be safe here. I'll make sure of it." Without waiting for her reply he closed the door behind him, leaving her alone with a single candle to keep her nightmares at bay.

CHAPTER 25
KYRA

K yra squinted, the sun bouncing off the freshly laid snow. The air was bitter, face burning as she pulled her knees under her chin and wrapped her arms tightly around her legs. The land surrounding the community truly was beautiful, even in the winter when nature was dormant, waiting patiently for spring to bloom. It was surprisingly quiet, peaceful even as the children screeched at the snowball war between them.

It reminded her of where she grew up, in a little secluded cottage by a bubbling brook. It too was quiet, but not as peaceful. Her parents had chosen it specifically so no one could hear her scream – before she'd learned not to.

She'd cherished her time with the small stream, bathing her feet when she was supposed to be tending the garden of poisonous plants that her father sold on the side. She could hear it too, from the darkness of her room. The water running freely through the rocks and stones of its bed.

That was where she stood as she watched the cottage burn, and for long after until the embers no longer glowed. Her feet frozen. The water washing her skin. Washing away her past. Her sins.

She hadn't looked back, and for several years she'd travelled on her own, learning and exploring. London called, a city of glittering skyscrapers and old historic buildings blended as if they were one. A city of possibilities and dreams, where Breed congregated and the place where she now called home.

She hadn't known her magic was banned under the Magicka law, had learned quickly to hide what she was. It was a chance passing that Frederick had sensed her and had known she practiced black magic. He'd given her a choice.

Death, or him.

She could feel Xander watching her, his attention a brand that seemed to scare away the cold and make the hostile stares of the adult Seers harsher in comparison. He'd said nothing as he settled himself beside her, the wind ruffling his pale hair. She turned her head to notice his stubble dark, almost as dark as his brows. The contrast of his pale hair would have looked strange on anyone else, but on him it was striking.

"You ready to get out of here?" she asked.

"They're whispering again," he said with a scowl, his lashes low to protect his eyes. "I clearly didn't scare them enough. Maybe I should have eaten one as a warning?"

She'd heard the Seers, their venomous words scrambled in the early morning wind.

"I don't know if you're aware, but I'm a dark witch," she said with a smirk.

He looked at her then, his scowl deepening.

"I'm used to being a pariah." When his face didn't budge her smile widened. "People unaffected by insults, make their enemies absolutely powerless."

He nudged her shoulder with his own. "You say that like you have many enemies."

Kyra shrugged, studying his strong jaw and the tattoos

that wrapped around his neck. She'd woken up beside the key to the manacle, and surrounded by candles. They'd been placed strategically in the corners, so there was nowhere that shadows could settle. Nowhere for anybody to hide. It was the nicest thing anybody had ever done for her.

"I've heard from my brothers and no one has been near your place, or your friend's."

Reality struck, and she tightened her grip on her legs before turning back to the field. "It's not my place anymore." She could never risk going back.

A finger brushed against her cheek. "I won't let him hurt you."

"He'll never let me go." Not when she knew too much. "It's funny. I have dreamed of being free, but I didn't think I would feel so lost once I was." Kyra climbed carefully to her feet, the children in the field shouting and giggling as some adults joined in with their fun.

Silence stretched between them, reminding her of his lips so deliciously close to hers.

'If I stay, I'm going to fuck you up against that wall.'

She hated it when her cheeks glowed, and that heat shivered down her spine. Her breasts became heavy, sensitive against the fabric of her bra. She imagined him doing exactly that, taking her against a wall. His powerful body moving inside hers.

A warmth burned in his eyes, his smile purely male, as if he knew exactly the angle of her thoughts. Her mouth opened, her tongue darting out nervously as he slowly bent down, closing the gap between them until she felt his breath against her lips.

A scream, followed by a shout of warning.

Xander shoved, a ball of arcane passing between the gap where they'd just stood. Kyra caught herself before she fell, blinking as she turned back to the field where a man stood with his wand pointed. He wore a long purple cloak, the lapels green with a metal pin engraved with three stars. An enforcer.

How did they find me?

"Get everyone back!" she cried to Xander.

The children shrieked, running to the adults who were also crying. Luckily the enforcer ignored them, striding across the snow with determination.

"Get behind me," Xander said, squaring his shoulders.

"No, go help the community!" Their worst nightmare was a witch, and because of her there was one attacking.

The enforcer's wand lifted, the end glowing so brightly she had to look away. Nothing happened, there was no strike from the front. Instead she felt it from her back, arcane tearing through her aura until she wrenched herself to the side. The magic had feasted along her in little bites, a warning rather than a deadly hit.

"Xander!" she cried. "Please, go!"

He ignored her, his own magic responding in his palms.

The witch at their front was almost on them, and she couldn't see the one at her back. "They're enforcers," she explained, hoping he understood the significance. "If you counterstrike, they'll kill you." They'd come to take her back to the Magicka. Back to Frederick.

Xander let out a steady breath. "They're not taking you." His sphere of arcane expanded, the tattoos that peeked out of his shirt pulsating with a white glow. He blocked the next shot from the wand at his front, baring his teeth as he waited with trained patience to make a strategic strike of his own.

Kyra felt the magic at her back, was able to throw herself to the side before the enchantment hit her. It had been a ball, a pellet of some sort that exploded into a fine dust against a tree.

Finally the other enforcer stepped into view, a gun held in one hand, and a wand in the other. "Get down!" he snarled, marching over to her with the gun pointed directly in her face. She wasn't sure what the spell was, the smell slightly bitter and no way earthen magic. Kyra risked a glance to the tree that had been hit, the bark bubbling.

In that split second he was on her, wrapping his hand in her braid and forcing the gun into her side. She hit out, her fist connecting to his throat with just enough weight behind it to give her a satisfied choke. But it wasn't enough.

"Get on your knees, bitch," he gasped, her chi on fire as if it was being painfully pulled. "If I feel you call to your magic, I'll shoot your pretty –" Xander appeared behind him, a heavy fist connecting to his head. He fell, but Xander didn't stop his advance as he swatted the wand from his hand as if it were a twig.

Kyra's hair was released. *"Incenduro!"* she screamed as the enforcer scrambled for his wand, her arcane flames searing across his hand in a burst of purple. The centre burned white, iridescent in the sun.

Xander grunted, and she turned just as arcane marked at his chest, the spell burning through his shirt. A gun shot, and then a pellet hit the same spot.

"No!" she cried, watching in horror as the spell began to eat away at his skin.

They were going to kill him.

Kyra screamed, the syphon on her arm vibrating as the magic she hated flowed. The arcane that had started in her palms grew until the flames were up to her elbows, the purple darkened, virtually black against the white of its heart.

She could feel the ghosts all around her, sparks of sentience and dread. She could feel the bodies buried beneath her feet, the ancient bones and half-rotten corpses.

Hundreds, maybe more that stretched across the whole of the Borderlands, and even beyond as her awareness spread.

She set her attention on the enforcer before her, his mouth snapping open as she saw her image reflected in his wide eyes. There was no heat from her arcane, only an endless cold that burned even worse. She could feel his thread, his life essence tethered by something so easily cut. But that wasn't what she wanted. No, it was the spirits that surrounded them, drawn to her like a moth to a flame. They came in their waves, thousands pulled to the field. They made no sound, no footsteps in the snow. She knew when they had reached the first enforcer, the one who fought Xander while his chest was still burning, melting.

His scream made her want to cover her ears, but she couldn't rip her eyes away as the spirits tore at him, clawing and tearing away at flesh that would never be theirs again.

They glittered against the surrounding white, a sea of souls that ignored Xander as he turned toward her in horror. His eyes widening in warning.

A weight hit her head, hard enough the world spun and she fell to her knees. Her hands were crushing against the snow with a wand was pressed to her cheek, the end sharp enough to cut.

"Call them off or I'll kill you!"

The spirits roared, a cacophony of deafening cries.

She needed contact. Her skin on his. Without a word she reached up to touch his hand with just her fingertips. It strengthened her connection, the essence that tethered his life heavy against her senses when she pulled it gently, like she was playing the harp. His soul sang to her, and then the pressure was gone, ripped away by a man of controlled fury. She couldn't focus, not when the souls had started moving to her. Wanting something more, wanting life that she couldn't give.

"Kyra!" Xander stood before her, his chest a splash of red.

She felt his thread, more of a silver woven rope and velvety against her senses despite there being no physical connection. His connection to the realm was strong, enhanced with something she'd never seen before.

"Kyra!"

His hands went to clamp down on her arms, ignoring her arcane that hissed and struck out like angry vipers.

"Don't touch me." It was barely a whisper, her voice lost against the spirits that surrounded her. So close they blocked out the sky.

"Ignore them!" Xander shouted at her. "They can't hurt you if you don't give them power."

"Don't touch me," she repeated. "Please, I can't control it." The spirits rippled across her chi, their energy thrumming until they began to merge with hers. The souls continued to reach for her, and she couldn't stop them. "Please, no, stop!"

"Kyra! Look at me!" Hands on her face, eyes of impenetrable ice. "Look at me!"

She blinked, drowning out everything else to concentrate on him. Only him. The edge of her peripheral darkened, the spirits disappearing one by one.

"That's it, look at me," he murmured, voice achingly soft.

Kyra trembled as her power cut off, the snow seeping into her bones. The cold registering against her skin.

"You're okay," he whispered. "You're okay."

You disgust me.

The enforcer to her side was face down, arm twisted at an impossible angle. His skin had been sliced open, the muscles and tendons exposed. She didn't know whether he was alive, not daring to check with her magic.

Xander lifted her into his arms, holding her against his wet, bloody chest.

"You're okay," he repeated. "You're okay."

She said nothing as he placed her in the car, securing her belt with a snap that set her on edge. She didn't know how long she stared into the distance, the scenery changing. The snow melting the further they drove.

"Pull over," she muttered, her hands trembling. "Pull over!"

The car screeched, and before it had come to a complete stop she'd thrown open the door to fall to her knees and vomit. It came out black, so dark it absorbed the surrounding light. Fingers in her hair, a warm hand pressed against her back.

Then the tears came, so hot against the seeping cold of her soul that they burned. Xander held her as she sobbed, her hands fisted against his chest when he pulled her closer, not caring about his own wounds. He mumbled something to her, his words not registering as all she heard was her memory echo.

You disgust me.

CHAPTER 26

XANDER

Xander faced Riley and Alice, his stomach clenched as he carefully described exactly what he'd seen. Kyra had been both beautiful and deadly, her raging scream when the pellet had hit his chest a siren's call to the surrounding ghosts who'd watched from a distance.

Dark energy had burned against his skin, an acid eating away as he'd gritted his teeth and ignored the searing pain to land blow against blow on the enforcer.

Not one, but two had been sent to take her away.

Fuck.

She'd destroyed them with a look of pure power, their souls ripped clean by the spirits who'd answered her pained call with eagerness. He'd watched, filled with horror as the spirits then swarmed on her. Touching her as she struggled beneath their need.

A Goddess of Death.

"The enforcers weren't sent by the Magicka," Alice said when she stormed in, lightning crackling between her fisted hands. "There's no open warrant for her arrest and my contacts can't find any evidence of Kyra being on their system. She isn't even registered."

"Her power was like nothing I've ever seen," Xander said. Her arcane had been devoid of any warmth, the black with a heart of iridescent white so cold it was like a dying star. "Her magic defies all logic."

"It explains why she's wanted so much by Frederick," Riley said.

"She barely has any control over her magic. She's not trained," Xander added. "She was like a child who'd only just realised they could call arcane. She could've killed herself."

Alice folded her arms. "Black witches usually train their children to expand their chi before they can walk. Her parents should have –"

"Have you heard back from the Council?" he asked as a distraction. He wouldn't share her secrets, not when she'd gifted the pain to him.

Riley scowled, dragging a hand down his face. "Edwards mentioned that the Council chamber's sealed until further notice."

Xander concealed his rage, unsurprised that the Council of other councils was unavailable. the Council ruled, but gave the illusion of control to the separate Breed organisations that governed their own.

"He mentioned needing to speak with you," Xander said, leaning against the wall. He was too worked up to sit, to relax while Kyra was alone upstairs. It took concentration to not go after her, to hunt her down and... He had no idea. "I assumed the Magicka aren't going to be much help either?"

Alice just snorted in response.

"It's our job to deal with Daemons, and Frederick's now an extension of that. Edwards is aware of the situation and has agreed to step in against his fellow Councilman if needs be."

"You trust him?"

"Of course not." Riley stood, pressing his palms hard against the surface of the table. "We need to find a way to trap Frederick. Maybe Kyra could —"

Xander's snarl ripped through the room. "No way is she going anywhere near him." Riley's beast teased his irises, and Xander responded with his own. "It's too much of a risk, we need to find another way to get to Frederick."

Alice placed her hand on her mate's shoulder, trying to calm him down. "Then we wait." When both the men turned to her she rolled her eyes. "Frederick made a deal with a Daemon, and that deal requires Kyra. He may be powerful, but he hasn't got the capability to match that type of magic without hurting himself greatly. He'll become desperate and make a mistake."

Xander's tone was harsh, leaving no room for argument. "Until Frederick's out of the picture Kyra stays here." His beast roared in agreement. "She stays with me."

KYRA

Kyra tugged back the blanket, blinking the sleepiness from her eyes. She froze, not recognising her surroundings as she took in the calming earthen tones and simple wooden furniture. Five lamps blazed, all different styles and patterns that didn't match the rest of the décor.

With a slight panic she searched for her syphon crystal, finding it flush against her upper arm like it always was. Her chi stretched. And stretched. And stretched. Her power a constant thrum beneath her fingertips, charged to the point she was going to burst. She had expected her aura to ache, but she felt nothing except pure energy.

Her body itself was tired, heavy as she swung her legs over the side of the bed. A leather jacket draped over the armchair in the corner, a pair of trainers placed messily beneath. A dagger lay on the seat, the tip sharp and gleaming as if it had been freshly cleaned.

She padded across the room in bare feet, finding a picture of three children smiling. It wasn't hard to recognise Xander, not with his hair and eyes. His grin looked so natural on the young, gangly teen. Even if bruises and small cuts did cover the majority of his face. His hands were relaxed around the shoulders of the two other boys, the knuckles red. They all, she realised, were bruised and broken. And yet they smiled for the camera, the bond between them clear even through the photograph.

An open doorway led to the bathroom, almost the same size as the large bedroom. The marble tiles were heated beneath her feet, so warm she wanted to curl on the floor and go back to sleep. The shower was open to the right, just a single glass pane separating it against the room. Kyra took a second to appreciate the sheer size of the bath built into the floor, with three steps leading down and could easily fit five.

Her boots were beside the toilet, and since there was a white towel folded neatly at the front she assumed at some point she'd probably been bent over, puking the effluence from her system.

Great.

She had no memory of arriving there. Or puking. Or going to bed.

The small window was endless black, the moon obscured by clouds making it night, or maybe morning.

She dared look into the mirror, knowing what the reflection would show. She reached for the dial for the shower, the bathroom immediately filling the room with steam.

Pulling at her clothes she walked beneath the scalding spray. It stung against her skin, but she didn't care. Not until the coldness that had settled in the centre of her chest began to ease. She released the tie from her hair, the water cascading down to free the black ooze that had stuck to the strands. The water at her feet was like rust, and she stood there until it ran clear.

The cold air kissed at her skin when she shut the water off, shivers rattling as she blindly reached out for the towel. It was large enough to wrap around twice, and warm as she stepped back into the bedroom.

Xander stood by the bed, lashes low. She couldn't read his face, his expression a carefully composed mask of calm which went at odds to the rigid lines of his body. He looked like he was going to snap, and clearly it was because of her.

Kyra remained where she was, her eyes instinctively checking his chest. He wore a t-shirt, hiding the damage she knew had to be there.

"Do you have my bag?" she asked, voice hoarse. Probably because of all the puking. "I'll get dressed, and then get out of here."

"Get out of here?" he repeated with a scowl. "Where the fuck do you think you're going to go at one in the morning?"

"I don't know," she bit back at his tone. "Anywhere else."

"Anywhere else?"

"What are you, a parrot?" she asked, the excess energy inside her slithering like snakes, uncoiling and ready to strike. "As soon as I'm dressed I'll be gone, and you can go back to whatever it is that you do." The magic inside her was wrong, noxious.

"You're not going anywhere."

She bristled at the sleek aggression of his threat. "You can't stop me."

"No?" A growl. A warning. "How's the chi feeling? You know, after calling on the fucking dead."

Kyra felt like she'd been slapped. "Fuck you!" the curse exploded out of her before she'd even realised, anger searing through her veins. "I never wanted any of this!"

"You keep saying that, and yet drama follows you everywhere."

"I did it for you!" She was screaming, her voice rising as he gave her a mocking smile. Kyra sucked in a staggered breath, trying to cool the anger that rippled through her before she accidentally released some of the energy. "I don't need to explain myself to you. I don't need to hear how *disgusted* you are by me. I'm leaving." She didn't care that she was wrapped in just a towel. She'd worn worse.

Xander blocked her in two strides, his movements as elegant as any dancer despite his size. "You're an idiot who called the dead because of me." A statement rather than a question. "I didn't need any help, Princess."

"Move." She tried to shove past him, but he was an impenetrable wall. She fisted her hands, feeling her chi respond. Her crystal scalded her arm in response to the power surge, and his eyes darted to it.

"If you leave," he said, slightly calmer. "You'll be vulnerable."

She lifted her chin. "I can defend myself."

"You could've broken your hand when you punched that enforcer. You have zero training in any defence moves, both physical and magical." He glowered, but was clearly trying to stay calm. "You almost killed yourself because you've never been taught control of your power."

"Maybe I should go back!"

Xander's face thundered, his rage an almost physical force.

"You saw what I can do," she said. "Maybe I should go back, it's probably what I deserve." She went to shove him again, but cringed away from his chest. "Now move!"

Xander noticed, tracking the focus of her attention. He pulled off his shirt in one smooth movement. His skin beneath was whole, normal with no discolouration or marks to indicate any damage. The beautiful tattoos undisturbed as if he'd never been hurt.

"Ho... how?" She reached forward without realising. Her fingertips brushed along his pectoral, the muscle beneath rock solid. She'd seen his chest open and bleeding, destroyed by the arcane.

"My tattoos," he explained, pressing into her touch until her whole palm branded him. "Are a specialised type of glyph, a syphon just like your crystal. But they don't block my magic. They concentrate it."

"I saw you... I saw you..." She looked up to meet his eyes, his rage melting to a simmer. "You were hurt."

"Your crystal's the same as my tattoos. They concentrate your magic, Kyra. It's probably the only reason you haven't killed yourself yet."

"No, they block the connection I feel to souls."

She wanted to snap her hand back, her power ready to strike. He sensed the tension along her arm, moving to hold her against him. His action had been a blur, so fast her eyes couldn't track it.

"No, they concentrate your powers elsewhere. It's why you were able to call those spirits to you in the field."

She could still feel those spirits, inside her. She needed to get away, to get them out.

Kyra tugged at her hand, his grip like iron. "Let go!"

The tattoos that she touched rippled beneath her palm, glowing. "I need to go, I can't be here!"

"At eight I was thrown into training against my will, along with Riley and all the others. We were forced to train. Forced to withhold more magic than our bodies could possibly hold. It would rip us apart, and many times almost killed us. And when it didn't, we were forced to hold even more."

His words came hot and fast, as if he didn't tell her quickly he might never tell her at all.

"The Archdruid at the time, Riley's father, wanted perfectly designed warriors. Ones who were capable of defeating a Daemon. But druidic magic wasn't enough, even though we were more powerful than any of our ancestors. Druids are of nature, and our magic generally isn't aggressive. So he made a bargain with Hadriel, a fallen angel, and the ruler of the Nether realm."

"The Nether?" Kyra asked. "As in the prison in Hell?" She hadn't heard of the place since her childhood, when her parents would gush about the dark power that could be found in the small but powerful realm.

"Hadriel cursed us, forcing our bodies to share themselves with beasts he'd created. And it fucking worked. We were suddenly able to take a lot more damage, and survive things not even a vampire could walk away from. We developed advanced strength, speed and agility, all designed to make us undefeatable warriors. We tattooed ourselves with the glyphs, the syphons enabling us to concentrate our natural magic without the arcane tearing us apart. We became exactly what the Archdruid had wanted."

Kyra couldn't help but react to Xander's pain. "You don't have to –"

His lips contorted into a grimace. "I was thirteen when I was forced into the ritual. Stepping out the other side with my own personal beast. We were all warned not to shift too much, otherwise we'd risked never being able to turn back into the man. So we kept away from temptation and strong emotions that would cause our beast to force control."

"What about love?" Kyra asked, emotions clogging her throat. "What about Riley and Alice?"

"He risked everything for her," Xander said, his voice softening. "He would have walked into Hell, and destroyed Hadriel himself for her." A quiet, secret smile. "We later found out it was all bullshit, lies told to us to keep us in line. We were never at risk of losing ourselves to the beasts, not if we fell in love. No, the curse that Hadriel put on us was to fight for one-hundred years, and then once that time was up we were to serve him down in Hell. Bound to him for all eternity."

Kyra gripped the edge of the towel with white knuckles. "Why are you telling me this?"

Xander's nostrils flared, his irises swirling into liquid silver. "Because you need to understand that I *see* you. That sometimes the Fates give you a shitty hand, and you do nothing but make it a bit more bearable. Being born a soul witch wasn't your fault, it doesn't make you *disgusting* or any less than anyone else. In fact, it makes you so fucking incredible that you have survived despite everything."

Kyra flushed, unable to look away as he bent closer, his lips open in invitation.

"Keep surviving Kyra. Don't let the darkness win."

She reached for him at the same time he slanted his lips over hers with a ravenous growl. He caught her returning moan, her hands exploring the width of his shoulders before dragging them down his pectorals.

She loved it when he lifted, pressing her against the wall so softly she barely registered the cold against her back. He pinned her with his heavier weight, the towel rolling up to the point she was very much aware of something hard and thick pressing against her stomach. His fingers gripped her thighs tightly, his thumbs moving in slow, teasing circles that made her core clench and breath quicken.

He released her lips, only to brush them gently against her jaw. She angled her head, waiting for the first stroke on the side of her throat. He paused when she tensed, hovering over her pulse.

"Please," she begged. She needed him to touch her there, to show her something other than fear. Her throat was one of her biggest vulnerabilities. One of her biggest triggers, but she trusted Xander completely.

With impressive patience he waited, his lips featherlight. "Stay with me," he whispered against her skin, her body trembling. His fingers teased closer to her core, distracting the dread that tried to steal the moment. "You have such a pretty pussy, Princess."

His thumb brushed against her clit, causing her to gasp.

"I can't wait to feel how tight you are around my cock."

His lips captured hers again, his tongue stroking, coaxing as he wrapped her legs fully around his waist. He walked them backwards to the bed, his knees hitting the mattress and forcing him to sit with her straddling his lap. He was far too gentle for what she wanted. Far too restrained.

Her towel began to slip, but before it could fall Xander caught it. "I'm trying to take this slow," he said, his voice deepening with his beast. "I've waited for you for far too long to lose control now."

Lifting her once more he flipped them so she was flat on her back. He held himself over her with a hungry expression, his lashes low as he settled himself between her legs.

Her breasts ached against the towel, an abrasive restriction she needed to remove. "What if I want you to lose control?"

He caught her hands when she tried to wiggle it free, moving them slowly above her head. "Keep them there," he growled, releasing her wrists and dipping his head to bite through the cotton fabric.

She squeaked, her core throbbing while her clit seemed to have a pulse of its own. When she went to tug at the towel again he simply moved her wrists back above her head. His grip was loose, just a slight pressure that shouldn't have caused her to panic.

"Say my name," he said, noticing her slight change.

Kyra remembered the restraints. The dark and pain –

He demanded her attention. "Say. My. Name."

Kyra blinked, tracing his face above her own. "Xander," she said, voice humiliatingly hoarse with the barest touch of dread. "Kiss me."

He followed her command without hesitation, exploring her mouth with teasing nips of his teeth. He pushed out his chi, brushing against hers in a full body caress that had her back bowing off the bed, the sensations overwhelming. Distracting.

She wasn't going to let fear win. Not this time. No, she was going to play with Xander until they were both exhausted and sated from such pleasure she wouldn't even remember her name. All she saw was him. His eyes. His face. His expression of pure lust, and not the violent echo of the past.

"That's right, Princess." A rumble of his chest, a vibration that went straight between her legs. "I bet you taste absolutely fucking delicious, all wet and ready for me."

"Fuck me." Kyra wanted more. "I need –"

"Tell me what you need, Princess," he murmured against her skin, looking up with eyes of liquid silver.

She felt no terror when she saw the beast through those irises, not when he released her wrists again to stroke down her body. He slipped beneath the towel, fingers dipping between her legs.

"Tell me exactly what you want." He didn't tease this time, his thick finger slipping between her hot, swollen folds in dominant little thrusts that had her clenching around him.

His thumb circled the bundle of nerves that craved his attention, her pussy aching to be filled with something bigger.

"Kyra?" He said her name as a question, asking for permission as he slowly pushed in a second finger.

"Please," she gasped, her back bowing and pleasure short-circuiting her brain. "I want you to fuck me."

She needed to feel something before she was forced to go back. Forced to do things that would slowly kill her inside.

She needed him to be the one point in her life that wasn't a mistake.

Unlike before there was no hesitation, not when she knew what she wanted. She wrapped her hands in his hair, pulling his lips down until she could savour his taste. Committing him to memory. Her next moan poured into his mouth, her tongue showing him exactly what she wanted as she raised her hips.

"Kyra," he growled against her lips. "I'm trying –"

Another thrust, his thumb flicking against her clit.

"Not to –"

His thumb pressed harder, making her squirm against the pressure she craved, so close to the edge she knew it would only take one more stroke.

"Rush." He pulled his hand back with a little smirk, slowly lifting his fingers to his mouth. His tongue flicked out languidly, tasting her so slowly she ached at the sight. "Fucking delicious."

Kyra shivered, pushing at his shoulders with a frustrated cry. When he didn't move she called a little arcane, the slight shock forcing him back. It gave her the room to wiggle, twisting the towel until it fell open to leave her bare to his gaze. Her skin burned at his visual caress, her nipples pebbling against the cool air.

"Off," she said, glancing down at his jeans while reaching up to cup her heavy breasts. "Now."

He ignored her, unable to look away from her hand. "More," he demanded, content to just watch. "Show me how wet your cunt is, Princess."

She moaned, her other hand travelling slowly down her stomach to dip into the heat between her legs. She played lazily, teasing herself while he watched with such raw hunger she could probably come just from him watching. Dipping a single finger inside, she arched her back. Chasing her own orgasm.

She enjoyed pushing him just as he'd pushed her, her thumb playing against her clit.

When he tensed as if to join she stopped, cutting him a glare. One that he returned.

"Kyra." An angry, frustrated snarl. She heard a rip, and then he was standing before her gloriously naked. He straddled her thighs, his cock gripped in his hand. He matched his strokes with her lazy movements, thumb rubbing across the pre-cum that glistened on the head.

Her fingers slowed, watching him touch himself while he watched her... Her orgasm uncoiled, so close she could almost taste the release.

Just as she was about to peak Xander yanked her down the bed. He stepped between her legs, keeping them open and ready.

"Xee!" She needed skin to skin. Needed to feel his pulse against her palms and his breath against her skin.

She needed to feel alive.

Xander hooked her knees over his hips, opening her further. She felt the blunt head of his cock at her entrance. She trembled with anticipation, but he didn't thrust. Instead he bent over her body, his teeth finding her nipple at the same time his finger circled her clit.

His cock sank only an inch deep, stretching her just enough for her to whimper, to beg. "Xander!" she cried, the sensations too much, her hips moving while his teeth and tongue tormented her breast. His finger teased her sensitive nerves. "I –"

Xander pushed into her body with one thrust, his finger finally adding the right pressure. The orgasm tore through her like a storm, so powerful not even a gasp escaped her lips. He stretched her to the point of delicious pain, her body clenching around his cock as it rippled in delirium.

"Harder!"

A mischievous smile, pausing for a few seconds longer until she was ready to burn him from the inside out. He held her gaze, making sure she was with him the whole time as he pulled back, and then slowly pushed inside her again.

She'd had enough, her core molten as she scored her nails down his back, urging him to go faster. "I swear to the Goddess –"

He pulled back only to thrust in hard enough it forced the air from her lungs. She only encouraged him, shifting her hips and crying out in pleasure with ever stroke. He fucked her like she'd asked, his cock pistoning so fast she was lost in desire.

His chuckle was dark before flipping them so she was on top, knees spread over his hips. The angle caused his cock to go even deeper, his hands clamping down on her hips. He lifted her as if she weighed nothing, only to pull her back down to take him to the hilt.

"Look how good you take me." His smile was smug, and she would've commented if he wasn't making her feel so good.

Every thrust. Every brush across her clit. He held her gaze through it all, the intimacy pulling another orgasm from her body for the second time in a matter of minutes. His thrusts became harsher, dominating from the bottom while still giving her control. She rode him through her peak, his cock thickening inside her.

He groaned, hips halting as he groaned out his own release. "I always knew your pussy was made for me, Princess."

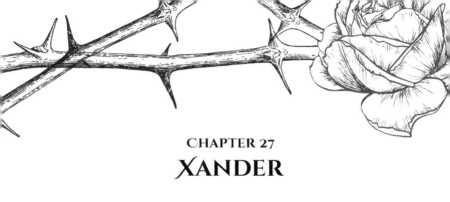

CHAPTER 27
XANDER

Kyra sat with Alice, expressions animated as they discussed ways to ostracise her excess energy. Xander had felt it even before she'd walked out of the bathroom in nothing but that towel. Those spirits had been absorbed into her aura, and until they discharged out of her system she was dealing with a dangerous level of power. It seemed to vibrate the air around her, an intense charge that reminded him of an electrical storm. He was definitely going to be struck by lightning.

She must have felt him staring because she paused her conversation to turn, her cheeks tinting at his unflinching gaze. Xander should have smiled then, put her at ease under his scrutiny. But instead all he could think about was how the same shade had flushed across her entire body. He could remember the little mewling sounds she'd made before she came, and he only wished he'd been able to actually taste her orgasm properly. He'd been too impatient, needing to feel her clench around him. He'd been too impatient the second time too. And the third.

Kyra's blush deepened, her lashes falling low as she turned back to her friend.

"You're making me feel sick," Titus muttered, crossing his arms as he watched from the corner. "I can scent your arousal from here."

"Fuck off." Xander scowled, still unable to tear his attention away.

He thought he saw Titus shoot him the finger in his peripheral, but he wasn't sure when Sythe appeared in his line of vision. His usually sickly happy face was creased into a scowl, his caramel eyes alert.

"What's happened?" Xander asked, noting the bruise darkening across his left cheekbone. "You look like shit."

Sythe's lips tipped into a smirk. "Someone left Kyra a present."

Xander cut off the growl that began low in his chest. "Present?" He'd sensed Kyra move at the mention of her name, her head appearing beside them a moment later. She eyed Sythe warily in such a way he couldn't help but smile.

"Tell me," she said, her tone like steel brushed with ice.

Xander moved to her side. Crowding. Pushing. She tensed beside him, flicking him a frustrated glare. He didn't care, not when she turned instinctively toward him, her hand reaching out to touch his arm.

"Well?" Alice prompted at Sythe. "What was it?"

A curse came from the hall, voices raised as Kace appeared in the archway. In one hand he gripped a sword, the end covered in blood while the other...

Kyra sucked in a pained breath, almost a cry.

Kace settled the woman on the table, or what was left of her. His sword clattered beside it a second later. He had no idea how Kyra was able to identify the blackened husk, the woman curled in on herself. The corpse looked delicate, as if a slight breeze would cause it to disintegrate. Her arms and fingers were twisted into impossible angles, those limbs scorched while her legs were missing entirely. Her face was turned towards her chest, eye sockets empty and a look of pure terror permanently scarring what was left.

Riley followed, mouth set in a grim line. "What happened?" he demanded.

It was Sythe who spoke first, his voice a fraction too excited for the situation. "We were guarding Kyra's place and this –" he gestured loosely to the woman, "literally appeared out of thin air."

"Adeline," Kyra said quietly. "Her name was Adeline. She was the High Priestess."

Xander pressed forward until she was flush against him, her hand hiding a slight tremble. "Out of thin air? Like a drift?" he asked.

"We didn't sense anything, not until she was already on the ground. Two – whatever the fuck they were – appeared as soon as she hit the carpet."

"Not many Breed can drift," Kace added with a growl. "But I've never seen anything like these two. They were like shadows. I caught one with my sword, but barely."

"Fae," Alice said, moving closer to examine Adeline. "You able to get anything from this?" Her question was direct, but her eyes were soft when she turned to face Kyra.

"Do what?" Xander asked as Kyra slowly nodded. Without a word she stepped out of his reach, moving until she was beside the corpse. Her shoulders were tight, tightening further when she noticed the attention she was receiving.

Alice blinked, her eyes glazing in the tell-tale sign she was looking through her third eye. It was something druids weren't able to do, and it had never bothered him until then. No, they could naturally see ley lines, but couldn't see auras.

"What's happening?" he asked Alice quietly, not wanting to disturb Kyra whose shoulders hunched forward.

"She's pushing her aura out from herself, concentrating it slowly over the body." She shrugged, as if that was explanation enough.

The corpse held no spirit, or if anything was left it was nowhere in sight. It was the only time he sought after the dead, their knowledge on how they died something helpful from a gift that caused him such a headache.

"She was killed by a spell," Kyra said, tears glistening on her cheeks. "The magic had reversed onto her because she wasn't able to withstand it." She reached up with a sleeve, rubbing at her cheeks.

"Not uncommon amongst black witches," Sythe commented. "Karma, I suppose."

Kyra moved towards Sythe, her face still wet but her gaze brightened with a defiant sort of despair. "Adeline may have been cruel, but she didn't deserve this. Don't ever believe those under Fredrick's rule ever had any other choice. They're just as trapped as I was."

Sythe blinked, hissing out a breath when Kyra's chi snapped out. He went to respond, but Xander stepped forward.

'*Careful,*' he warned his brother.

Sythe sneered, his eyes hardening when they met his. '*You're fucking whipped, Xee,*' he responded in the same way, their beasts growling at one another through connected minds. Despite the anger that rippled beneath his skin, his beast itching to get out, a smile tipped his lips.

"Where specifically was the witch found?" he asked aloud, surprised his voice wasn't gravel-rough when the beast was riding him so hard. He dared not look towards Riley, not when his control was fracturing the longer he was around Kyra.

"Outside the door," Kace responded. "Literally in the hallway."

Kyra's face paled. "Eva?"

Sythe snorted, and Kace shot him a warning glare. "That woman must have been a Valkyrie in a previous life. She completely ignored Kace as if –"

"Shut the fuck up," Kace hissed.

"– he wasn't there," he continued, sounding unrepentant. "She also made me cookies. Kace, did you get any cookies?"

Kace glowered, but didn't comment.

Sythe grinned. "Eva's fine, she wasn't even home when it happened. Other than her concern for Kyra, nothing seems to bother her."

"She wasn't supposed to be aware that you were guarding," Riley said with a scowl.

"Have you met the fucking woman?" Kace growled. "And you call me crazy."

Sythe nodded in agreement. "Axel and Titus have taken over for now. We'll continue to protect her, so don't worry about any threats."

Kace crossed his arms. "Hopefully she'll hit *them* with a fucking cooking utensil instead of me."

Riley ignored the comment. "The dead witch was a warning, one we can't ignore. According to reports Frederick has recently become uncontactable, and Daemonic activity's been quiet."

"Too quiet," Jax said as he entered the room, Lucy waltzing in behind without a care in the world. He winked at Kyra, and Xander had to clench his fists to stop from reacting.

'*Settle down,*' Riley said, his voice calming the beast. '*It gets easier.*'

Xander took a second to respond, making sure none of the other Guardians had connected to the mental bond. '*What gets easier?*'

"We need to pull Frederick out from where he's hiding," Riley said aloud without responding. "He's dangerous even without having Daemonic knowledge. But a Daemon with the resources Frederick could provide would be catastrophic."

"Dirk won't be working alone," Lucy added, his tone bored. "I doubt he's more than just a pawn in the plan."

"What plan, exactly?" Kace asked, the words seemingly ripped from his tongue. He had become stone when Lucy had entered the room, his gaze low.

"Gain a councilmembers trust, and then stab them in the back?" Lucy shrugged. "How am I supposed to know? We don't exactly meet up for a girly chat and gossip diabolical plans over cocktails and fucking manicures." He promptly looked at his hands, his nails freshly painted black.

"We need to draw Frederick out," Alice said. "We can use him to expose Dirk."

Kyra nodded. "I have an idea."

KYRA

"I don't fucking think so," Xander said, his voice dangerously quiet. "If any of you agree that we use Kyra as bait, I'll fucking gut you."

"We're giving them exactly what they want," Kyra said, keeping her voice steady, controlled despite her chi pulsating. "We will plan it —"

"No." His tone left no room for argument.

Kyra let out a sound of frustration. "I'm not going to just cower and sit by while he's hurting people."

Xander's gaze smouldered. "Let me make myself

fucking clear, Princess. The whole world can burn to the fucking ground for all I care. You're not going anywhere near that prick."

"He'll find a way to get what he wants, even without me."

"Then let him do it without you," he said as if that fixed everything.

Anger burned in her chest. "I'm an adult. I make my own decisions." She looked towards Riley, whose lips were set in a thin line. "There isn't another option, not unless you want innocent blood on your hands."

Xander snarled, fury in the set of his jaw. "I don't care —"

"Well, I do!" Her voice broke. "I care, Xee! I'm not stupid, I knew the risks when I left. I would sacrifice myself a thousand times over if it meant someone else could survive. Stop trying to control my decisions, otherwise you're no better than them."

Xander's eyes froze over, his face becoming a mask of cool contempt. He said nothing as he turned and left, his footsteps silent despite the anger that clenched his fists. She watched after him, her arms coming up to wrap around her chest as if she could keep herself from falling apart.

A few moments passed, and when the silence stretched so taut she quietly repeated, "There isn't another option."

Riley pinched the bridge of his nose. "Xee's right. You're not disposable, Kyra."

"We need to think of something else," Alice added softly. "Anything else."

"We don't have the time." Her eyes drifted back to Adeline, her gut clenching at the sight. She had screamed as she'd died, the emotion so strong it left an echo. "You said so yourself, the resources Frederick has at his fingertips could be catastrophic if Dirk got hold of them."

Riley let out a steady, controlled breath. "Kyra, we're not risking it."

"And I don't need your permission." She met his eyes, fascinated in the way they swirled to liquid silver. A beast's trait, it seemed. "I will not sit and do nothing when others are being hurt. Do you really believe Frederick will simply forget about me?"

She didn't wait for an answer.

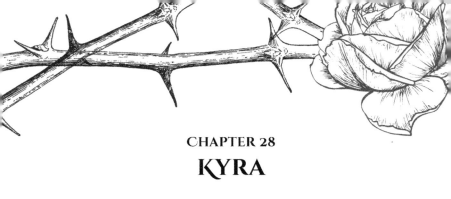

CHAPTER 28

KYRA

S torming out would have been more dramatic if she knew the layout of the house. Not even a house, more of an estate by the sheer size and surrounding greenery she could spot through the oversized windows. It seemed each Guardian had a suite, with their own bedroom and bathroom. Private, but also close to one another. She understood why Xander preferred to stay there compared to the empty flat he kept. It was probably convenient for him to keep, for uses such as hiding an illegal soul witch.

Kyra brushed her hand on the wall as she walked, each room so light and airy in the early morning sun. Everything was decorated in shades of ivory and sand, accented with hints of navy blue. Very different to where she grew up. The rooms were warm and lived in, with books left open, waiting to be read and a coat draped over a chair in the hall. A left shoe was forgotten in the corner, the right nowhere in sight while decadent rugs, mostly in blue or various patterns of grey, broke up the clean but scratched wooden floor.

She knew she was stalling. She didn't care about the art that draped the walls, or the carpets even though she stood and studied everything for longer than necessary.

240

She needed to find Xander. To explain.

"That was cruel," Kace said from the archway that led to the kitchen. His voice was like sandpaper, but she turned to face him anyway. He leaned carefully, dark red hair brushed low enough it obscured his eyes. "He didn't deserve that."

She knew he was right. "I –"

Glass shattered, Kyra's ears popping as if something went boom.

Kace stiffened, his head turning at the same time as Kyra. "What the –"

Neither of them had noticed the knife, nor the flash of silver as it sliced across his throat.

"Kace!" she hoped her cry carried throughout the house. A shadow solidified, a thin, bony arm appearing beneath a dark cloak. Pale features were obscured by a hood, but she knew it smirked as she threw herself forward to try and catch Kace as he fell. He choked, his hands scrambling up to touch the wound that sliced his neck in two.

Xander could heal, surely Kace could too.

The bleeding didn't ease, that tattoos that wrapped around his arms and shoulders pulsating against his skin and causing a glow against the shadow who watched from a few feet away. Footsteps echoed, but another bang vibrated the house, followed by more shattering.

Kyra called to her power, the syphon on her arm cracking beneath the surge. She could bring people back from the dead and force souls in and out of bodies. Surely she could heal mortal wounds?

"Incenduro!" She flung arcane at the shadow, the power hitting it square in the chest, hard enough for it to crash against the heavy bookshelf. "Please, please, please," she begged for help, hoping someone was close enough to hear.

She pulled Kace's palms away from his throat, replacing them with her own. The blood was slick between her fingers, coating the wood beneath them both red.

Kace spluttered, gasping for breath.

She ignored everything around her, her gaze concentrating on the wound. Imagining it closing. *"In morte vita,"* she whispered, her chi flowing down her arms, across her palms and onto Kace. She pushed everything she could into her hands, the magic flickering at her fingertips.

A sharp pain started on the left side of her throat, a reflection of his injury.

She knew there was a cost for both life, and death.

Kace grasped for her, his grip surprisingly strong on her upper arms as the shadow staggered to its feet.

She reached with her chi, flinging it across the room as she pressed harder against the blood that still pumped hot. She didn't know if it would work, the spirits that rode her aura howling inside her head. They were pushing, craving vengeance for their deaths.

She could taste it, the shadow's chi like ash on her tongue. She felt it try to break free from her grasp, its life essence delicate to her senses. But it wasn't the essence she was after.

"In morte vita!" she screamed this time, amplified by the spirits.

The shadow dropped to its knees, those skeletal fingers scratching at its own throat as the skin divided on its own to reveal muscle and bone.

Kace sucked in a staggered breath, his skin slick with both blood and sweat. His eyes were closed when she finally broke her concentration, pain creasing his brow. But he was whole, not even a faint line remaining.

"Very clever, Kyra," a familiar voice said. Bane stepped

through the wall, his body solidifying enough that she could make out the lack of emotion on his face.

"Bane?" she choked out, scrambling to reach the knife that was left by the fallen shadow. Her fingers brushed the metal, but a heavy foot landed on her hand.

"Did you really think we wouldn't find you?" He sounded bored, his attention barely flickering to Kace who'd begun to roll on his side.

"You haven't been alone in years. There's always one of us with you, watching everything you do. Eating, showering... fucking." A hollow laugh. "Frederick would never have allowed his prized possession such freedom." He pressed harder on her hand, the bones protesting at the pressure.

Kyra hissed out in pain.

"I told him those threats wouldn't work."

Realisation dawned on her. "You? You were the one behind those notes?"

"I knew you would never have agreed to move into the bastion and give up your *privacy*." His foot released, but he leant down to wrap his hand around her braid. "Even if you were threatened, or attacked." His eyes glittered, and she remembered phantom fingers squeezing.

Kyra flared her power, reaching for his essence but was met with a sharp sting.

"Uh, uh, uh. I've learned of your little trick." A band around Bane's wrist crackled, absorbing her magic. "I'll never understand why you chose to leave. Think of the power you could have learned, the spells and enchantments that no other witch is capable of controlling. You had the illusion of freedom, something Frederick believed would make you more compliant, more grateful to him for sparing your life. And yet you fucked that up for what? A male?" He yanked her up to her feet, her scalp screaming.

"No," she spat. "I chose myself."

"Interesting..." Another twist of his wrist, her neck bending at an angle. "I wonder if I killed your friend, would you be able to bring him back to life?" His attention skirted to the dead. "Shall we find out?" Bane said, the first sign of emotion rumbling his voice.

"Kyra?" Xander skidded to a halt, his face smoothed into a lethal calm.

A shadow shimmered in the corner, a skeletal male stepping out. He held a knife, identical to the one she'd tried to reach.

Kyra tried to shout, the words cut off when Bane's free hand slammed across her mouth. She watched with horror as the dagger stabbed deep into his back, so hard the handle snapped. She screamed, but she was already shoved out the door and into the hands of eight Magicka enforcers who waited out front.

XANDER

Xander felt the silver pierce his skin, Kyra's muffled warning giving him the time to turn. It was enough, the blade missing his heart. He grunted at the pain, his fist knocking the wraith before he could become ethereal. He hadn't sensed the bastard at all, not until the last second when it stepped out from beyond its glamour.

A flash of light, and then Kace was there with serrated claws extended and rage burning in his eyes. His markings glimmered darkly within his grey fur, a reflection of the tattoos on the man.

Xander took in the situation with one quick sweep. Kace, the screaming wraith, and another dead by the bookcase, its throat cut from ear to ear. He scented both sulphur and smoke, and from the great thunders he'd felt only moments before he suspected that the dead witch had hidden an explosive surprise.

Xander saw the slight glimmer in the air this time, catching the blade as it thrust towards him. With a quick flick he broke the wraith's wrist, catching the knife as it fell and shoved it into the Fae's gut.

"Xee?" Riley called, a heavy sword held in his hand. His gaze flickered to Kace, who had begun to eat the now dead Fae. "What happened?"

Xander couldn't speak through the cold rage that burned his chest. His beast rippled beneath his skin, their minds essentially merged as he twisted the blade.

"Kace!" Riley shouted, pulling at the great beast as if he were a puppy. Kace snarled, lips pulling back to reveal thick fangs tainted red. Riley stared him down, even as the beast roared a warning. After a tense second Kace huffed, stepping back.

Xander pulled the knife free, the urge to keep stabbing strong. Instead he knocked the wraith to the floor, beside the mess that was left of his friend. Riley pinned him to the wood with his sword.

The wraith flickered, struggling to disappear while impaled with the metal.

"Fun fact," Riley rumbled. "This sword has iron through the centre." Iron being an irritant to Fae folk, the same way silver upset shifters.

Luckily Xander was neither, the blade still stuck in his back nothing but a fucking nuisance. It was Jax who noticed it, his brow furrowed as he appeared at his side. Soot covered half his face, the skin beneath red and blistered.

"Fuck sake," he grumbled, pinching the blade between his fingers. The knife slipped out as easily as it sliced in.

"Who's our friend?" he asked with cool disdain, tossing the blood-coated dagger onto the floor like it was a toothpick.

Xander finally found his voice, the low timbre devoid of everything but pure ice. "I have no idea, but he's going to tell us exactly where they've taken her."

CHAPTER 29
KYRA

Kyra's hands twisted nervously beneath the table, the handcuffs on her wrists unnecessarily heavy.

Frederick sniggered from his position in the centre, the bruises across his face a shade of sickly yellow. Her skin was much worse, even if her colouring hid the nastier of the marks. She would heal, and have even more scars to add to her growing collection. The enforcers hadn't been kind.

She met his gaze head on, hoped he could read the hate as she straightened in her seat. His smile tightened slightly, but they would never believe her word against his. He knew it, and so did she.

Fight or flight, that was the instinct, and she was tired of running.

"Kyra Farzan, how do you plead?" the first Triumvir witch to Frederick's right asked, glasses perched at the edge of her nose as she stared with critical eyes. Her face was cruelly pinched, her too long nose thin and slightly upturned which only emphasised her withered lips. Kyra couldn't help but compare her to the children's horror stories, and had to fight the nervous giggle when she imagined the woman in a black witches hat with skin painted green.

Kyra in return knew she looked feral, her hair wild and blood still soaking her front. They'd arrested her to immediately travel to court, not giving her a chance to wash or change. She wasn't allowed a representative, or a solicitor to plead her case. Or to even ask what happened to Xander, remembering the knife sinking into his skin.

"Miss Farzan?" The second Triumvir witch to the left prompted when she remained silent, his face young, too young to be one of the head witches for the Magicka. He barely looked older than Kyra, which for some reason made the situation worse. "You've been accused of practicing black magic without a license, how do you plead?"

Kyra knew she had a valid license, but it looked like it was recently revoked.

Frederick grinned, knowing her train of thought. The other two didn't seem as excited, more indifferent as they waited for her reply.

Judge, jury and executioner. The Triumvirate, three witches who would decide her fate because of the magic she practiced, and one who'd forced her into it.

Her chest tightened as Frederick chuckled, but she remained silent. They sat themselves on tall podiums, positions of power with Frederick in the centre. He touched the thread detailing on his velvet cloak, fingers crooked. Broken.

"If you remain silent, we'll rule without a plea," Frederick said before gesturing to the woman.

The female Triumvir pursed her lips. "Then as per the laws of the Magicka, to protect our Breed, Kyra Farzan you have been found guilty of practicing black magic without a license."

"The sentence," Frederick added with a poisonous smirk, "is death."

Kyra closed her eyes, not caring as someone gripped her arm tightly, yanking her from her seat. She knew the risks, and was surprised she didn't feel more upset that her life was at an end. No, she was angry, angry about all the stuff she'd put up with in her twenty-eight years that had led to her death at the Magicka's hands.

"Come on," the enforcer sneered quietly into her ear, his breath an unwanted intimacy as he dragged her from the court and towards the holding cells. The walls turned to stone as he guided her, a chill teasing her ankles as her t-shirt stuck to her skin.

"Through here," another enforcer said, gesturing to an open chamber. There were three in the hall, and he wanted her to go into the one on the furthest right. "We'll transfer you to the prison later today, where you will wait until we have a date set for your execution."

Kyra stepped inside, stiffening as it clicked closed behind her.

"Arms!" one of the enforcers barked, unlocking her handcuffs when she passed her hands through the gap in the thick metal door. As soon as she pulled her hands back the gap slammed shut, leaving her alone in the small metal cube. There were no windows, only an artificial light that burned too brightly for comfort. There was no bed, no sink or toilet. Not even a single chair to sit. Nothing but three-sixty metal with anti-violence enchantments lasered into every surface, the space so small she could stretch and touch each side.

She couldn't feel her chi, which wasn't at all surprising. Her aura ached at the loss.

Sweat beaded down her spine, and she fought the darkness that was invading her vision. She took a steady breath, trying to calm her racing pulse.

She was trapped.

Breathe.

She blinked past the panic, staring at the door. She would not die there. She refused. But there was no lock to pick, the metal created so there was barely a seam where the door met the wall. The only indication that there even was a door was the slight bump of the hinges, the surface smooth to touch.

The enchantments reminded her of the bastion, the runes burning like orange embers in her peripheral, but darkened to coal when looked at head on. She knew the patterns, the tight swirls and hard lines. She knew exactly how to disconnect them.

Her shirt squelched when she pulled it off, the scent of copper thick. Wringing the fabric between her hands the blood dripped heavily onto the floor, giving her a puddle. Dipping her finger she carefully touched the first rune, ignoring the biting sting as she carefully traced the divergent pattern across the top. She had no idea how long she was drawing for, the blood beginning to dry as she came to the edge of the first wall. The anti-violence enchantment flickered, and then the embers turned into polished metal.

A bang against the door, so hard it vibrated on impact. There were no other sounds, the room airtight. Kyra waited, hoping they knew she'd disarmed the spell and would open her door. But then what?

Bang.

Kyra pressed herself into the corner closest to the door, ready for when it swung open. She held her breath, legs tensed and ready to strike.

Bang.

The door opened faster than she'd anticipated, a shadow taller than the frame appearing in the threshold.

"You miss me?" Dirk grinned, his face smeared with blood when he bent his head into the cell. His red eyes glistened when they dipped to her bra and bare stomach, his hand snaking out to pull her towards him. His grip was wet when he pulled her back into the hall. "Look at what you've done."

Body parts decorated the floor, more limbs than she could account for making the floor slick and shiny.

"You should never have run, my Little Black Witch." His hand tightened as smoke erupted around them.

Kyra had decided she no longer cared for drifting, not when it took precious seconds for her molecules and mind to settle. It didn't give her time to steady herself before she was thrown forward onto her knees and palms, knocking hard against the floor with an audible crack.

Frederick sat in an armchair, his leg draped over the other and his face masked with fury. A large black cauldron lay beside him, in front of the cold hearth that she recognised despite the room appearing different. The glamour had disguised the area into a cramped bedroom, the four-poster bed in the corner rumpled and even the stained sheets half fallen on the corner.

"You look pathetic," Frederick commented as he stood, the floor beneath his feet creaking, uneven. "How does it feel to have killed all those innocent people?"

"I didn't kill them!" she snapped, stress making her voice sharp.

"Oh, but you did," Frederick mused. "That's what the Magicka will believe anyway. The dangerous black witch escaped and killed everyone in her way."

Kyra tried to shuffle back when he stepped towards her, but she came into contact with Dirk. He kicked her down, keeping her on the floor.

"This was all your fault," Frederick continued. "If you hadn't run, I wouldn't have had to resort to such extreme measures."

"Naughty Little Black Witch," Dirk smirked as he moved around her, settling himself on the bed with his head rested in his palms. "I had to punish Frederick for your disobedience."

Frederick tried to hide his recoil, his bruises making sense. "You should've told me that all you needed was cock, I would have happily arranged something."

Kyra flicked her gaze back to the bed, and to where Dirk winked. Horror froze her blood as she tried to make herself appear smaller. Frederick knelt to her level, her attention settling on the thick band on his wrist. It was the same type that Bane had worn when she'd tried to cut his thread, and failed.

She didn't bother to disguise her disgust when he gripped her jaw. Or the fear that soured her tongue when he forced her head up, his fingers pinching.

"Silly little bitch. You really believed I would give you all this freedom? Your own home? Your own privacy?" A dark chuckle. "I own you. I control where you live, I control if you earn money, and I definitely control who you fuck."

She hadn't noticed Dirk move, but she felt cold fingers brush her throat before something locked tight around it. Kyra tried to twist, but Frederick's grip kept her immobile.

No, no, no! She swallowed her panic, blinking past the memories that threatened to destroy her. Her breathing became uneven, chest aching as she tried to claw at it, unable to find a fastening against the solid metal choker.

Her last one had been simple, only needing an iron key that had been kept in her father's pocket. But the one she wore now pulsed with magic, so much so that it crackled against her skin, stinging.

"That's your punishment for running. Because of you Adeline had an... accident."

Fire burned in her veins, and before she realised what

had happened her fist hit his smug face. Her knuckles hit solid bone, the shock reverberating up her arm to the sound of Dirk's laughter.

Frederick's head shot back, his angry shout joined with a splash of blood. His hands flapped to cover his face, and before Kyra even thought about running the choker tightened, strangling the breath from her lungs. She fell back to her knees, black invading her vision before the choker released.

"Fucking bitch!" Frederick screeched, his fingers delicately touching his nose. It was clearly broken, the bridge crooked. "You'll pay for that."

Kyra concentrated on her breathing, not even making a noise when Dirk lifted a heavy foot and kicked against her ribs. She kept herself flat to the floor, looking up through the hair that had escaped her braid. She flared out her awareness, but she couldn't feel any life. Her power thrummed beneath her fingertips, charged but weaker than before. They'd replaced one magical restraint with another.

Shit.

"You'll be good, won't you?" Dirk asked. "Won't you?" he repeated when she remained quiet, his smile growing.

"Yes," she croaked, her ribs protesting.

Frederick stepped back towards his armchair. It looked at odds with the rest of the room, the green velvet bright and luxurious compared to the surrounding shades of dirty brown. "Tell me, Kyra, what is Chaos magic?"

"I don't know," she said quickly. She slanted her eyes to the side, watching Dirk as he stood with his arms folded, eyes bright with excitement.

"Of course you don't know I forget, you're uneducated," Frederick sniggered as shame burned Kyra's face. "Chaos magic is the foundation of all magic, the conception of what we are all now. It's what originally powered the veil between the realms, before the birth of witches. Over years magic has evolved, but Chaos is always there, named because of its violent force and destruction. You're only the second person I've ever been able to track down that's able to manipulate it without succumbing to the force, and you weren't even aware of it."

"I'm not hurting people for you," she hissed.

Frederick smiled. "Do you really think you'll have a choice? Dirk was less than pleased when he found out you'd run, and into the arms of a Guardian of all people. The only way I've been able to calm him down was to offer you to him." His eyes mechanically appraised her body. "All of you, and not just as insurance."

"Fuck you!" she spat.

Dirk grinned. "Is that an offer?"

"Did your Guardian teach you that language?" Frederick said. "Honestly Kyra, I truly believe you're one of the most ignorant bitches I've ever met. Do you even know who those men are? Savages. They know one thing, and that's how to kill. Especially tainted people like you." Frederick's smirk grew, eyes flickering to Dirk behind her before returning with an extra glint. "Maybe that was their plan, to trick you into one of their beds and then carve out your black heart. You're tragic enough to believe anything."

The choker tingled against her skin, but was no longer painful. She slowly moved to her feet, conscious that Dirk remained only a step away. "If you give me to him, you'll never get what you want. You need me." It was the only option she had left.

"You really think I would give you up entirely?" A click, and the room morphed around them. The dirty brown walls transformed to the stone of the bastion. The uneven floor straightened, plush rugs breaking up the expensive oak. The bed had changed into a desk, an ink dipped quill writing across several sheets of paper before twisting in the air, and then starting again. The cauldron disappeared by the hearth, the fire roaring to life only seconds later.

The bedroom before had been a trick. A threat.

"We can only hope the Guardians come to play," Dirk purred behind her.

Frederick tilted his head, his hair brushing forward to cover his brow. He stepped closer, and Kyra tightened her stance. Her hands were clammy at her sides when he stopped before her. His lips were thin, too thin for such a long face and his eyes glittered with victory despite the newly blossoming bruises.

"Dirk may have you physically, but it's your magic I need. And if I make you my familiar, I can take that anytime I want."

Familiar. He wanted to force her into a familiar bond, pulling on her magic whenever he wanted without fear of the repercussion. That had always been her true fear, the one thing that could shatter her mind. It wouldn't matter if she suffered, because he would pull her magic from her, over, and over again.

"Get the ceremony ready," Frederick demanded over her shoulder as the door behind her opened, awareness prickling down her spine. "We need to have the bond active."

Kyra stiffened, Dirk moving a step closer to Frederick.

"Bane, that was an order," Frederick snapped before his face paled, his eyes widening. He staggered a step back, arcane burning up his arm. "What do you think you're —"

Dirk swung his arm and Frederick's words became gargled, blood spluttering out of his mouth.

Kyra didn't have time to react before Dirk was before her, stepping over Frederick who'd collapsed to his knees, his breathing laboured. Wings slowly erupted from his back, the click, click, click of his bones nauseating as they rose high above his head. The arcs were spiked, the horns dangerously sharp as he rolled his shoulders.

Dirk's pupils dropped to her choker, his smile turning sordid. "This is going to be so much fun."

She struggled, unable to move as something cold coiled in her gut. He had a serrated knife on his hip, the end covered in blood. If only she could reach.

Her tongue darted out to lick her dry bottom lip, Dirk's eyes following the movement. She let herself fall forward, landing heavily against him as her hand snaked against the cool handle in her palm. She would have sliced it into his stomach, but he caught her before she was even unable to unsheathe the weapon. His eyes darkened, annoyance furrowing his brow as he spun her in his arms and clamping her tight against his chest. Her head was wrenched to the side, face forced forward.

Bane stood at the threshold, and with each step he slowly stripped out of his glamour.

His face was whiter than bone, cheeks hollow with the indents of his teeth visible against paper-thin pale lips. Dark, shoulder-length hair draped around his shoulders, the same obsidian shade as his large eyes. His nose was sunken, leaving a slight crater that only emphasised cheekbones so sharp they could cut.

His form rippled, ethereal, and then corporal as he settled his attention on Frederick. His voice was deeper when he spoke, harsher as if screams echoed in every word. "You're arrogance is your own downfall."

Frederick wheezed in a breath. "What is this?"

Dirk bared his teeth, his growl vibrating against her back. "Prick of the many useless titles. You really shouldn't have given away your hand so easily." His arm tightened around Kyra, his long nails moving to cup her breasts. "Our summoning names can never be removed, they're part of the deal when we ascend to our new power. You're either ignorant, or just fucking stupid to believe you could trick me."

Bane drifted forward, and Frederick shrunk back, not knowing who was more dangerous in that moment.

"Dirk and I have come to an agreement," Bane said with an eerie calmness. "He gets the witch who has the power to help him, and I get to go home."

"It's impossible," Frederick stuttered. "The doorways have all been sealed to Far Side. There's no way through, otherwise the Fae would have found it already."

"A year, that's how long I've waited for you to help. Well over a year since the veil that separates our realms has been fortified."

Frederick's face tightened, lines appearing around his thinned lips. "It's impossible. The Light and Dark Courts themselves have shut it down, you know this to be true."

"Not all of them, the original doorway floats across this godforsaken realm."

Frederick dropped his fingers to the wood beneath him, his fingers coated in red. "It's supposedly untraceable, a rumour that Liliannia herself has never confirmed!"

"Dirk and his kin have been trapped in that prison for several millennia. Now he is free to pass through the veil between here, and the Nether as he pleases. If anybody is able to help me get back home to Far Side, it's them."

Frederick's eyes widened, a strangled sound coming from his throat. "You know who I am!" his voice quivered with an underlying current. "You can't do this!"

"Years I have served you, and everything you say is lies. It makes you weak. Absolutely worthless." Bane hit out, and Frederick's eyes rolled into the back of his head. Kyra flinched at the crack he made when he hit the floor.

Arms tightened around her, and it took everything in

her not to panic. She squeezed her eyes closed, concentrating on not passing out as her lungs filled with cement and dread tightened her muscles.

"Kyra," Bane whispered, closer than before. "You're not going to be a problem, are you?"

His fingers were like ice, a bitter sting against her skin. Those same fingers, longer, slimmer than they were only moments ago were iron around her wrist.

"Kyra?" he asked more forcefully.

She opened her eyes then, meeting ones of pure obsidian. She remained silent, the only bit of control she had left as smoke teased her ankles. Bane smiled, revealing a row of sharp, pointy teeth. He looked exactly what she expected Death to look like.

"Think of the power you're going to learn. I'm so proud. You were born for this."

CHAPTER 30
KYRA

Kyra knew she wasn't alone, keeping her breathing slow, as if she were still in sleep. The bed beneath her was rock hard, the sheets rough against her palms. Her jeans uncomfortably clung to every curve and angle, dried blood flaking off with even a subtle movement.

Bruises decorated her ribs, as well as down both her arms as she had fought with all her strength. Which admittedly wasn't much compared to the wraiths that had visited her room. Her nails dug into the sheets involuntarily as she thought about the shadows who'd watched her for years, who were probably in the room at that exact moment, concealed.

Dark laughter from the corner.

Kyra blinked open her eyes, the familiar cracked artex ceiling greeting her. Panic began to swell, but she was able to swallow the reaction as she slowly sat up, her eyes drifting past Dirk who leaned in the corner to sweep across the room.

A single bed and a locked door. No window, because it had been boarded up with thick planks of wood and enforced with metal lattices. The walls were cold, damp to touch with mould growing in all corners. The floral paper had peeled on every wall, revealing worn plaster beneath and the carpet was threadbare. Something must have once adorned the walls, maybe shelves, or a large painting considering the holes were left without thought or care to the aesthetic.

"You going to co-operate today?" Dirk said, his smile teasing enough she knew he wanted her to resist. To fight back. "Or am I going to have to be forceful again?"

Kyra remained silent, knowing it pissed him off.

It didn't take long before he snarled, the bed dipping before his hand fist into her hair. His face was creased with frustration, probably at both her silence and blatant dismissal of everything asked of her. Kyra would've smiled, but she knew it only resulted in more punishment. The choker around her neck tightened, only slightly, a gentle reminder that she had no control.

"Bane's furious. Three of his men still haven't returned." He slowly reached for her cuff, tapping on the crystal before brushing across the top of her breasts. She didn't react, even as her pulse thundered in her ears.

How long had it been? Two, three days? Possibly more. It was hard to track time when she spent the majority of it knocked unconscious when punished. She needed to know about Xander, but was too scared to ask. If he was alive he would be used against her, and she couldn't risk him, not even to save her life.

Dirk's nostrils flared as his head tilted to the side, his fingers playing with the edge of her bra. Mighty wings rose over his shoulders, spreading across her peripheral until she saw nothing but him. "We're not that much different, Kyra," he whispered against her.

"I'm nothing like you," she finally said with a hiss.

Dirk grinned in triumph, pulling back slightly. "My kin

and I are the druids biggest secret. We're the ancestors that chose black magic, and in return for the power we evolved into Daemons. We're hunted because of what we are. Because of fear and ignorance. Tell me, how does that make us that different?"

His wings snapped back, and she flinched at the sound. "I don't hurt people."

"You keep telling yourself that," he said. "Our magic isn't rainbows and sunshine. Death and blood is what makes us powerful, you should never apologise for it."

"What do you want from me?" she asked when his red eyes narrowed. "What can I do that you can't if we're the same?"

"Not many of the pitiful druids choose the Rite to evolve, which is why we've had to resort to force. Unfortunately, not many are strong enough to accept the transition."

Which meant they'd died during the process.

"Druids are already rare, so we've tried over the last few centuries with shifters to create a hybrid," he continued. "The majority failed, and now there are less than fifty Daemons left in a realm of billions. I'm sure you can understand our concern."

"Maybe part of the evolution is extinction," Kyra said before she was slammed against the wall. The bed was propelled across the room, tipping on its side from the force.

"Careful," he warned. "We believe that during the transition our souls change, adapt." He pressed harder, eyes glowing. "It makes the survival rate... disappointing. Which is where you come in, my Little Black Witch. I need you to make sure their souls remain exactly where they're supposed to be until the transition is complete."

"And if I don't?"

"Then I'll continue to punish you, and innocent druids will die." His smile felt like spiders crawling along her skin. "What were you saying about being nothing like me?"

"Dirk, I suggest you get the subjects ready," Bane said as he stepped inside the room, disguised in his basic glamour once more. "I'll prepare Kyra for the Rite."

Dirk's tongue snaked out to lick along her jaw. "Looks like you're up, my Little Black Witch." He released her without warning, her legs collapsing at her own weight. "I'll be seeing you real soon," he chuckled, his heavy footsteps fading, only to be replaced with quieter ones.

"Come on," Bane said, reaching down with an open hand. "The more you participate, the easier this will be."

"Easier?" she croaked, tipping her head back to look up at him. Even his clothing choice was mundane, blue jeans and a white t-shirt that matched his forgettable face. "He wants me to hurt people."

"No, you're saving them. How do you not see that?" He reached down to grip her arm, pulling her to her feet. "You're filthy, come with me."

He gently nudged her towards the connecting bathroom, the sink and toilet smudged with grime. A shower was placed in the corner, the surrounding glass long gone.

"Clean up," he said calmly. "You'll feel better once you're not covered in blood."

Kyra crossed her arms.

Bane sighed, pinching the bridge of his nose. He reached over to the shower, turning the dial until water trickled out. "Clean up. Once you're refreshed we'll talk through my expectations of you."

"No."

"Kyra." He said her name like a warning. "I'll not discuss this again. Take your soiled clothes off, and clean yourself." When she hesitated, wild magic creeped against her skin. "I don't want to hurt you, not when we need each

262

other. But I will. You have no choice, not now the Magicka's actively hunting you. You'll never be free. Not unless you do exactly what we say."

"I'm not undressing with you here."

Bane pursed his lips, and then with a blink he was gone. Kyra stared into the space, as if she concentrated enough he would appear again. That was how he'd watched her for all those years. She pushed out her exhausted chi, searching for him and felt... nothing. To all her senses he wasn't there.

Kyra clenched her fists, but stepped back into the spittle fully clothed. It was freezing, the shivers rattling her bones as her teeth chattered together. The basin was obscured by slime, the water more of a rust colour than clear liquid as it soaked into her bra and jeans.

Bane became corporeal, reaching for a towel and handing it over. His eyes roamed over her exposed skin, the fabric of her bra plastering itself to every curve. Her chest clenched, but there was no heat in his gaze, no attraction.

"I've made note of your reluctance."

Kyra patted the towel against her jeans, trying to absorb the excess water. "I did what you asked. I'm clean."

"We both know you'll never be clean, your aura's tarnished." His eyes narrowed. "Tell me exactly how you were able to transfer that wound from one man, to another?"

Kyra held the towel to her chest. "I don't know, I've never done it before."

"It should be impossible, the same as when you saved that bird," he commented, stepping forward to grip the towel between them. "Tell me what else you can do."

Kyra didn't hesitate. "You know everything, there isn't anything –"

"Do not lie to me," he said, giving her another fierce stare. "Matilda's grandson had some interesting information for me when you departed. Something about the vampire being afraid. You were able to control him, how?"

"I don't –"

The towel was ripped from her grip. "Eva Morgan will be on stage within the hour. Wouldn't it be a shame if someone was to hurt her?"

"I don't know how I do it!" she snapped in panic. "If I concentrate, I'm able to feel their true age and sometimes I'm able to freeze them, but that's it, I swear!"

"Interesting," Bane muttered. "Chaos magic is of both life and death, which is why you have the ability to hold and remove souls. Vampires are neither dead nor alive and it's widely believed they have no souls. And yet you held one immobile. I wonder if you would be able to control one entirely?"

Kyra said nothing, the water cold as it dripped from the ends of her hair. The power didn't work with any other Breed, only with vampires. She'd figured out that ability when she was ten, and her parents had invited vampires to come play.

"I guess it's a theory we can work on another time." Bane's upper lip twitched, head turning as Cassandra appeared in the doorway.

"Dirk says they're ready," she purred, her gaze brightening when they met Kyra's, her smile full of poison.

Bane nodded. "After you," he said, gesturing for Kyra to step out of the bathroom.

His hand was a heavy brand as he guided her out of the bedroom and down the hall, the floral wallpaper turning into stripes and the carpet frayed to the point it revealed the scratched wood beneath. They never let her linger too long in the old house, most of the rooms obstructed. The windows were blocked off in the same way as the one in her bedroom, giving no indication of natural light. There were no stairs, at least, none she'd seen in her limited walk-through. Dust covered every surface, the frames that decorated the walls in the hall either damaged or missing photos entirely.

There was nothing to pinpoint her destination.

"You'll do as you're told," he warned as he pushed her through a door to her right, the old house turning industrial, nondescript grey concrete. The new hall was slim, Bane's shoulders scrapping the walls as he pulled her in front so she was leading.

"Keep moving."

On the far right there was an arch which led to a wide open space, a warehouse she guessed, the expanse empty other than Dirk who stood in the centre. Fluorescent bulbs hung from the high ceiling, a faint buzz as the furthest one away flickered on and off with a whine. At least there were windows, the outside a pitch black so dark she couldn't look into its depths. Bane read the sudden fear along her muscles, his hand tightening before he shoved her forward. She had been too distracted with the darkness that she stumbled, barely able to catch herself.

"Where's the rest of the coven?" Kyra asked, realising Cassandra hadn't accompanied them into the room.

"Dead," Bane replied without a hint of emotion. "Adeline wasn't the only witch who tried to tame Chaos magic." He waved his hand and Cassandra stepped into the room from the same hall, dragging something behind her.

A muffled scream, followed by a choked sob.

"As you can see," Bane continued. "Cassandra offered her services."

Cassandra released the squirming man, his legs and arms bound together, connected with a single chain. A thin band of glyphs were tattooed around his wrists while a cloth covered his mouth, filthy and stained brown. Tears stained his young, pale skin, barely out of his teens.

He scrambled back as soon as Cassandra stepped away, the concrete beneath his feet cracking open with an eerie light that highlighted his slim frame and hollow cheeks.

"What are you doing?" Kyra cried, trying to reach the man before Dirk's hand twisted around her stomach, yanking her back. "How long have you had him?"

The concrete continued to break, the cracks circling around the man who sobbed until he was completely enclosed. Kyra tried to jerk away, shoving against Dirk as she struggled in his grip.

"He doesn't get a name yet," Dirk said as she tried to call her arcane to her palms. "Not until after."

The choker at her throat prickled against her skin, halting the access to her magic.

The man's eyes widened, his words stifled by the fabric thrust in his mouth.

"He would've already ascended if a certain witch hadn't made it more difficult." His voice held an echo of dark, painful promises. "Now we're having to rush things. But that's okay, if this one dies, we can try again until you get it right." His eyes gleamed. "You ready?"

He didn't wait for a reply before he threw her into the circle.

XANDER

The darkness called, the spirits glistening with an ethereal glow as they slowly found him. Even the moon hid behind the clouds, the stars nowhere in sight as if they knew the violence he barely suppressed.

Xander crouched, the wind whistling through the surrounding trees as he concentrated on the spirits, filtering through their voices. Many were cries of help, some with fear, and others full of anger at their passing. He didn't care about their problems. No, he needed to hear something in particular.

Come on, he thought. *Where are you?*

Riley moved beside him, head turning a second before Sythe stepped out of the shadows. Xander hadn't sensed him at all, in much the same way he'd never sensed the fucking wraith. It was a vulnerability that infuriated both the beast and the man.

He fully faced his brother, the darkness seeming to cling to him even though his arm was bare to the night, the glyphs tattooed there black against brown skin. A few of the Guardians had their own unique abilities inherited from their mothers, and heightened by their curse.

'*I can't get any closer without detection,*' Sythe said inside his mind, his voice the deep grumble of his beast. '*But there are no longer any watchers.*' His tight leathers glistened, and Xander scented the richness of blood that coated him.

Riley nodded, which meant Sythe had spread the connection to include both Riley, and Kace. '*We'll take it from here,*' Riley replied the same way. '*I need you back home.*'

Sythe hesitated, but still stepped back and disappeared with a sharp nod. It was a trick he'd learned as a kid, and it fascinated the surrounding spirits much as it did when they were all children. It wasn't a drift, but he could become part of the shadows to the point even their beasts could no longer feel his presence.

'*Alice won't appreciate the overprotectiveness,*' Kace muttered, followed by Riley's deep chuckle. '*That woman is*

267

a force of nature, I don't know how you convinced her to stay at home.'

Riley smiled, and even in the dark they could see it was the one reserved for his mate. Xander would have given his best friend a snide remark if he wasn't so worked up himself.

'She agreed too easily,' Riley said. *'Which means she's up to something.'*

Kace smirked then, teeth flashing white as his need for violence vibrated the air around him.

Xander drowned them out, the spirits whispering again, coaxing. They were his eyes and ears across the many acres of land recently purchased under a fake name. It would have been a needle in a haystack if the wraith hadn't sung like a canary, but only after Xander had broken every single bone in each of his hands. And then kept going. Kace usually dealt with that aspect of interrogation if the situation needed it, but he couldn't help himself.

Kyra had escaped the Magicka, at least that was what those fuckers believed. He was thankful Kace enjoyed keeping his prey alive after torture. If Xander had listened to his beast and sated his desire for death they would've been fucked.

Now, all he needed was for the spirits to do their thing.

He was famous for his patience, but right then he was ready to explode.

Xander couldn't stop it as his gaze drifted to Kace's throat, the skin whole, but covered in blood he'd refused to clean off despite it being days. They had almost lost a brother, and the only reason they hadn't was because of Kyra.

'She'll be fine,' Kace said, reading the direction of his stare. *'She can handle herself.'*

Pride swelled, but it was quickly replaced with dread.

268

He didn't understand his reaction, but right then he didn't care, not when he felt such vicious rage.

His beast pressed against the inside of his skin, ready, waiting. A predator.

"Where's my family?"

"Am I dead?"

"Why am I drawn here?"

The spirits whispered and shouted, their voices a singular hum.

Find her.

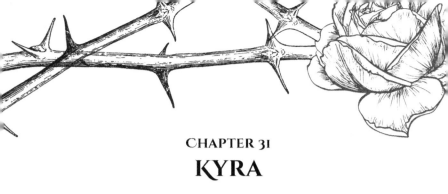

CHAPTER 31
KYRA

His soul kept slipping, her hold on his life weak as she tried to keep him as still as possible. Liquid salt wet her lips, the light around them so bright she could barely see while the man violently surged, his back bowing at an impossible angle. His wrist broke, hand slipping through the chain with a wet crunch.

Kyra went to grab his flailing arm, to keep him immobile despite his scream echoing so much pain. Her fingers barely touched before he hit out with a strength that surprised her, knocking her back hard enough she bit through her lip.

"Careful!" Dirk snarled, his dark presence behind the barrier of light. The thin shroud of magic burned across her aura, a type of circle she'd never encountered before. There were no markings, symbols, or elemental anchors she could see on her side. Only the bright light that leaked from within the cracked concrete. "I can feel your chi through the necklace. You're not even trying!"

Copper coated her tongue, her hands rubbing against her now dry jeans. "I've never done this before!" she cried, the young man's soul slipping once again. She didn't know how to hold it, her magic strangled by the choker that pulsated around her throat. She'd only ever pulled the thread, she'd never tried to keep it tied together.

She didn't even know if there truly were threads, or if that was something her subconscious envisioned when her parents pushed. She didn't really care, not when she forced her awareness out to wrap around the essence that had frayed, to keep it anchored to the earth. Anchored to her.

The man screamed once again, his body twisting in such a way something else cracked.

"Stop moving!" she pleaded, hoping he could hear her through his delirium. His eyes were wide open but empty, the fabric that had been tied around his mouth long gone as blood stained his teeth. Veins strained beneath pale skin, black and throbbing so hard it was only a matter of time until they burst.

He was going to die, and there was nothing she could do to stop it.

"Please!"

His head shot to her, lips pulled back in a roar as he launched forward, taking her down beneath him. The momentum had pushed them flush against the circle, the light barrier searing against her aura. His hands tore at her skin, the fabric of her bra ripping beneath his nails. They sliced and cut before reaching up to wrap around her neck, fury lining his expression. His movements weren't a warning, or a way to scare her. He wouldn't torment and mock as she thrashed beneath him. No, he had one purpose, and it was only the choker that blocked him from destroying her trachea.

There was no point begging, not when nothing sane looked out from dark eyes rimmed with red. The choker creaked at the pressure, and she stopped struggling.

The circle flickered, Dirk a dark silhouette against the bright light that started to lash out, her aura throbbing against the onslaught. The man's skin began to pucker, splitting open to reveal a splash of crimson before it darkened to black. He was closer to the circle, nearly touching the barrier.

The choker cracked, she could feel it in the increased stress of the metal.

Just a little more.

The circle dropped, and the man was torn away with a feral cry. His hands had curved into claws, nails covered in blood she only just felt drip down her chest. His animalistic screams continued while Dirk gripped him tightly, Cassandra walked up to blow a pale powder in his face. He immediately stopped fighting, going limp. He was still alive, barely, but he was not the same man he was before.

"I see that went well," Bane commented from the corner, his glamour still in place.

"He's alive, that's already progress," Dirk said, dark eyes gleaming with exhilaration as he hauled the man onto his shoulder as if he weighed nothing. "That's only the first stage."

Kyra couldn't drag her eyes away from the man, the veins that had appeared were a toxic spiderweb beneath pale skin slick with sweat.

It took her a second to register Dirk's words. "First stage?" she repeated, her voice just as tired as the rest of her.

A humourless smile touched his lips.

"Dirk?" Bane interrupted with an eerie calmness, a slight shimmer in the area beside him.

Was there another wraith here? she thought.

"I think Kyra should be excused for the moment," Bane continued. "I have something privately to discuss."

The Daemon held her gaze, upper lip twitching before he faced Bane. "We've only just started."

"We can continue –"

"I'm sorry, who do you think's in charge here?" Dirk's wings rustled at his back. "I say when we're finished, not you."

"You've made that pretty clear," Bane said, his tone hardening despite his relaxed expression. "But I highly suggest you pause for the moment and let her recover, otherwise your next stage may not go as well."

Dirk laughed, the sound a sharp bark. "Cassandra, take Kyra to the lower level, and make sure she stays there until I'm ready. I'm sure she'd appreciate meeting the others."

Anger brightened the black witch's gaze, her eyes flicking towards Bane in reassurance.

"Now, Cassandra." This time Dirk spoke, it was a command.

A little pout of her lips, her hand brushing against her braids that tingled as the beads beat against one another, but the irritation was still there. She produced a wand, the implement meant to enhance the force of arcane.

"After you," Kyra said as Cassandra pointed it in her direction. Out of all the coven it was Cassandra she liked the least, not that she really spent time with any of the others. She couldn't blame their abhorrence towards her, not when they were forced to stay at the cottage while she was allowed her own place in the city. Privacy, and her own life. Or at least, that was how it seemed. Now she understood it was all a way to manipulate her, to make her believe she had a choice. Easier to control.

Cassandra was the one witch who'd really enjoyed the death. Enjoyed the physical kill when animals were required for sacrifice. She seemed to savour the high, craved it even. The others had always kept their expressions neutral, while she'd never tried to hide her hunger. Other than Adeline, she was one of the longest serving witches. There longer than Kyra, and had seen many witches come and then disappear once they were no longer useful.

"Come on," she snapped, the end of her wand digging into her back. "It's just through here." She gestured down the same hallway Kyra had walked earlier, but instead of turning into the house she forced her through another doorway, one with stairs that lead down.

The basement at the bottom was relatively small compared to the floorplan of the house above, made smaller by the crudely constructed sections at the back. Metal bars had been added horizontally, thicker than her wrist and so close together Kyra had to squint to see inside. Two men cowered in the corner, naked other than a pair of tattered shorts.

Kyra stopped, pressing herself closer to the bars. "What's this?" she asked, her voice making the men flinch, their heads turning to look. "Cassandra, how long have they been here?"

Cassandra's laugh brushed over the back of her neck, the wand stabbing forward until it pierced skin. "Don't get all superior on us now, Kyra. The only reason they're here is because of you."

Kyra whipped around, not caring as the wand sliced her skin further. "How long have they been here?" she asked again as one of the men moved closer. His lips were sliced, face swollen. His eyes moved to her choker, then up to meet hers briefly.

Cassandra blinked at the men, tongue darting out to lick her lips. "Dirk brought them here a few days ago. Before that? Who knows."

"Why are you even here?" Kyra squared her shoulders, stepping to the side and forcing Cassandra to echo the movement. It put Kyra towards the door, and Cassandra against the bars. "Like you said, they're here because of me and what I can do. So why are you here?"

Cassandra's smile tipped into a snarl, the end of the wand sparking. "Shut up and get in there." She gestured to the other cell, the door slightly ajar. The lights above flickered off, leaving them momentarily in pitch black.

"You never answered my question," she said, hoping her voice didn't shake as the lights turned back on with a pained whine. "Why are you not dead like the others?" In the darkness the other man had moved forward, his long fingers squeezing though to wrap around the bar, tattoos decorating the digits.

"Because I'm not a fucking fool like the others were, blindly following orders from that Supreme arsehole and the Triumvirs." Her featured hardened. "Bane promised me the freedom to practice spells as I see fit. I won't be restricted by rules created by some old men who believe black magic is inferior because they can't control it. It should be people like us who control the Magicka, witches with actual power. Not some superior arsehole."

"Is that what you want?" Kyra sneered, needing her riled up. "To take over the Magicka?"

"Death is the way of life. We shouldn't be treated like shit because we embrace that." Cassandra eyes brightened with a mixture of excitement and fury.

Kyra couldn't hide her disgust. "You've just swapped one monster for another."

"You say that like you're not a monster too," Cassandra spat. "Your fake tears make you worse, at least I own my actions."

She couldn't use her magic, not without Dirk knowing. "I'm so much better than you. It's why I'm actually needed, and you're nothing but the help." Kyra laughed, the sound strained. "Tell me Cass, do you really think you could better me?"

Cassandra's snarl echoed against the concrete. "Shut up or I'll kill you!"

Kyra's stomach tightened, but she still forced a smile. "I very much doubt that."

The wand tip brightened, and Kyra barely managed to keep the cry of pain to herself as the first hit of magic seared. The spell was dark, Cassandra's words muffled as blood rushed in her ears.

Kyra pushed herself forward, ignoring the burn as her chi reacted to the attack and shoved with all her strength.

Cassandra's eyes widened as she fell back, and before she could recover the men caught her, their fingers gripping anything they could. Kyra moved, grabbing the wand and feeling Cassandra's power thrum through the wood. It heated against her fingertips, and before another spell could be cast Kyra lifted a fist and hit Cassandra square in the face. Her head cracked back, connecting to the metal bars with a heavy thump.

Kyra fell to her knees at the same time Cassandra collapsed, the wand falling from her palm. Kyra couldn't control the trembling as she concentrated on the black magic working its way across her aura, searching for a weakness. But that was one secret she'd always been able to keep to herself, and even Frederick wasn't aware of her natural immunity to black hexes.

"Hello?"

Kyra ignored the whispers, keeping her gaze downcast. She fisted her hands, waiting for the trembles to stop completely even as her nausea rose.

"Are you okay?"

She needed to repel the murk, but right then she swallowed down the bile and looked up to find the two men crouched, waiting. They gasped, and she knew her eyes had bled to black, encompassing even the whites. It was a side effect of her aura breaking down the dark charm, and from the pain she felt in her bones the spell had been more than a simple incapacitation. It had been deadly.

Cassandra had tried to kill her, and thank the Goddess that the choker around her throat hadn't interfered with her resistance. She paused a minute, frozen as she waited to see whether Dirk had felt Cassandra's magic. Her fingers brushed the cool metal, but she wasn't able to remove it. A horrible taste coated her tongue, and when she lifted her hand to her mouth she found blood, so dark it was almost black.

"Key?" she managed to ask, her voice throaty.

The two druids remained silent, staring at her with open horror. The one on the left blinked, as if he finally understood what she'd asked. "We don't know," he replied, his voice equally as rough, unused. He seemed older than the man who'd just passed the first stage, his face lined with age.

Kyra managed to crawl forward, her fingers hesitant when she touched the large solid lock. It was basic, with no enchantments other than simple reinforcement that she could see. In the years she'd been free, she'd spent hundreds of hours learning to pick locks. She could do it both manually, and magically, but she didn't trust there wasn't a charm hidden that would set off a silent alarm if she forced it open with a spell. She knew logically she should've spent those precious hours learning how to defend herself, but then the memories of herself trapped in a cage and unable to escape had won.

"Stay quiet," she warned, keeping her own voice low.

Reaching for the discarded wand she broke it in half, exhaustion making her muscles quiver. She placed both sharp ends into the hole, closing her eyes as she felt for the pins. Her hands shook, so much so she pushed out a breath, trying to calm herself. The final click made her heart skip a beat, the lock snapping opening. When she looked back up both men were crouched only an inch or so from her, frozen. The door opened against Cassandra, the gap large enough to squeeze through, but they made no move to escape.

Kyra dropped the wand pieces, scooting back to give them space. They remained where they were. She wanted to give them some type of encouragement, but the words died on her tongue. She couldn't tell them it was safe, because it wasn't.

Her knees protested when she climbed to her feet, stepping towards the doorway to peer outside. When she turned back the men were exactly where she'd left them.

"If you stay here you'll die," she said, bending to pick up Cassandra's leg. She pulled, moving her across the cold floor until she was at the threshold of the other cell.

"If we leave, we may die," the one on the right said.

Kyra nodded, and with a nudge she shuffled Cassandra fully inside the second cell, closing the door and locking it tight. "I wouldn't blame you for staying." And she wouldn't, not when she understood how hard it was to overcome fear, the emotion so strong it had paralysed her muscles to stone on more than one occasion. "Only you can decide which is best for you. But I can't stay here."

"Will you come back?" the left man asked, attention flicking to the blood smear left by Cassandra.

"I will." And she meant it. "I'm going to try and find a safe way out, and I promise I will do everything I can to come back for you."

Her words seemed to satisfy them, and without another glance she moved towards the stairs.

The door at the top was quiet when she gently pushed it open, the hall empty. She could hear nothing, the surrounding doors blocked with furniture or locked tight. The air was heavy, thick with dust as she tried to open the first door, but found the handle broken.

Keeping her panic contained she tried the next door, and then the next. She slowly climbed over the blockades, carefully moving the furniture to the side. The house was larger than she'd first thought, the main hall breaking into smaller corridors with even more possible escapes routes. Pushing a bookshelf, she paused at the screech it created across wood. Her pulse was a violent beat inside her skull as she strained to hear any movement. But there were no footsteps. No breathing other than her own.

She pushed it a little more, the gap small, but enough for her to squeeze through. The door behind it was unlocked and lead into a kitchen, the stench immediately forcing her to breathe though her mouth. She took a second, the light from the hall scarcely penetrating the small room.

She barely glanced at the table, or at the four decaying corpses that lay face down on the surface. Their mottled skin had been nibbled, eaten by vermin while the food had been left to rot. Flies hovered, a faint buzz that had her searching for a hole, for anything that lead to the outside.

There was no other door, the kitchen cabinets hanging off their hinges as Kyra carefully pulled herself onto the counter. The sink was full of brown water, the tap dripping every few seconds in an inconsistent patter.

Drip. Drip. Drip.

The window had been covered with wood, but there was no metal lattice like the others. Feeling a twinge of hope, Kyra tried to claw at the panels, her fingers unable to get beneath a single plank.

Please, she begged whoever would listen.

A floorboard creaked, and before she could turn she was yanked from the counter and thrown against the opposite wall. The tiles at her back cracked, the air stolen from her lungs as a man appeared an inch from her nose. His eyes were lavender, his ears pointed as he snarled.

On instinct she kicked out, her foot connecting with his knee hard enough she was able to shove past him. She ignored the decaying bodies, trying not to think about how long they'd been there, forgotten. Her hand searched through the rotten food and decaying flesh, pressing forward until she felt something cool against her fingertips. This time when she was wrenched back she didn't fight it, and the knife slipped into the man's chest with zero resistance. He looked at her with disbelief. Her face likely echoing the same expression.

"You sure you need to be rescued, Princess?"

Kyra gripped the knife harder, looking over the Fae's shoulder to be met with familiar eyes of frost.

CHAPTER 32

XANDER

He had no idea what to expect, but Kyra with her hands wrapped around the handle of a blade wasn't it. And especially not in her fucking bra. Her skin was pulled tight on her knuckles, the knife piercing clean through the man who stood very still, not acknowledging his presence.

"You sure you need to be rescued, Princess?" His gaze roamed over her, making note of every cut and bruise. Her face was pale even in the darkness, blood a stark spatter across her skin. Her hair was unbound, loose around her shoulders with the ends curled as if it had been recently wet.

She met his eyes then, her dark amber irises and whites replaced with a black so dark it absorbed the limited light. She tightened her grip, the Fae hissing out a pained grunt. A type of faerie was his guess, but he could never be sure with the Fae.

Xander let out a growl, unable to stop the sound as he stepped forward. Without dropping the eye contact he lifted his Glock 17 and put a bullet through the side of the man's head. The Fae fell backwards off the knife, hitting the floor with an audible crack.

Kyra made no sound, her hands still wrapped tight around the cutlery. He didn't care, needing to touch and reassure himself she was there, alive. His fingertips brushed her cheek, as light as a feather as he waited for her to react. To do anything but stare with foreign eyes. She hadn't even flinched at the gunshot.

He wasn't sure if that was a good thing or not.

"You're okay?" she asked on a rushed exhale, her arm shaking as the knife wavered. "I thought..." Her voice broke as she blinked several times, the tears that escaped tinged with black.

"I should be asking you that." Xander carefully removed the knife from her iron grip, gently settling it on the table before he reached up to brush away her tears. She was alive, and he needed to get her the fuck out of the shithole farmhouse in the middle of butt-fuck nowhere.

"You're okay?" she asked again as if she wasn't the one who'd been taken by a homicidal Daemon, and being forced to do fuck knows what for the last forty-eight odd hours.

"Kyra –"

She launched herself forward, arms wrapping around his neck to pull him down to her lips. There was no hesitation, no gentle teasing as he opened for her, the need to devour and mark her as his overwhelming. He wasn't sure when his hands had reached for her hips, or when he lifted her until her legs wrapped around his waist.

The scent of death and decay was thick in the air, and it didn't matter as she melted beneath his touch. He kissed her hard, a punishment for going with the enemy, for leaving him. He knew it wasn't her fault, and yet he wanted her to feel exactly how angry he was that she dared put herself in danger.

282

Xander reluctantly pulled back. "We need to go," he said as he gently placed her back on her feet.

She nodded, her blush deepening, giving her back a little colour. "Kace? How's –"

"Fine. Everyone's fine," he interrupted, annoyed at the jealousy that knotted his stomach.

Why the fuck was he jealous?

"We're not so easily killed." Actually a lie, they had almost lost Kace, and for that alone he would be forever in her debt.

"I don't... I don't know how," she stuttered, her hand absently brushing against the metal choker around her throat.

Anger kissed his bloodstream, but he kept himself calm as he replaced her hands with his own. There was a crack at the front, blood smeared by thumbs if he went by the prints left behind.

"What happened?" he asked quietly, ideas racing of what he would do to every single person who'd put their hands on her. His beast grinned inside his mind, just as bloodthirsty.

Kyra sucked in a breath, looking up through thick lashes.

Guess he couldn't hide his anger after all.

"It strangles my chi," she said. "Dirk can feel my magic through it."

Which explained why she'd used a bread knife against the Fae. It also meant he needed to remove it, and fast.

"Tell me if this hurts, okay?" He added a little pressure to the crack, feeling the metal strain beneath the force. Kyra let out a strangled cry and he stopped. "Kyra?"

Her dark eyes glittered. "Just do it."

Xander added more pressure, a little at a time as he watched for her reaction. They needed to leave as fast as possible. They weren't sure how many men walked the halls of the farmhouse, or the attached warehouse that wasn't supposed to exist. Sythe had taken out five men around the perimeter, and Xander had removed two Fae inside, not including Kyra's. It was more men than they'd expected, and that worried him.

The Daemons had only been free for just over a year, when the veil that separated the realms fractured. It was repaired quickly, but in that time the gate that kept them within the prison of the Nether had opened. It had tethered their magical chains, giving them freedom from what was essentially Hell.

The Order had received reports from other sectors that the Daemons had split themselves across the world, but the ones that had settled in London were becoming an increasing pain in their arses. The city had one of the largest Breed populations in the northern hemisphere, and they were making their presence known by brute force.

They were planning something, but they had no idea what.

The crack deepened, the metal bending dangerously close to her skin. It had weakened, so when Xander pulled at the sides the choker split. He immediately discarded it, tossing it in the corner before he handed her his pistol.

"Don't shoot me," he joked.

She held it awkwardly. "I've never used one of these before."

Xander repositioned her right hand, moving her finger. "Point and click."

Kyra's brow knitted together. "I can't use a gun."

"Would you prefer to be up close and personal with a knife?" His tone hardened as he said it, knowing he would never allow her close to anyone who'd cause her harm. "A monkey can fucking shoot. There's a reason guns are illegal on the streets, Princess."

Kyra glanced at the knife on the floor, and then to the Fae.

He reached for her free hand. "Come on, we can't stay here." He turned to leave, but Kyra gave a resistant tug.

"There's druids, two in the basement and the other one..." Her tone was rushed, the words tumbling together.

"We'll take care of it," he said before he reached for his brothers, opening a joint connection, the mental bond immediate.

'Druid hostages in the basement. Two, with a possible third.'

He didn't wait for a reply, pulling her back towards the door and out into the hall. The dark interior was covered in white powder, and when Kyra's eyes widened at the sight he couldn't help but smirk.

"Powder bomb," he shrugged. "Great at detecting something that we can't see." It also made footprints visible, giving him some advantage against the invisible bastards. "Kace's handy with this type of shit." Or explosives in general.

Their shoes crunched against the powder, Kyra rigid beside him with eyes so wide he could finally see the whites peeking through.

'This place is fucking huge,' Kace growled inside his mind. *'There's three levels beneath the warehouse still under construction.'*

'Take images for our records,' Riley added. *'Then plant the charges and get outside. Our cover's been blown. They know we're here.'*

Xander drowned them out as they continued towards the front door. He wasn't surprised Kyra hadn't been able to find it, not when the farmhouse had been arranged like a bloody labyrinth, with random doors and halls leading to nothing. The front door had been sealed shut with paint, and then blocked off with wood. He hadn't cared about the noise as he kicked it open, the almost physical need to find her driving him forward and making him careless.

"How did you get in?" Her voice was barely a whisper, and yet she held his beast's entire attention.

"A door."

Kyra's lip twitched, and even more of the black in her eyes had receded, hinting at the amber irises beneath. He wanted to kiss her, to press his lips against hers until she felt nothing but him. Thought of nothing but him.

Fuck! he thought, shaking his head. *Concentrate!*

Xander paused, pushing them both flat against a wall. He cocked his head, listening for an indication they weren't alone. Sound didn't seem to travel too well throughout the farmhouse, but he knew from the aerial view Titus managed to create that the entrance to the warehouse was close, his brother a genius when it came to computers.

Xander didn't want her anywhere near the warehouse, not when they had yet to find Dirk or Bane, the wraith prick. He knew about Daemons, having been trained to fight them for twenty years. Fae, on the other hand were a mystery, especially fucking wraiths.

"Do you know the layout?" he asked quietly.

Xander had quickly searched the available rooms, each more dilapidated than the last. The dust was so thick he knew it hadn't been used in months, at least until he *felt* Kyra like a spark across his chi. He'd followed that feeling until he found the smallest gap behind a bookshelf, the room beyond a void.

Kyra shook her head. "I was kept in one of the rooms in the other hall."

He was surprised to find her there, or in the large house at all compared to the strong structure of the warehouse beside it. That was built with a purpose compared to the crumbling building around them, and despite the number of men that they'd taken down the whole operation felt unfinished.

'*Watch yourselves, this place reeks of a trap,*' he shot down the joint connection. He finally released Kyra's hand, pulling one of his blades from its holster, the weight familiar in his palm.

Xander picked up speed, retracing his steps to find the front door he'd previously broken. Kyra followed quickly behind, both hands around his gun as she kept it pointed towards the floor. He'd never had a fantasy, but a beautiful half-naked woman holding a gun was something he was going to remember forever.

"Everything okay?" she asked with a frown.

He should've offered her his fucking shirt. What an arsehole.

"Let's get out of here." He carefully opened the door with a boot, throwing out one of Kace's new handmade toys through the threshold. The small bomb exploded with a soft pop, and white powder shot in all directions. Kyra lifted her gun at the same time Xander moved forward, slicing with his dagger as three men were revealed. Only one was a wraith, the other two wearing clothes designed to blend into the night.

It was an ambush.

What a fucking surprise.

His blade sunk into the closest man, the life behind his eyes vanishing within seconds before he moved on to the next. The moon high above gave little illumination, but enough to notice the glitter in the powder. Kace was an unpredictable bastard who loved pain, but you couldn't say he didn't have a sense of humour. Or Lucy had gotten into his shit again.

Snarls and grunts carried across the wind, and Riley fought against a hound in the distance.

'Get your arse to the surface, K!'

Kace's return was a simple snarl.

Xander turned, throwing his knife into the head of the man who tried to grab Kyra. It sunk in deep, and in the same movement he unsheathed his sword.

The air prickled, his beast brushing along the inside of his skin, wanting to play. To tear and shred.

"I think that's enough," a dark voice sniggered. "My Little Black Witch, what present have you brought me?"

Xander steadied his stance, tightening his grip on his sword. Kyra stood beside him, her breathing laboured as her arm trembled.

"You must be Dirk," Xander growled, his tattoos rippling to life beneath his leathers as Riley joined them. Thick cuts sliced across his shoulder, his body repelling the venom from the Shadow-Veyn's bite. It dripped from his wounds, hissing as it dropped against the grass.

The Daemon stood across the field, his hand resting on top of the head of a young druid, Dirk's long nails curling around to break the skin around the man's face. There was no awareness in the man's eyes, no indication of pain. His chest was bare, revealing thick veins pulsating beneath almost transparent skin.

The Daemon inclined his head, his smile cruel. His other hand reached across to the man's throat, pressing a thin blade against the skin. "And you must be a certain Guardian My Little Black Witch has been telling me so much about."

Kyra stilled beside him, the wind whipping at her hair.

Dirk's gaze flickered to Riley, and then to behind where

Kace appeared from within the farmhouse. Death clung to him like a second skin, his beast the closest to the surface.

"Ah, it looks like it's a party." Dirk's smirk disappeared, eyes hardening. "Kyra, come here."

"I don't think so," Xander snarled.

Dirk moved his gaze between the three Guardians before cutting back to Kyra. "Give me my witch, or I'll kill him right here." He sliced deeper into the man's neck, drawing blood.

"No, please!" Kyra cried.

"Don't," Xander warned her as she stepped closer.

"He'll kill them all if I don't," she whispered, her eyes glittering when she turned her head. "Please, you need to trust me."

Xander stiffened, forcing himself not to reach forward and physically stop her.

'You sure about this?' Kace asked, his voice more of a deepened rumble.

Riley was silent, his anger an almost physical heat by his side.

'No.' Xander clenched his jaw, his beast raging as they watched her walk the short distance across the grass.

Dirk grinned as Kyra stepped closer, the blade that kissed the druid's neck slicing before he released his hold. He grabbed Kyra around the hair, yanking her towards him. It caused the gun to fall from her grip, landing by her feet.

"She's such a good girl, doing exactly what she's supposed to," Dirk purred, kicking at the fallen druid, blood pumping from his jugular. "Tell me Guardian, what was it like to have fucked someone who always planned to betray you?"

Kyra struggled against the hold, but Dirk pulled tighter and her face paled in pain.

"Come on precious, we can tell him now." Dirk's lips

brushed against her ear, his powerful wings widening to block out behind him. "Tell him how your dark magic helped that innocent druid through the first stage of the transition."

Kyra stopped fighting entirely, her hands resting against Dirk's. She met Xander's gaze, lips opening slightly before the Daemon screamed behind her. She threw herself forward, breaking his grip and dropping to her knees beside the gun.

Xander was already moving, racing across the distance. Dirk's cry shut off, replaced with an angered howl as Xander swung, slicing across the Daemons chest with ease. He shot forward, readying his sword before a bullet zipped past, hitting Dirk in the shoulder. The momentum caused the Daemon to spin, and Xander took the opportunity to slice down his wing in one clean sweep, Riley tearing at his other side.

KYRA

Kyra had never shot a gun before, and that was evident in the fact she'd missed Dirk's head. She'd tried to pull his soul, but the connection hadn't been strong enough.

"Kyra!" Kace roared as he moved beside her. "Give me that before you shoot Xee, or Ri." His eyes were a deep green, darkened around the edges when he turned to her. His hair was pulled from his face, the skin at his throat perfectly smooth, but his front was drenched in blood, both old and fresh. He handed her a knife, smaller than his own but fitting perfectly in her palm.

Kyra opened her mouth, her words drowned out by the rumble of the earth beneath their feet. She was shoved back just at the first crack appeared, a paw clawing through. Kace seemed to burst from his skin, a bright light cutting through the darkness before a large beast stood where he once was. The dark green eyes were replaced with liquid silver, watching her warily before he turned and shot towards the crack where a hound crawled out.

Kyra stood there, unable to take her eyes away from the beast that was so similar to Xander's, except his fur was a light speckled grey compared to pure white.

Someone grabbed her arm, and she turned with her knife before her wrist was caught.

"Fucking bitch," Bane said calmly as he pulled her back with him, taking the blade with little effort.

She jerked, panic beginning to tighten her lungs. He released his grip causing her to fall forward, the grass cold and wet beneath her palms.

"Look at the mess you've caused." He forced her head up to watch the three hounds circle the Guardians. Dirk had lost both his wings, but his moves were precise and strong when they connected, his arcane a bright scarlet with a heart of black.

Bane unwrapped his hand from her hair, allowing her to sag against the cool earth. She dug her fingers into the dirt, using it to calm herself. Bane stepped into view, his glamour stripped as his natural appearance emerged. Kyra watched him through her hair, her heart beating so loud it drowned out the snarls and clang of heavy metal. Bane wore all black, a stark contrast to skin so white it was paler than bone. He flipped her knife between skeleton-like fingers, his smile pulling such thin lips they almost split.

"My kind are rare, and tonight has been a great loss." He knelt in front of her, the flat of the knife resting against her cheek. "One day I'll make you pay for killing my brethren, but until then I'll make sure it hurts."

Kyra knocked the knife, her hand brushing across Bane's arm to grip at his withered skin. She stretched out her awareness, feeling the roughness of his essence and pulling it with all her strength. The blade nicked her as he screamed, but his essence didn't break, the band he wore around his wrist hindering her grasp.

"You fucking bitch!" He punched her, knuckles snapping her head painfully to the side. Her eyes settled on the druid, the one who now stared blankly at the sky, his lifeblood soaking the same dirt she was pressed against. With tears burning she called to him, feeling her magic roar to life as the crystal on her arm burned against her skin.

She could taste it, the Chaos, both life and death.

It was raw, feral as her chi pulsated, embracing the power she was born with. She no longer wanted to hide from her magic, the once untameable Chaos bending to her will.

That was what she was. Life, and death.

Another punch connected, but she could no longer feel it, or the fingers that pressed against her windpipe. Arcane burned from her palms, the purple so dark it was almost black, but the centre was a shimmery white that seemed to sparkle.

Life, and Death.

She could give life, and she could also take it.

A perfect balance.

Bane's essence was in her grasp, and she was on her feet with no memory of how she got there, his skin on hers. Her arcane wrapped itself around it like vines, feeding from his life through such a thin thread. That was all that secured Bane to his soul, to his life, an essence as weak as he was.

Bane cringed, fingers tightening as she gently tugged, feeling his soul sing to her in response. She felt resistance, a spell fighting her hold. A spell that was weakening with every passing second.

Kyra smiled, watching Bane try to disappear from her grasp by calling the shadows around them. But he struggled as fear and desperation creased his features.

The druid glittered in her peripheral, his spirit answering her call. His eyes were white in death, hollow as he looked towards Bane with nothing but pure, unedited fury. He stepped closer, hand moving slowly until it gripped around Bane's wrist.

Bane's head jerked to the side as his wrist broke with a crack, his fingers releasing her windpipe. She sucked in a staggered breath, not realising how long she'd been without air. Her lungs burned, her throat dry as she watched the spirit ravage the man who'd watched her for years. Who'd violated her privacy.

She would have fallen, the Chaos that surrounded her anchoring her feet to the earth.

This time when she tugged at Bane's thread, it broke with an almost embarrassing ease. As she watched the life behind Bane's eyes fade, the crystal that had once helped control her magic shattered.

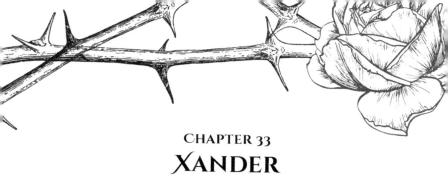

CHAPTER 33

XANDER

Xander felt Kace shift, his own beast howling for the switch. It took effort to keep his beast at bay, effort needed against his fight with the fucking Daemon. His grip was tight on his sword, blood dripping down his brow as he slowly backed Dirk towards the warehouse. He needed to remain in control, to savour the kill.

"You'll never stop it!" Dirk teased, his grin strained despite the arcane that coated his hands. "Join us in the new age. The one where we rule."

The power in his palms spluttered and spat, Xander's chi already aching from the onslaught. His own arcane coated his blade, an icy blue that matched the frostiness of his irises.

Druids were of the earth, their magic natural, but limited, which was why the ancestors looked for other ways to strengthen it. They bargained with dark magic, corrupting themselves until they were able to manipulate blood and death much like black witches. Along with their own natural abilities, they made themselves more powerful. Reborn as Daemons.

It was why the Guardians were created, a penance to

pay for the sins of the ancestors who'd chosen the dark, and all the madness that came with it. Forced into a ritual against their will, because pricks like Dirk wanted to be immortal.

Except nothing was immortal, and Xander was about to prove that.

A flash of silver in his peripheral, a knife shooting past as Xander twisted slightly to the side. It caught his chest, cutting a clean slice before it disappeared behind him. He hadn't seen where it came from, but from the pained shout only seconds later he guessed Riley had.

Tendrils of black magic tainted the area around him, strangling his lungs and coating his tongue in fur. Xander blinked past the blood dripping into his eyes, his night vision perfectly clear as he quickly swept the surrounding area. The dead druid lay on his back, his front covered in a stark red against pale skin. It was clear he'd started the transition, Xander had witnessed enough bodies over the years to see it in the lines indented into his face and in the veins that continued to squirm even in death.

Druids alone were one of the rarer Breeds, taking up only five percent of the population. According to the Order who ruled across the entire Breed, there had been only five-hundred successful Daemon transitions ever registered. Five hundred because the success rate was less than one percent. Candidates died, their bodies not designed to withstand that type of magic.

Except before Dirk had sliced the man's throat, he'd been very much alive.

Dirk laughed as realisation narrowed Xander's eyes. Kyra had been able to keep the druid alive, which meant Dirk wasn't leaving there with breath in his lungs.

Not that there was really any other option.

"She's magnificent, isn't she?" Dirk purred. "I've never quite tasted power like hers."

Xander dodged Dirk's quick strike of the knife, his returning swing strategic as he closed their distance.

"But not as tasty as the little place between her –"

Xander moved without a conscious thought, his beast pushing for blood, for the blade to pierce skin. It was an error, Dirk's words chosen specifically to torment. Dirk's arcane struck against his arm, weakening his grip with the sword.

Xander threw down his weapon, launching himself forward with a clenched fist. His knuckles hit bone, and as Dirk's head whipped to the side he landed another. Rage was a storm in his veins, numbing the pain as nails raked deep down his side.

Something sharp brushed his skin, the discomfort harsh before he gripped it, ignoring the sting across his palm.

A heavy weight knocked him to the wet grass, rancid smoke strangling his lungs before fangs clamped down on his shoulder.

"Fuck!" he grunted, gripping the limited fur of the hell-hounds scruff. He yanked back, ignoring the amount of his own flesh that came with the teeth before the hound closed down on his forearm, tearing and thrashing.

A flash of pale grey, Kace colliding with the giant hound. His brother snarled, the black markings along his thick fur brightening as he launched a deadly attack.

Dirk smirked, his red eyes bright as they flicked behind him. A man screamed, the sound piercing before it quickly changed into a furious snarl.

"Looks like our Little Black Witch is having some fun of her own," Dirk said. "Don't worry Guardian, I'll share her once I've broken her in properly."

A blade glistened in the grass, Xander's own blood

coating the severed edge. Dirk noticed, his smile dropping as they both launched toward it at the same time. Red arcane seared across his chi, eating away at his aura before his palm touched the coolness of the handle. The tip pierced straight into Dirk's heart. It wasn't a killing blow, not against someone as powerful as him but still Xander smiled at Dirk's pained howl.

"Say hi to Hadriel for me," he snarled, stepping back. Dirk tried to remove the blade, but Xander lifted his heavy boot and kicked the handle perfectly, pushing the Daemon towards Riley's waiting blade.

He didn't need to watch as Riley expertly separated Dirk's head from his body, trusting his brother to finish the job. Kyra stood, the derelict farmhouse an ominous shadow against the arcane that coated her palms, the magical flames dancing. A grim reaper looking Fae lay dead by her feet, several spirits surrounding Kyra in a thrall, their eyes pale and hungry.

"Kyra?" he called as he closed the distance, ignoring the spirits who turned their dead gaze to him in a single, quick movement. "Kyra?" he called again when she stared blankly with eyes completely black, hair whipping violently around her face. There was no warmth from her magic, the power so cold it ached against his skin.

Spikes at his nape, his beast snarling a second before something dark attacked his back, the magic a mist that moved to wrap around his chest. It stole the air from his lungs, filling the space with a thickened sludge.

Kyra turned her head, the spirits copying the movement before they shot across the field. Xander called on the strength of his beast, the black magic wrapping its spell tight enough phantom thorns pierced into his heart.

A black hex, one that fucking hurt and was likely killing him. He locked his knees, stopping himself from collapsing as he reached for Kyra, her face just as empty as the spirits. A scream echoed behind, and he savoured the sound as the magic released him with a pop. His lungs opened, the sludge disappearing along with the ache in his heart.

"Kyra?" He ignored her arcane, the icy flames caressing against his skin, but not harming as he gently touched her cheek.

There was nothing. No recollection behind those eyes of obsidian. Nothing but endless death, the spirits using her as a conduit. He looked over her shoulder, spotting waves of the dead in the distance. Moving towards her like a magnet. An army.

"Kyra."

"I'm sorry," she whispered, her voice distant, lost. "I can't stop it."

Xander brushed his hands down her arms, the crystal shattered in her overlapping bands. "Princess, listen to me." He made his voice hard, a vicious strike. "You can do this, you're in control. Not them."

Tears burned down her face, the liquid black.

"Xee?" Riley called, but Xander ignored him, not wanting to look away from the woman who was both the light, and the dark. One who he'd hated on sight because of his own prejudice, and then hated himself for wanting her anyway.

"Fuck!" He slanted his lips over hers, breaking her sight of the spirits that moved to surround them. Leeches attracted to the life she represented. He kissed her with everything he could, his lips full of desperation and need. He showed her that she was there with him, and not lost to the enclosing darkness. It took a second, her body rigid before her lips finally moved, and Xander praised her with a flick of his tongue. His hands pulled her more easily against him, kissing her as if he was a man starved. As if he'd waited his entire existence just for her.

Kyra pulled back, her breathing rapid as she blinked at him with familiar amber eyes, her chi no longer electric. The spirits still stood in his peripheral, watching. But they no longer marched.

"Mine." His beast howled in agreement, and then he kissed her again, crushing her against him so she knew just how much he wanted her.

How much he craved her.

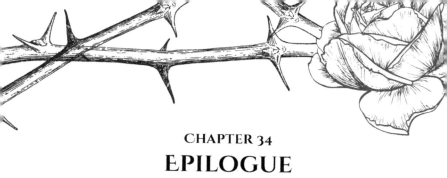

CHAPTER 34
EPILOGUE

ONE MONTH LATER
XANDER

Xander's hands were sweaty, slipping against the leather steering wheel of his car. His heart rate had increased, and if the butterflies in his stomach didn't fucking stop soon he was likely to stab himself.

If Kyra realised his reaction, she didn't let on as she stared quietly out the window, watching the snow-covered trees blur past.

Why was he so nervous? Xander didn't get nervous, especially not when he'd had a month to plan. To figure out how he could ask for Kyra's heart. Or beg if he had to.

Kyra slid her eyes to him, concern glistening in them.

Fuck the Fates. When did he become so pathetic? He'd taken down hounds, Daemons, and Shadow-Veyn three times his size, and yet the thought of asking the woman he loved about being officially his was what brought him to his knees?

He hoped none of his brothers ever saw him like this, he'd never live it down. But then again he *had* asked them to help, so they were probably all sniggering back at Blood Bar. He'd left to drive Kyra an hour outside the city's limits without an explanation.

Shit. She probably thought he was kidnapping her, or something.

"Almost there," he said, giving her a weak smile. The steering wheel squeaked beneath his grip, knuckles white.

Kyra's returning smile brightened her face, easing the slight tightness in his chest. "Are you going to tell me where we're going yet?"

Xander swallowed, returning his attention to the road. "No."

The plan was stupid. Who thought that driving her at the dead of night was romantic?

KYRA

"Are you planning to kill me?" she asked as Xander guided her up another snowy hill, the city glittering in the distance. "Or is this trip ominous for a reason?"

"You'll see," he said, his lips tipped in a crooked smile when he turned his head, the moon casting a glow against his sharp features. He was nervous, and trying to hide it. "I promise it'll be worth the walk."

Kyra tightened the coat around her shoulders, much to Xander's amusement. Weeks had passed, and despite knowing both Dirk and Bane were dead she still had nightmares. She'd woken up covered in sweat, her breathing laboured before an arm would wrap around her waist to pull her against a hard chest. She panicked when the arms tightened, but Xander was patient, helping her through her triggers until she'd sighed and relaxed back into sleep against his warmth.

It had been worse in her flat knowing Frederick was still out there, so after only a single night Xander had convinced her to stay with him instead. It had hurt to say goodbye to her only home, even though it was tainted. It had been her one place she'd called hers. Her sanctuary.

She was only supposed to stay with Xander for a few days, yet she found herself there after all these weeks not wanting to leave. She knew she would have to eventually, to figure out what the next stage of her life was now she was no longer wanted by the Magicka.

Kyra waited as two thirds of the Triumvirate had taken their seats, ignoring the vacant space in the middle where Frederick should've been. She didn't blame them for their hostility, not when they'd barged into the building and demanded a meeting. She wasn't in a court this time, but a conference room with a large table, enforcers ready and waiting behind the glass wall.

There had been an incident when she'd been pushed into her seat, but as Xander barked a warning Kace had already punched the man out cold, and was promptly ejected from the room. The other enforcers had shared a look, and from that point they kept their distance. It had made everyone on edge, including the remaining Triumvirate. But oddly enough, it had calmed Kyra.

She wasn't alone.

She'd always been alone.

'You need to trust me,' Alice had whispered to her only moments before. 'I have a plan.'

'You never plan,' Riley had laughed. 'You just go in full guns blazing and hope for the best.'

It wasn't a glowing endorsement, but Kyra had two options; to run, and hide for the rest of her life. Or to live. Hopefully.

"You have us here," the female Triumvir said, her tone like steel. "I'm very surprised, but also interested in what you have to say. You took a great risk in returning here." Her actual name was a mystery, as was the male who looked between the few Guardians, and then Alice who'd joined her. They'd never introduced themselves other than their titles, and Kyra never asked.

"My name is Kyra Farzan, and I'm a dark witch."

The man nodded, but the woman frowned. "Miss Farzan, do you understand what you've just said? The Magicka do not take kindly to those who practice black magic. The punishment is severe, as you very well know."

"I understand," she replied, hoping her voice didn't waver. "I'm guilty of practicing black magic because I have to, to survive. It's something I'm born with, and have to practice to stay balanced."

"You deal in blood and death," the man commented with a raised brow. "Look at what happened when you were in our custody."

Kyra ignored the growl at her side, not wanting to break the eye contact. "I never hurt any of those people." She reached beneath the table, finding Xander's hand.

"We're aware of your statement," the woman said. "And the evidence that has been handed to us."

Kyra looked between them. "Then you understand I am innocent of everything but my birth. I will not apologise for something I can't control."

The female Triumvir pursed her lips. "There are laws for a reason."

"Outdated rules that don't reflect the newer generations. I have never intentionally hurt anyone, and yet I'm treated like a monster."

"Because black magic is too dangerous," the man said. "It could never be sanctioned."

"I'm not asking that," Kyra replied quickly, speaking before Alice could cut in. "I'm asking that if a witch born with the signs of a black chi, that they should be trained rather than ostracised, or even murdered. Only then should they come before the Magicka, after being given the opportunity to be educated."

The two witches glanced at one another, her fate in their hands.

"Despite the evidence of your innocence, and the accusation against the Supreme, the law still remains," the woman stated. "Your admittance to practicing black magic is concerning, but not surprising. I would even say it was brave, considering your situation."

"I agree with the laws being outdated, and it's a shame that according to those same laws there's only one choice," the man added, his eyes flicking across the Guardians who were present in the room, and then the ones who waited behind the glass wall to her right. "If you would let us confer."

The two witches faced one another, their voices quiet.

Kyra felt attention prickle her side, turning to find Xander staring at her. She met his eyes of frost, watched them thaw as something else she couldn't read flashed across those pale irises.

She smiled gently, hoping he understood that she had no choice, and she knew there was always a risk in returning to the Magicka. He'd shown her even in their limited time together that she was worth her life, even if she was born from the darkness.

His dark brow raised, his fingers tightening against her own.

"Because the Supreme is indisposed, we have come to a joint decision," the man continued, forcing her attention back to them.

Kyra held her breath, blood a roar inside her ears.

"You've shown us the severe corruption within our own organisation, and because of the evidence you've provided we've decided you're not guilty of the deaths suffered around your escape. You'll not suffer the death sentence."

Xander pulled her from the chair, his arms wrapping around her shoulders.

"However," the woman said with an almost sad smile. "Black magic is still banned within the law unless specifically licensed, so you must have your magic graded within the Magicka and recorded. Upon inspection, we will decide whether you can continue to practice safely, and within boundaries."

"We'll take your advice under advisement," the man added. "But we're a long way off from welcoming black magic so openly. You'll forfeit your services to us, an advisor of sorts, and maybe together we can come to an understanding."

Kyra's legs would have collapsed if she hadn't gripped Xander like a lifeline. "That's fine," she mumbled, unable to believe she'd been given back her life.

Kyra blinked away the memory, finding Xander watching her carefully. She offered him a small smile. "You going to tell me where we're going yet?"

"And spoil it?" He tugged her until his body blocked the icy wind, his lips brushing the side of her neck. She waited for her mind to react, for her body to stiffen. But instead she settled closer, tilting her head so his lips had better access. "If you carry this on, you won't get your surprise," he gently whispered before releasing her. "Come on, it's just at the top of that hill."

Kyra followed the direction he pointed, noticing a gentle glow between a thicket of trees. They had driven to the outskirts of the city, leaving the car at the edge of the national park. The grass crunched frozen beneath their feet, the snow only a thin layer as she struggled with the steepness.

Xander had been right, the cold walk had been worth it. She felt his eyes tracing her face, watching her smile grow as she noticed the picnic blanket, covered in a gentle white dusting. Candles surrounded the square fabric, protected from the wind by glass.

"This is..." Emotions clogged her throat.

"That's not the surprise," he said, pulling her down to sit on the blanket, his body tense beside her, nervous. "That is."

Kyra hadn't realised that in the distance was the Magicka castle, the hill overlooking the grounds without restrictions. She could make out a crowd, and someone on their knees within in a circle. She leaned forward, trying to get a better look, unable to tear her attention away as she recognised the green velvet coat.

Nobody could find him, the enforcers only discovering blood smears at the bastion, Frederick's whereabouts a mystery. It had been at the back of her mind that she would never truly be safe, not with her looking over her shoulder for the rest of her life.

"It seems Alice had her own grudge against him," Xander said quietly beside her, his eyes a brand. "She found him cowering in Wales. His trial was private, but Titus hacked the system and found out he was found guilty of

306

treason, as well as black magic. He's to be sentenced to fifty years in prison, and for his chi to be permanently suppressed. After that, he'll fall to the same law he threatened you with. Poetic-fucking-justice."

Snow fluttered around them, so gentle in contrast. The wind didn't carry his cries, but Kyra was sure he shouted his innocence, Frederick's body twisted with rage as he fought whatever hold they had on him. Two witches stepped forward, and even from the distance she could just make out the faces of the other two Triumvirate.

Kyra laughed, the sound echoing around them. But she was still unable to speak. Not yet, not while she watched the man who'd controlled her for so long be tortured with a punishment worse than death.

It was fitting. Frederick had craved power, and would do anything to obtain it. Now he would suffer for the rest of his existence without it before suffering a painful death.

"I wanted to show you that he can't hurt you anymore."

Kyra turned to face Xander, his face relaxed but eyes guarded.

"You're safe to do whatever you want. Go wherever you want to go," he continued quietly. "You're free." He spoke as if he was unsure. As if she'd leave, and never look back. Maybe before that was what she'd have done. But not now. Not after him.

Kyra threw herself forward, pulling his face down as tears covered her cheeks. Their relationship had started out rocky, and she understood the reasoning behind his hatred. But as his lips parted, salt mingling with the delicious taste that was just him, she couldn't be happier.

"Thank you," she said with a sniffle, the tears coming harder. "Thank you for everything."

"Kyra," he groaned, his hands coming up to pull her fully into his lap. "I'm sorry how I was, I didn't –"

She silenced him with another kiss. She didn't need an apology, not when he'd shown her more care and consideration even when he'd hated her than most people had in her entire lifetime.

His fingers pushed beneath her jumper, freezing against her skin. She didn't care, needing more skin-on-skin contact. Tugging the hem she pulled it over her head, the air cool against her bare skin. Snow gently landed on her shoulders, only heightening every touch, and brush of Xander's fingers. His lips moved to her breasts, teeth nipping at the cup of her bra.

"Off," he growled, and she couldn't unfasten it quick enough before he was biting her soft curves. She could no longer feel the cold, not when her entire existence was concentrated on the heat between her legs. On the hardness that pressed expertly against the apex of her thighs, despite the barrier of fabric.

Xander seemed to be just as desperate when she tore at his jeans, lifting her slightly so she could easier reach the zipper to release his hardening cock. His shirt was removed, lights dancing across his tattoos as she settled back on his lap, thankful for her skirt and knee-high socks.

Her underwear tore, and then he was inside her, stretching her to her limit in one powerful thrust. Her cry echoed the area around him, and in the back of her mind she hoped the sound travelled down to Frederick.

The thought instantly vanished when Xander's thumb reached down to rub against her clit with exactly the right pressure, his lips claiming hers as she began to lift herself, and then drop back down. Their movements were rushed, frantic as her orgasm exploded out of nowhere, tightening her internal muscles.

"So wet for me, Princess." His hands dropped to her hips, taking over as she rode through the aftershocks, her breasts pushed against his chest. His speed picked up, and just as she felt another tightening Xander flipped her gently onto her knees. "Beautiful," he rasped, stoking over her hip.

His thrusts were slower than before, the angle deeper but no less feral. He'd turned her towards the castle, letting her watch Frederick's demise with his cock forcing more pleasure than she'd ever experienced. She came with another cry, her body clenching around him so hard he groaned, his cock pulsating his release. Xander gently pulled her onto his lap, wrapping part of the picnic blanket around them before pressing his forehead against hers. Kyra laughed, unable to stop the manic sound. A weight had been lifted off her shoulders, the realisation that she could do whatever she wanted.

Be whoever she wanted.

She pulled back to better look at his face, their bodies slick in the most intimate way. "Xander, I –"

"Kyra, It's always been you." His pale eyes searched hers. "I felt it the moment we first met, and I was a fucking idiot to think I could fight it." His fingertips brushed across her cheek.

"I love you," she said before she lost the nerve.

Xander's smile brightened his entire face. "Good, because you're mine, and I'm not letting you go."

His next kiss was full of promise, full of laughter and happiness as the snow continued to flutter around them like a rebirth.

It was the start of her new life, and she wasn't alone.

A shiver of anticipation rippled through her.

She couldn't wait.

KACE

Kace wasn't sure why he'd decided to step inside the Dollhouse, rather than waiting in the cool air. He had no interest in the dancers that graced the stage, and definitely not the greasy crowd who watched, believing they were hidden in the shadows. Yet his beast pushed inside his mind, patience a virtue neither of them possessed.

"You'll never get anyone better than me," a voice echoed, drawing his attention to the bar, and to the vampire who gripped a woman's arm tight enough to bruise. "You're just a slut who can –"

Kace reacted without thought, wrenching the Vamp to the side and crushing him against the wall. "Apologise," he growled, pressing closer until he was almost nose to nose. "Now." He cared very little for anyone who willingly hurt those weaker than themselves. And almost everyone was weaker than a vampire. Except him.

The Vamp snarled, fangs elongating past his lips. "Fuck you!" he managed to squeeze out, the sound strangled.

A deep chuckle, fire surging through Kace's blood. "Careful, fang face."

"Put him down." A hand brushed his shoulder, and for once he didn't recoil. "He's not worth it."

Kace turned his head to the side, watching how the one fucking woman who'd crawled beneath his skin sucked in a breath, recognition flashing across her features.

"You know this guy?" the Vamp asked, catching himself

on the bar when Kace released his grip. "What, you fucking him too?"

Kace remained silent, waiting to see whether a blush darkened Eva's skin at the thought. Was strangely disappointed when her complexion remained the same.

"Who I fuck is none of your business anymore!" she said, anger vibrating her voice.

Kace caught the fist seconds before it hit his jaw, the bones in his hand groaning at the power behind it. The strength would have killed a normal man. Luckily he wasn't a normal.

"Hey Red, we got a problem?" Marshall, the man he'd been waiting for appeared. "This guy giving you trouble?"

"I've got it," Kace muttered, tightening his grip until the Vamp hissed. He didn't catch the rest of the conversation, didn't care as he started moving towards the exit. All he cared about was killing the fucking vampire who'd had his fingers around Eva's arm.

"Wait!"

Her voice jerked him back from the rage, the crimson around his vision gradually residing until he could think past the need to kill.

"Fuck off," he snarled to the guy he held, grip loosening enough for the vampire to break free.

The Vamp hissed. "Or what?"

Kace smiled, a cruel twist of his lips. He'd already shown mercy once, he wouldn't a second time.

The vampire blinked, black eyes flicking between them. "I'll see you around, babe," he shouted towards Eva before quickly disappearing down the street.

She quickly turned to face him, tension visible along her shoulders. "What was that? Why did you have to make it so much worse, *Red?*"

He wasn't sure how he felt about her using his fighting name.

"Don't bother helping next time."

His eyes snapped to the mark on her upper arm. The earlier rage returned, but he kept it suppressed enough to reply. "Sure."

"What the hell?" She moved closer, but he stepped back, wanting to keep distance between them when the beast was riding him hard. "What are you even doing here?"

"I didn't realise you owned the city," he said, the words edging towards a growl. "I'll remember to ask permission next time I want to speak to an acquaintance."

Eva let out a frustrated scream. "You're such an arsehole!"

"Noted."

He watched her face pinch with frustration, her eyes slowly sweeping across his face, before dropping lower. Anger slowly bled from her gaze, replaced with something else, something that made heat surge through his stomach.

"Careful," he said, his tone deepening at her attention. "We don't want a repeat of last time."

EVA

"You wish," she said in a suspiciously husky tone. "You couldn't handle me."

Fuck. Me. Sideways. It had sounded like a challenge, and that was not her intention. What the fuck was with her attraction to hot, dangerous guys?

His eyes narrowed, and she hoped like god that he couldn't read her mind. She didn't wait for a response, instead turning to jog towards her car. It was late, and even

312

in a city that never really slept it didn't take her long to get to her building, parking in a space that was surprisingly close to the entrance.

Even the distance hadn't dampened her embarrassment, nor the arousal that just made it that much worse.

"What's wrong with me?" she groaned, settling her head against the leather of the steering wheel. Kace was a mystery, a grumpy arsehole who scowled at her more than smiled. So why was her body ready to climb him like a mountain?

With a dramatic sigh she opened her front door, the automatic light in the corner flicking to life when she moved inside. She was acting like a woman in heat. Dropping her keys on the side table she headed straight for the kitchen in the back, placing the leftover lasagne into the microwave and setting the timer before grabbing one of her homemade muffins.

If it could be baked, Eva would make it. It was different to dance, but it was something else she loved to explore and experiment with. It was just a bonus that at the end she got something delicious to eat, well, most of the time it was delicious.

A loud bang, her front door slamming open with a crash.

"You stupid cunt," Lucas snarled, hands wrapping around her arms in an iron grip. "Do you really think you could ever be with anyone other than me?"

He threw her across the room, her stomach connecting to the sofa hard enough the whole thing knocked onto its back, taking her with it. He kicked at her ankle, and Eva let out a scream as she felt the bone break. He reached down to grip her throat, pulling her up as if she weighed nothing, her lungs screaming for air.

Eva pulled at his fingers, scratched down his arms but

nothing moved his clutch. His face was void of the humanity so many vampires wore, his once warm brown eyes completely black with rage, his lips pulled back to reveal large fangs.

"I marked you from the beginning," he spat at her. "And now I'm going to make you mine, forever."

He's never wanted anyone... until her.
Ready for Kace & Eva's story? Order now:
https://mybook.to/TouchofBloodBOB

Want more of Xander and Kyra?
Enjoy this free bonus sexy epilogue! Download!
https://BookHip.com/DGTXKMM

Please take a second to rate and/or review. Reviews are super important, and help readers discover this series. Thank you from the bottom of my disturbed heart, Taylor

P.S. Want a fun, safe place to chat about my books with others? Join my exclusive reader group, Taylor's Supernatural Society!

Keep in touch with Taylor Aston White

Instagram
@tayastonwhite
TikTok
@taylorastonwhite
Facebook
/taylorastonwhite
Website
www.taylorastonwhite.com
Bookbub
www.bookbub.com/profile/taylor-aston-white
Goodreads
www.goodreads.com/taylorastonwhite

Sign up for Taylor's newsletter mailing list to receive updates, exclusive content, giveaways, early excerpts and much more.
Plus there's a free short story!
www.taylorastonwhite.com

ABOUT THE AUTHOR

Taylor Aston White loves to explore mythology and European faerie tales to create her own, modern magic world. She collects crystals, house plants and dark lipstick, and has two young children who like to 'help' with her writing by slamming their hands across the keyboard.

After working several uncreative jobs and one super creative one, she decided to become a full-time author and now spends the majority of her time between her children and writing the weird and wonderful stories that pop into her head.

Printed in Great Britain
by Amazon